BRITTLE SCARS

EMMANUELLE
USA TODAY BESTSELLING AUTHOR
SNOW

Smart Lily
Publishing

LOVE
WILD & COUNTRY
HOCKEY GAME

Brittle Scars
Emmanuelle Snow

First edition - November 2022 (V_1) (2025 update)

ISBN eBook: 978-1-990429-66-8

ISBN paperback: 978-1-990429-68-2

This book is part one of the Breathless duet.

Editors: Shalini G. and SLE

Cover: SMART Lily publishing inc.

Published by SMART Lily Publishing inc.

———

Emmanuelle Snow
emmanuellesnow.com

CARTER HILLS BAND UNIVERSE
(SUGGESTED READING ORDER)

Carter Hills Band series
False Promises

HEART SONG DUET
Blindsided
Forevermore

Whiskey Melody series
Sweet Agony

SECOND TEAR DUET
Cruel Destiny
Beautiful Salvation

BREATHLESS DUET
Wild Encounter
Brittle Scars

Upon A Star series
Last Hope

Midnight Sparks

Love Song For Two series
Lonesome Heart Duet
Fallen Legend
Rising Star

Two of Us Duet
Snowbound

Wicked Love

All titles available at
emmanuellesnow.com

For the best experience, read in the order as shown above

TRIGGER WARNINGS

Disclaimer

My books are realistic and emotional love stories.

I'm an advocate for mental health, and some topics could be sensitive for certain readers since they are portrayed as close to real life as possible.

I've listed the potential trigger warnings for each title on my website.

Be advised that those trigger warnings could potentially be spoiler alerts for the storylines.

Those sensitive topics have been written with the utmost care and respect. Please reach out if you have questions or comments.

All books contain sexuality, mature content, and language not intended for people under 18 years of age.
For other readers' sake, please avoid spoilers in your reviews.

Thank you and have a wonderful day!

Emmanuelle

emmanuellesnow.com

BECOME A VIP

TO NEVER MISS A THING

Snow's VIP

Join **Emmanuelle Snow's VIP newsletter** for all the cool stuff, promos, new releases, giveaways, and gifts.

emmanuellesnow.com

Snow's Soulmates

Join Emmanuelle Snow's Facebook VIP group, **Snow's Soulmates**, to chat with her and other readers, get updates, and more bonus content.

facebook.com/groups/snowvip

Chapter 1

Addison

Mrs. Ellis was right about something. I hadn't eaten all day, and now I felt weaker than I ever had. Two strong arms caught me as I was about to collapse to the ground.

Tucker.

My heart jolted back to life when I opened my eyes and saw him standing there, the trench across his forehead deeper than before.

"Huh…thanks," I muttered.

"Wilde, enough already. Seriously, you're starting to freak me out. You almost fainted just about now." His grip around my waist tightened. His low voice, barely above a whisper, tickled the side of my face. "What's going on?"

"Food. And water," I said as he held me up, pressing me against his chest—my safe haven—his heartbeat rocking me into calm and bringing me much-required comfort. I took a deep breath in, hoping to send blood and air back to my brain.

"Come," Tucker said, his voice reassuring, laced with noticeable concern. "I've got you, sweetheart. I'm here. Lean on me." Never letting go of me, he led me to a shadowy corner of the yard, where sunlight was gentle enough not to overwhelm me, and pulled up a chair. "Wait here. I'll be right back." He pressed a kiss to my forehead and hurried away.

A tiny piece of my heart healed at how he cared for me, and another one hurt as he put more distance between us. My gaze stayed glued to him. Tension had taken over his upper back, and he kept rubbing his nape as if to loosen the knots that had developed there.

A few seconds later, he watched me from a distance, and our stares fused. I tried to avert my eyes, urging myself to look away, but I couldn't break the eye contact—the magnetism emanating from him reeling me in, powerful and impossible to resist.

Tucker came back a moment later, carrying a plate of finger food and crudités with dip, along with a glass of water, and took a seat facing me. "Here. Eat."

I nibbled a carrot stick in silence, unsure if my stomach would hold it in, washing down the small bites with sips of water.

"How are you feeling?" He traced the curve of my cheek with his knuckles. "You're pale. Something is off. Don't bullshit me."

I pressed my lips together, avoiding his piercing dark irises.

"What did Dahlia's mom tell you? You seemed upset after she left."

"Huh…no. I didn't… I… Anyway, it doesn't matter."

Tucker lifted my chin with a finger to study me, and my heart rate picked up.

Could he read me as much as I could read him? I glanced down for a long second, praying that he would miss my despair.

Instead of letting it go, he continued, "It matters to me, Wilde."

My shoulders slouched and I sank into the chair as fresh tears prickled the back of my eyes. How could Tucker Philips be so in sync with my feelings? If I wished hard enough, could I disappear right now to avoid spilling the truth to him?

"Tell me," he pressed.

I lifted my fleeting gaze to meet his. A *don't fuck with me* expression lingered in his dark one. My pulse kicked up another notch. "It…it doesn't matter. Really. She talked nonsense." I shrugged, bringing a stick of celery to my mouth.

"Wilde. What did she say? If it's nasty, I'll chase her down. I don't care how old she is or if her daughter is royalty."

A tiny smile peeked through, curving my lips. I squeezed his strong forearm, feeling the cord of his muscles twitching underneath my palm.

"Stop. Don't go all Chicago on Mrs. Ellis. She's a fan of yours. She couldn't stop praising you," I said, avoiding his eyes.

Tucker dipped his head down and searched my face. His voice lowered as he continued, "Then tell me, Wilde. What did she tell you? It affected you, and I won't drop it."

I inhaled. I didn't have to tell him, right? Dahlia's mama had no idea what she thought she knew. A little *what-if* hovered over me, and I feared she could be right after all. No, she was wrong. So wrong. But Dahlia's mama had more experience than I did. Ohmygod. My hands quivered. All the thoughts jumbled inside my head. Tucker moved closer, erasing the distance between our heads, his warm cheek now resting against mine.

"Talk."

He cupped my bouncing knee with his big muscular hand.

I pinched my lips together. Dahlia and Nick's wedding wasn't the time for all the drama.

"Wilde." Tucker's voice grew impatient. Insistent.

Why did he have to push the subject?

"Talk. I know you're hiding something. If I did anything that hurt you, I'm sorry. But I can't fix it unless you tell me what's wrong. Is it about last night? I didn't wanna push you. I thought we were on the same wavelength. I had no idea you changed your mind. Truth is, I'll never talk about us being together like this again if that's what you're afraid of. I promise. Now be honest with me. Please. We said *truth always*."

I spewed the next words, closing my eyes, not ready to face the emotions that would flood his grave expression with shock. "Tuck, I don't need to be fixed. I'm not some project you gotta tackle. Since when do I owe you something? We're not even a couple, so stop acting as if you're entitled to know everything." My voice cracked. "Anyway, it's nothing. Already told you."

I cupped my mouth as more sobs rocked through me. Tucker did nothing wrong. He didn't deserve my venom, or to bear the brunt of my moods.

He cleared his throat, his next words like shards of glass piercing my fragile armor. "Don't try to push me away by using harsh words, Wilde. It's unlike you to talk like this. I've gotten to know you well enough over the past month or so to call you on your bullshit. I'm not letting you off the hook until you confide in me. I know you don't owe me anything, but I can't stand seeing you sad."

I remained silent.

"Suit yourself, Wilde. We're staying here until we get to the bottom of this. I'm being your friend right now. Deal with it."

Fury bubbled up inside me, and I groaned, refusing to speak in case I said something I didn't mean.

He moved closer, squeezing my hand.

I sighed, unsure how long I could keep the storm of doubt front and center in my head under control, or pretend nothing was wrong when everything could really be all wrong. I shut my eyes and silenced the voices in my head as I delivered the news, not knowing the best way to do this.

"She thinks…she thinks I'm pregnant."

I pushed a hand over my mouth, hoping I wouldn't throw up as the words flew out of my lips before I could catch them back. After all, being dramatic was my most endearing quality, no? That was what Phoenix, my twin brother, used to say growing up. He'd be so proud of me right now, because I just about aced the drama.

Tucker froze beside me. His grip on my knee slackened. His throat worked as his breathing quickened. He pinched the bridge of his nose, and tilted his head back.

He said nothing for the longest time, while I fidgeted with my fingers. After what felt like an eternity, he returned his gaze to mine.

"Wilde, is she right? Fuck. Tell me the truth. Here and now. Don't sugarcoat anything. Are you pregnant? Is Mrs. Ellis right?"

I shrugged. Because I had no clue. What Dahlia's

mama said added up, but my upcoming period could explain most of my symptoms too.

"Wilde. Are you pregnant? I deserve the truth. Be honest with me." This time, his voice carried more urgency.

I would never be able to lie to him.

"I-I don't know. It didn't cross my mind until she suggested it. My cycle is always all over the place, so nothing unusual here. Adding to the fact I'm under a lot of stress—"

He framed my face with his large hands, his palms hot against my skin, calming the tremors in my body. I could have fallen asleep right there, knowing nothing bad could ever happen to me with him watching over me. Tucker Philips was not only irresistible, but also protective and caring, every side of him appealing to me.

"I've got you, sweetheart. No reason to panic over it if it's nothing. We'll get a test and figure this out, okay?"

I nodded, lifting my eyes to stare at him, knots loosening in my stomach at the idea he'd take the lead.

Something softened in his expression. Why wasn't he freaked out by all this? How could he be so calm? Inside, I was a storm. A volcano about to erupt, set to devastate my life. A freaking ticking time bomb, ready to blow.

"No matter what, we'll do this together. I have your back. Always."

I nodded again. Like a robot. What else could I do? I must have looked so dumb.

"I have question, though. The morning-after pill…can it…can it fail?"

"No idea." I twisted the golden chain around my wrist between my fingers. "I followed the instructions. It's supposed to be effective if taken within seventy-two hours. I took it well before that. I swear I did."

"Stop. Don't blame yourself, okay? I would never blame you. I believe you. Addison Wilde, I trust you." His lips molded to mine. Warm and soothing. Soft and comforting. Protective. "I love you, sweetheart. We'll be fine."

My lungs idled. Air couldn't reach them anymore. I swallowed. My pulse raced. What did he just say?

"Whoa. W-what?" I escaped his grip, but Tucker held me there, inches away from his face. "You're out of your mind. Are you crazy? This day is surreal. I'm sure I'm dreaming. What the fuck, Tuck. You don't love me. We spent like a dozen days together at the most. Are you high?"

My breathing returned. I inhaled a big gulp of air, needing to wake up my numb brain.

"Stop squirming, Wilde. Listen to me. For once, just listen. I've never said those words to anyone before. There's something about you. I-I never planned for this to happen. You woke up something in me. The time we spent apart made me realize many things. While they made you rethink everything, they cemented something inside me. Lately, you've become my best friend. The one person I can't live without. Don't ask questions because I don't possess the answers. How you did that is still beyond me, but you took a big slice of my heart home after we went our separate ways the last time. Every day, you're all I think about. The only person I wanna call at any hour, just for the pleasure of hearing your voice."

The gears of my brain overheated. "Tucker, you can't love me. I told you I'm not screwing things up again. You and I, not happening. We can't. It's not… It is not…"

He squared his shoulders. "It's not what, Wilde? It happened when we were in different states. I spend all day waiting for our daily call. Everywhere I look, you're there. I dream of you every night. Slowly, each time we had one of our late-night conversations, you anchored yourself deeper into my heart. Believe me, I'm as much in shock as you are. I had no idea what it meant either…until I saw you last night. And the more I think about it, the more I'm sure I'm in love with you, Wilde. If it isn't love, then tell me what is this feeling? Because I have no idea how to get you out of my mind. You live under my skin. I want to be with you all the time. Kiss you even if everybody is watching. Hold your hands and dry your tears. Bury myself so deep inside you that no one can tell us apart. It was killing me to see you sad earlier without being able to touch you or comfort you. It was as if my own heart was bleeding and I couldn't stop the hemorrhage."

He scratched the side of his head while I sat there, speechless, the words locked inside.

"I never thought I'd ever feel this way about anyone. But here we are. This isn't how I imagined breaking the news to you. And by the way, I should run away. I know it, and with any other woman, I would have already bolted far from here. And I'd be in denial. For some reason, with you, it's different. I can't hurt you, and I can't comprehend why I'm so fucking calm right now. Wilde, if you're pregnant, I'm pregnant. No way will I ever let you go through all this by yourself. And when you're sad, I'm sad. Please explain what spell you've cast on me because I'm bewitched by you. And it's powerful. I'm not sure I want to break free from it."

He lowered his head until his lips caressed mine with unsaid words.

I held my breath. Nothing he said made any sense, yet for a moment, his words soothed the tsunami raging inside me.

"We spent two weekends together physically, but

hundreds of hours together over the phone or video chat. Sometimes over six hours or more at a time. Don't lie to me or to yourself. It's a lot of time to connect and to get to know somebody."

"But—"

"No but."

"There's something else…"

"Tell me."

"Always the truth, remember?"

He nodded.

"I lied to you last night…and…huh, it's eating me up from the inside. I'm horny all the time when I think about you. I have no idea where it comes from," I said against his lips.

"See? That wasn't so hard," he whispered, his lips curling against mine. "We'll be all right."

Tucker molded his hand to the back of my head and crashed his mouth on mine, tasting me. Owning me. The same way he did that first time in Nashville. This time, it hit me harder. Like I truly belonged to him.

I placed one hand over his heart, relishing the strong beating under my palm.

He sucked on my tongue, battled my lips for the upper hand, awakening flutters inside me. I fisted his dress shirt, keeping him close.

"Let's find out. We'll get a test. Nobody will notice we're gone. It will only take fifteen minutes. We'll be fine. I promise."

I nodded, deepening the kiss, taking all he could give me right now because it calmed the throbbing in my heart, and my overactive mind.

Words I kept inside emerged on their own. "I'm sorry I pushed you away last night. I didn't want to. I thought I was protecting us. From falling too deep…from getting attached."

"What is going on?" The sudden interruption ruined the most intimate moment I'd had since… well, forever.

Breathless, Tucker and I broke apart and turned our heads, our foreheads still pressed together.

Nick stood there with wide eyes, Dahlia hot on his heels.

"Tuck, what's going on? Man, we agreed on two rules." The groom shook his head, a million questions dancing in his eyes.

My heart leaped in my throat. I squeezed Tucker's hand, hoping he'd understand I would stick by his side.

Tucker dragged a hand over his face. "Fuck. None of this is going down the way it should."

I sucked in a cleansing breath at his words, not sure what he meant.

Tucker shook his head and took a deep breath before addressing his friend. "It's not what you think. I love her, man."

"Tuck, stop saying that," I said through clenched teeth, narrowing my eyes at him.

"Wilde, it's true." He dropped a chaste kiss on my forehead. "I love you."

"You what?" Nick blinked.

Dahlia stopped at his side, her gaze sweeping between Tucker and me.

"Addi? What's this all about?" My best friend studied me, crinkles forming around her eyes.

Tucker turned around to glance at me. "I love her. I love you. And we might, or might not, be having a baby together."

Nick's lips parted, but nothing came out.

"Tuck—" I breathed out his name, bit it sounded more like a request.

A yelp exited Dahlia's mouth. "A baby?"

Nick blinked, faster this time, watching us as if we spoke another language.

"Addi?" Dahlia's silken voice brought me out of my trance. "Speak."

I raised my hands and let them fall to my thighs. "We…we have no idea. It's something your mama said. Anyway, it's a long story. I'll tell you more once I know for sure, okay? Sorry to rain on your parade, guys. You weren't supposed to find out. Not this way at least." I stared down, feeling a bit ashamed. My heart beat so fast I expected it to jump out of my chest.

"Addison Samantha Wilde, look at me." Damn it, my friend meant business when she used my full name.

As if it hurt to do so, I slowly moved my eyes in her direction.

She watched me with an expression I had never seen before. "Are you guys like *together* together?"

"We are," Tucker said at the same time I said, "No."

Both our heads swiveled until we faced each other again. For a moment, I was tempted to believe him when he said, "Trust me."

Dahlia continued. "Are you guys happy? There's so much we missed. Last night, you two—" She sighed. "We'll talk about it later." Her gaze bore into mine. "Do what you gotta do. I'm here for you. Always." She moved closer and enveloped me in her arms. Because Dahlia Ellis was the best. Always had been. And would forever be. "Go, get a test. And let me know if I'm going to be an aunt as soon as you find out, okay?"

I nodded against her shoulder.

"And while you're at it, touch up your makeup. You

have mascara stains down your cheeks. You look terrible." She winked, and both of us burst out laughing. Yeah, I would be all right.

Nick traced his eyebrow with a fingertip, lost in his own mind. He snapped out of his stupor with a shake of his head. "Keep us updated. Whoa. Never saw this one coming. When I think about it, I'm not even surprised..." He sighed. "Spare me the details of how this happened. You two are… Wow, I miss the words right now. Babe, we should have bet on it." He secured an arm around his wife. Devotion and unconditional love passed between them. He brought his attention back to Tucker and me. "Do what you have to do. I'd say wrap it up, but I think it's too late."

"Come on," Tucker said after they exchanged one of their one-shoulder man hugs, helping me to my feet and lacing his fingers through mine. "Let's get out of here."

Dahlia snaked her arm through her husband's. "If we had, I would have won," she whispered.

I shook my head, unable to hide my smile.

"Let's go. I wanna dance," she added.

Nick's stare focused on his best friend for a few seconds before he led his bride away and kissed her as if nobody else existed in their world.

Hand in hand, Tucker and I sauntered away, following in their footsteps.

"Wilde, no matter what, I'm not going anywhere. Lean on me."

Chapter 2

Tucker

In front of the bathroom door, I paced while Addison peed on a stick. Full breath in. Full breath out. In the last hour, I'd lost the ability to inflate my lungs on my own, without having to remind myself. All my thoughts were a tight, disordered weave inside my head. My heart must have done a dozen flip-flops in my chest in the same amount of time.

I not only had proclaimed my love to the woman who might be bearing my child, but also announced my feelings in front of my best friend. Dahlia and Nick promising to love each other forever earlier had turned me into a sappy version of myself.

Fear crawled along my spine. I was just getting my head around being in a steady relationship, and now I had to consider that I might also become a dad.

Every word I spoke to Addison earlier sent my heart

into overdrive as I replayed them in my head. On a loop. I meant them, but it didn't mean they didn't terrorize me.

It wasn't normal for me to be this obsessed with a woman. Being in love and all the sentimental shit was Nick's thing. It had never been mine before.

I snapped out of my restless state and focused on the door.

For how long had Addison been in there? Who took more than one minute to pee?

I rapped on the wooden panel with my knuckles. "Wilde, come on. Give a man a little reassurance. I'm dying here. Are you okay? Do you need anything? Can I come in?"

Not a word. Nothing.

Resting my forehead against the closed door, I pleaded, "Addison? Let me in. I wanna be there for you. No matter what it says."

Still nothing. Some heavy breathing sound—kind of a leaden snore—reverberated from the other side.

My pulse throbbed. "I'm coming in, sweetheart. You ain't keeping me in the dark any longer."

The doorknob turned in my hand, and I stepped inside the room.

The sight before me turned my blood to ice. Addison was curled in a ball on the tiled floor, her maid of honor gown spread around her in a chiffon puddle. At first, I thought she was crying, but then I realized she was actually asleep. My blood warmed up and my heart swelled at the realization.

She was beautiful beyond words. Half her hair was braided in a fancy updo. A rosy flush covered her cheeks. Long, mascara-coated lashes rimmed her eyes. She resembled a doll. Her full lips formed a pout, one I was dying to tug between my teeth. And kiss senseless.

Black streaks lined her cheeks.

Fight had left her, and she now seemed at peace after going to war.

With my back against the wall, I slid down until my ass hit the floor, lifting her limp body into my lap. She stirred but didn't wake up. We stayed there for a long time while I brushed her hair away from her delicate face, my mind spinning. In her hand, Addison was clutching the stick. Carefully, I tugged at it, the urge to know what it said too strong to resist and wondering if life was about to send me on a ride I had never seen coming. One I wasn't sure I was prepared for.

She let go of the test when my fingers curled around it, and I pulled it free. A dark pink line appeared in one window. My throat closed, and it pained to swallow the lump growing there. My gaze scanned the second window, where I noted an almost invisible pink line. Was my vision playing tricks on me, or was it really there? That was the moment I stopped breathing. The moment I got dizzy and pressed the floor beside me with one palm to keep my balance, as if I were at risk of falling into a bottomless well and never seeing daylight again. I dragged a hand over my face. Fuck. I had no idea how this thing worked, but my gut told me my apprehensions would turn out to be real. With an extended arm, I grabbed the packaging set on the counter. Even after reading the instructions twice, I still couldn't confirm with certainty what the almost-invisible line meant. Deep down, I was aware I did know the meaning, but it was like my brain refused to acknowledge it.

Relishing her presence and craving her touch, I cradled Addison's body to my heart and closed my eyes, resting my head against the wall behind me.

With my eyes shut, I prayed the entire day was a

dream, and Nick and Dahlia's wedding hadn't happened just yet. That I'd get a do-over. To make everything right.

"Here you are," a male voice said, bringing me out of my slumber. Did I fall asleep too? It took me a few seconds to realize the voice had addressed me. As if glued to my skin, I pried my lids open, briefly wondering where I was as my vision returned. The sight of Addison, still deep asleep in my arms, dressed in her yellow gown, rebooted my brain. I stretched my neck, perused the room, and met my best friend's gaze.

He cleared his throat and sat before me. "So?"

I shrugged. "I can't tell. It's ambiguous." I pushed the stick I'd been strangling in my hand into his and watched him as he rubbed his jaw and twisted it between his fingers.

"How do women understand this?" he asked with a frown.

I sighed. "No idea. I read the instructions several times. I'm still not one hundred percent sure."

He sighed, looked at me, and breathed out. "Do you love her for real? What I mean is, what's going on between you two?"

"It's complicated." My eyes drifted to Addison, and I studied the pattern of her breathing. A lopsided smile grazed my lips. "There's something strong simmering between us. We've spent some time together. The connection is real."

"Wow. But I thought she annoyed the shit out of you."

"She does…most of the time. Or rather, she used to. Now I can't resist her. I thought I'd seen everything, but she's wilder than me, man. I never believed it could be possible. Her kind of crazy unleashed mine. I don't know how to explain it. It isn't just physical. It's chemical. I spent all my evenings at home in the last six weeks, waiting for her to call. One weekend, she surprised me and flew to

Chicago. When she left, I missed her scent on my pillow, the way she tied her messy hair after she woke up, or her heartbeat when I held her at night. We spent another long weekend together in Nashville. A jerk was all over her, and it drove me nuts. Never felt that kind of jealousy before. We met with Barry and the guys, and even they fell under her charm. She's special. All this time, it wasn't even about sex. So, yeah, I think this is real." I paused to order my thoughts. "Jesus, listen to me. I'm turning into you, man." I ran my free hand over my face as realization set in. "Damn it."

Nick furrowed his brows and offered me a pointed look. "Is it such a bad thing? Being me, I mean. Look, I'm happy. I just got married today to the most amazing woman I know. I have a family of my own now, a great business, an incredible little boy, friends. Being me is great, actually."

I tilted my head back and let out a silent chuckle. "Yeah. It could be worse… I guess." My laughter died. "What am I gonna do? I'm clueless when it comes to women."

Nick smirked. "No, you're not. You've been studying them for years. I think you'll figure it out. Just be honest if you can't commit, okay? She doesn't deserve to be misled."

I shook my head. "I would never. She's the first woman I'm not thinking about getting into her pants every time we see each other. Well, yeah, I do, obviously, but I like that we can chat for hours about other things. That our connection is even stronger outside the bedroom. It's not only about sex all the time. Just so you know, I may have broken rule number one back in Nashville six weeks ago, but in my defense, I have no memory of it whatsoever."

"How so?"

"It's a long story, but we kinda bet we would each bring

a woman back to the hotel the first night. I have no idea how it happened, but when we woke up the next morning, we had hooked up together. You know the morning you barged in—"

"Fuck. She was the woman you trashed the hotel room with?"

"Yep. And neither of us could recall anything."

"And that unbelievable shower story?"

"That was part true. I helped her with her speech, we fell asleep, and I had to drag her into the shower to wake her up. Full disclosure, we spent the next day together. In bed. That's the only time I broke the rules willingly. Sorry I lied to you."

Nick flicked his hand. "You're both old enough to make your own decisions. I shouldn't have given you those rules to start with. It just… I don't know. Somehow, I feared the day you two would meet. You're very much alike. Dynamite. Amazing people. Loyal friends. But sometimes, unpredictable." His eyes trained on us for a moment. "For what it's worth, Dahlia said you two are a match made in heaven. I have to agree. No pressure, man."

I snickered and shook my head.

"Anyway, it's almost dinner time. We would very much like for you two to join us. If Addi feels all right. She looked exhausted earlier. Heard pregnancy can do that."

"Give us a few minutes. I know she'll request some time to fix her makeup and stuff." I held my breath. "And I have no idea how she'll react to this," I said, pointing to the pregnancy test still in Nick's hand with my chin.

My friend handed it back to me and moved to his feet. "If you two are meant to be, I'm glad you're the one for her. She's amazing. And you're my best friend." He stopped on his way out and spun around. "Never would I have thought I'd see you sitting on a bathroom floor one day, caring for a woman with stars in your eyes. Somehow, it suits you."

He mumbled something else I didn't quite catch and left.

I blinked, still wondering if this entire day had been a dream after all.

———

Addison and I joined the rest of the wedding party, still unsure if she was pregnant or not. After she woke up, she read the instructions herself and stared at me with doubts in her eyes. Instead of panicking, we'd decided to take another test the next day. Besides, there was nothing we could really do about it tonight.

We sat by our best friends for dinner. Gave speeches. Stole glances. Kissed. And danced under the stars when the band started playing one of Carter Hills's hits. *Our song.*

I pressed my hand to her lower back, enjoying the feel of her body nestled against mine. "Whatever the test says, I'm not going anywhere. We'll find a way to be together. To work it out. If that's what you wish too."

Addison nodded against my chest as my lips skimmed the top of her head. "Thanks. For being here with me," she whispered.

My insides clenched at the sound of her voice. "Are you feeling better? I'm glad you ate something. Mrs. Ellis warned me to keep an eye on you."

"She did, huh? She worries about me. But I'm fine. Or I will be. There's still something bothering me, though."

I lifted her chin with one finger. "What is it? Ask me anything. I'll be your loyal servant."

She detached herself from me and rose to her tiptoes

until her lips grazed my earlobe. "I'm still horny. For you. Are you coming home with me afterward? My nap felt amazing, and now I'm ready to have some fun. And there's no point in avoiding you any longer. All my arguments are pointless now."

"Wilde, you sure?"

She nodded, her irises swimming in lust.

"You won't have to ask me twice. I'll be whatever you want me to be as long as you'll have me." I kissed the tip of her nose and pulled her closer to my chest, wondering what would happen next, and whether our lives would be forever entangled—and irrevocably changed—by the next morning. "Two weeks without you was pure torture. I'm obsessed with that pretty mouth of yours." I slapped her ass, and she yelped. "We've somehow managed not to tear each other's clothes off for over a month. I've been patient so far, but every second I'm not inside you is agony."

"I know. And I'm aching for you too."

"That's what I'm talking about, sweetheart." I held her hand in mine and brought it to my crotch. "Feel the effect you have on me."

She grew flustered, her eyes flaring. "Take me home, Tuck. I need you tonight. I don't wanna be alone. Rumor has it I might have a surprise for you," she said, mischief shining in her eyes.

Around midnight, Addison could barely stay up on her feet. We said our goodbyes before climbing into my rental car. As I pulled away, my hand instinctively went to her thigh, giving it a soft squeeze.

Addison rested her head on my shoulder, and I felt whole again. For the first time, the fragments of my life seemed to belong together.

I parked in the driveway of Dahlia's old house and turned off the engine. Unable to resist the maid of honor for another second, I pulled her to me over the console between our seats. My mouth found hers, our lips taking their sweet time, memorizing every detail. I curled a hand behind her head, holding her in place as my mouth devoured hers.

She purred before pushing back, one hand splayed across my chest. "Gimme five minutes, okay? This surprise I told you about… It's…it's my best man gift to you. Something I put together with you in mind."

I arched a brow. "I thought it was that T-shirt?"

A heartfelt laugh broke free. "Yeah. And this. You'll see. I swear, you'll like it…very much."

She exited the car and waving at me, entered the house, turning the lights on as she made her way to the second floor.

I caught a glimpse of my ridiculous grin in the rearview mirror and shook my head in disbelief. I was becoming everything I'd always sworn I wouldn't. And somehow, right now, that thought didn't scare me. I even found it… thrilling.

My smile widened, and my heart's frantic thump softened.

When the longest five minutes of my life ended, I made my way inside and locked the door behind me. I followed the trail of lights to the master bedroom upstairs.

In the doorway, I swallowed. Hard. And swallowed again. Addison looked like every man's wet dream, all sexy wearing the skimpy red lingerie I'd gifted her, tied to the bed, a selection of accessories lying around her barely covered body. I had no idea what the rules of the game were, but now that I got sight of the playground, I couldn't wait and was more than ready to have some fun.

Like a hunter, I stalked my prey. The one I remembered the taste of, as it was still lingering on my tongue even after over a month. Her red-painted lips, resembling juicy berries, looked enticing. And forbidden.

My dick twitched in my pants. *Easy, boy.* I pushed it down with an open palm to tame its eagerness as desire coursed through me, unrestrained.

"Wilde, you're something else. I thought I'd seen everything." I pulled my shirt off, nearly tearing it to shreds, the fabric burning against my skin, and held my breath.

Unable to look away, I padded toward the siren lying on the bed, losing myself in the mesmerizing blue depth of her eyes.

"You can't ask a guy not to think about you when you do shit like this, sweetheart. You're perfect, and I can already predict we both won't be getting much sleep tonight." I blew out a long breath as I neared the bed, letting my knuckles trace along her jaw. "I thought you were tired?"

She shrugged. "I was. But my need for you is stronger."

Now bare-chested and about to combust at the seams, I smoothed her bottom lip with my thumb, taking the time to make sure she was speaking the truth and that a little exercise wouldn't tire her any more than she already was. Addison shivered on the bed and moaned, making her even more irresistible, and confirming she really wanted to do this. A guttural groan left my mouth in response. Jesus, I was so weak when it came to her. She sucked my finger into her mouth, her tongue playing around the tip before she released it with a pop. A ripple of sensation surged up my spine, tightening my balls and firing through my body.

"Ready to play with me, *Tuuuck*?"

My throat worked as I tried to form coherent words. I hadn't realized how badly I'd missed that flirty, playful side of her until now.

My voice, sounding more like a growl, sent fresh,

wicked twinkles to her eyes. "Tell me the rules, Wilde. It's been six weeks. I'm more than ready for a do-over… To be honest, I've been ready for a while." I leaned forward, my lips finding hers, my hands locking on her hipbones, holding her in place as she wiggled beneath me.

She bit my lower lip, almost sending me over the edge with the simple gesture, and I blinked as reality hit me. It doused the burning desire inside me. "Wilde, we can't do this." I stumbled backward, trying to escape her magnetic field. With her hands tied over her head, there wasn't much she could do to keep me from stepping back.

Addison's lips pursed as she watched me, hurt painting her face. "Tuck. Don't go. We can talk about it. I thought… huh…it doesn't matter. We can just sleep. Or cuddle. Be with me tonight. Don't go."

Was she under the impression I didn't long for her? That I wouldn't do anything, short of selling my soul, to be with her? To get a taste of her? I scratched my temple and sat beside her, brushing her hair back with my fingers. I didn't have enough eyes to admire her the way she deserved to be. And the way I craved to.

"No, it's not that. I-I haven't changed my mind, but if you're pregnant, we'll hurt the baby… *I'll* hurt the baby."

She studied my face for a beat, but soon her clear laughter broke the silence of the night. "Tuck, if it does exist, it's like chickpea size." She brought her thumb and forefinger close together above her head, as if indicating something tiny. "It would be like this big. And even when it gets bigger, I don't know a lot about babies, but I know sex can't hurt them. No matter how impressive your manhood is. Stop fighting this."

I huffed, wondering if she spoke the truth. Amid everything that had been going on today, I hadn't had time to look up safe sex during pregnancy.

"Tucker. Listen to me. You can't poke the baby. And there's a reason why pregnant women are horny all the time. It wouldn't be fair if we couldn't indulge in sex. Let's play now, okay? You can't leave a woman all tied up on a bed and do nothing about it."

A naughty grin formed on her lips, and it broke my restraints. Forgetting all about my fears for a few hours, I plunged forward, intent on rocking her night and making up for the things we hadn't done since the last time we had sex.

Later, entangled in the shower, our bodies were still vibrating with lust and endorphins—and contentment.

"Where did you learn to do that thing with your finger?" I asked Addison, still mesmerized by everything we had just done.

She shrugged. She'd just given me the most erotic experience of my life, and she fucking shrugged. I shook my head, the tip of my spine still tingling, and my chafed cock aching for more. Usually a straightforward lover, I wasn't used to sex with toys, but Addison made the game both enticing and exciting.

"In college, I experimented a lot," she said, motioning to the bedroom. "Hope I didn't traumatize you."

"Sweetheart, it'll take more than some balls and chains to scare me away. You should know that by now." My tongue trailed kisses down the length of her throat. "I think I could get used to this. With you."

She spun in my embrace and looped her arms around my neck, her eyes glistening. "Want to go for a second round? We haven't tried the hot candle wax yet."

"We should get some sleep. Never thought I'd say that, but my dick is begging for some rest. You should rest too. Today has been quite an emotional ride."

She stared at me and sighed, her smile never faltering.

I kissed her pouty mouth as flashes of everything those lips had done to me in the last two hours danced before my eyes.

"We'll have a re-match tomorrow. I'm in town for another week at least."

"Tucker Philips, are you taking a vacation?"

I snickered. "Trying to. We'll see how it goes. Nick suggested I stay here for some time. I wanna indulge in a change of scenery. They say mountain air is addictive… I think it's time I test that theory."

"Awesome. Because, technically, I'm here for two more days. You better be a man of your word. I'm not done with you just yet."

My squeeze around her tightened. "Watch out, Wilde, or I'll fall for you." I winked, and we both grinned.

"I thought you already had?"

I palmed my chest with one hand. "Touché."

"Tuck, you don't need to sweet talk me. Or promise things."

"I'm not. I just want to be there for you. With you. No matter what, don't fight it."

I twirled her around and enveloped her with my arms, resting my chin in the crook of her neck. I lowered my hands to cup her breasts. "I think these bad girls missed me too."

"Go ahead, keep boosting your ego, big guy." Addison playfully slapped my arm and tilted her head. I leaned in, meeting her lips halfway, and the world outside this shower disappeared.

For now.

Chapter 3

Tucker

The next day, we woke up at ten and lingered in bed for hours, surviving on nothing but sex and snacks, our bodies tangled in the sheets. Addison lay by my side, still naked, her legs intertwined with mine, her head propped on my chest, and her bright blue eyes staring straight at me. She nibbled her thumbnail, a habit I'd learned over the last month meant something was bothering her. I stayed silent, waiting for her to sort out her thoughts.

"What are we going to do?" She blinked and refocused her gaze on me, as if trying to read my mind. "If we're having a baby? I live in Atlanta, and you're in Chicago. I can't ask you to move across the country, and I'm not sure I'm cut out for the chilly northern winters. How would we even co-parent? How would that even work? Flying up and down the country every week with a newborn? That makes no sense. This is the worst-case scenario. How could a night we can't even remember lead to this? Maybe it's just a false alarm…and now I'm rambling. I'm Addison Wilde. I don't ramble. See? These hormones are already affecting my brain—and my sanity. I can't live like this for another eight months."

She closed her eyes and took a deep breath in, held it for a second or two, then let it out.

When her eyes roved back to mine, I held them. "We don't need to make all those decisions just yet… Not before another test or a doctor's appointment. But to answer your question, yes, I would move across the country to be with you." I pushed myself to a sitting position and lifted Addison with me, keeping her nestled against my chest, my stare trained on her face. "Wilde, in the time we've known each other, you've become a huge part of my life. Things have been off—almost strange—on my end for a while now… Hard to explain. I've been feeling like my life is passing me by, with no idea how to fix it… Somehow, everything lately has lost its appeal. All my friends have moved on. I've forgotten how to be content….until you came along.

"Every time we're together and you're beside me, it soothes all my doubts…all my insecurities. I don't feel so lost anymore. And…I can't believe I'm saying this, but I worship the ground you walk on. I can't explain the effect you have on me. Whenever we're together, or even when we talk, everything falls into place. It feels like rediscovering my true self…like I no longer have to hide behind expectations or pretend to be someone I'm not. That I can be myself and it's enough. Whatever it means. No one— not even my best friends—has been able to make me drop the act. Only you did."

A single tear rolled down her cheek, and I caught it with the pad of my thumb.

"Don't cry, sweetheart."

Addison watched me as if I held answers she didn't possess, and my heart waltzed behind my ribs at the sight.

"Marry me."

She blinked slowly. "What?"

I cupped her cheek with my hands and leaned in to catch her lips between mine. "Let's get married. You and me. Make it official."

"But I may not be pregnant, Tuck."

I searched her gaze. "See, I don't care. I want you. All of you. Now. No matter what the test says. Let's not get influenced by the result. I love *you*."

Addison blinked again, as if to make sure she was awake and that this wasn't some dream. "And I thought I was the impulsive one?"

A loud chuckle broke free. "I have my moments."

"You're still in shock about the pregnancy scare. Let's not rush things, okay?"

"Nick once told me, when you know, you know, when he was talking about Dahlia. This is the first time I under-stand what he meant that day. Because what we share is real...and rare. Wilde, you're the only person who can tame my ways, who makes me yearn for more." I brushed my nose against hers. "If you weren't aware by now, I'm a smart guy. Nothing I do or say is always as spontaneous as it sounds. Most of the time, I have plans. And rules. Or at least, I used to. Not anymore. You shattered them all. You freed me from some invisible ties and stole the best friend title, Wilde. I don't see it changing anytime soon. You just get me. You don't require a manual to understand how I work. It all comes naturally to you."

"Wow. It-it's a big commitment. You've become one of my closest friends too, Tuck." Her lips searched mine. "Truth is, I've talked to you more in the six weeks we've known each other than to all my friends combined in the last year. And Dahlia and I talk a lot. Seriously, we talk a *loooottt*." The ghost of a smile formed on her lips, still pressed against mine, her breath sending shivers through me. "I can't believe I'm actually considering this. Am I awake?"

"Yes, I promise you are."

We kissed before she pulled back.

"Let's say we were to do this. Would you want a ceremony or to elope?"

I shrugged. "Anything that would make you happy. Since we never do anything half-assed—or like most people do, whether it's big, small, or messy—I'd vote for Vegas. You, me, Nick, and Dahlia. Your parents if you want them there. And we could throw a reception later. For everyone else we didn't invite. What do you think?"

She nestled against me, and we sank into the mattress, my arms holding her close. "I love how you think. The best of both worlds. Why am I excited about this?" She let out a contented sigh, her happiness impossible to hide. "Let's do this. Tomorrow we'll pick a date."

With a single skilled motion, I caught her wrists and rolled her onto her back, getting lost in the blue sea of her eyes. My cock sprang wood, and while I busied myself kissing the shit out of my *fiancée*—was that how I should call her from now on?—I pushed two fingers inside her, relishing the way her back arched and her legs opened to make room for me.

I trailed kisses down her throat, along her collarbones, in the sweet spot under her earlobe. I traced her jawline with my tongue and found my way down to her perky breasts. I laved one nipple with circular strokes and sucked on it as she cried my name, her breathing quick and unsteady, as if begging me not to stop. With one hand curled behind my head, she positioned me over her other breast. Her hsilent plea made me cherish her second nipple the same way.

I lowered myself until I could kiss her belly and traced the seam between her thighs with the tip of my tongue. Her body trembled, and I moved back up, unable to wait another second before sliding my dick home, where it belonged.

Home. That was how being with this woman made me feel.

In perfect rhythm, we moved together, Addison whimpering each time my length slid in and out of her. No doubt her fingernails left marks on my back as she shifted the angle of her pelvis, deepening our connection.

With hooded lids and rosy lips, she looked fucking fabulous.

"Mine," I said between slow thrusts, trying to lengthen the pleasure, not ready to be done just yet. "Addison Wilde, you're mine." My mouth found hers, our tongues entwining in an erotic number.

Something had shifted between us. I could feel it in the way our bodies communicated. In the way we kissed. And the way we touched.

I nuzzled her neck, letting the fruity scent of her imprint on all my senses. Using my elbows to support myself, I leaned closer, every inch of me aching to touch every inch of her.

"Oh God, don't stop what you're doing." Her hips buckled and rolled with every plea leaving her mouth. She reached for my hand, and we linked our fingers as I increased the pace. She locked her other hand around my nape and drew me closer. Until I almost crushed her under my weight. "Don't you dare stop."

A raw, shuddering cry spilled from her luscious lips,

and it almost brought me to a point of rupture. I had never felt this way before. My entire self had a hard time comprehending the shift taking place within me. Without breaking eye contact, I pounded into her until we both went over the edge, undone and satiated.

I had never made love to a woman before, yet this moment, what we'd just done, felt like nothing else could capture the depth of our connection. The way I felt. The bubble we found ourselves floating in. The love enveloping us.

———

"Want me to go get a test now?" I asked as Addison and I snuggled in bed later that afternoon. Except to grab food and use the bathroom, we hadn't left the bed all day.

She shook her head. "Nah. I still haven't got my Tucker fix. Don't go right now. Stay with me a little longer."

"I love Jamie for a girl," I said. "And Lucas for a boy."

She twisted between my arms to kiss me. "Baby names? Really?"

"Why not?"

"Because we know nothing yet."

"Just a thought. I'm restless. My brain is thinking… analyzing…"

"I can relate. So many unanswered questions keep holding my thoughts hostage. If we're doing this, then I agree with Jamie for a girl. And I love Jamieson for a boy. Anyway, let's not get ahead of ourselves. I'm not even late yet."

"Doesn't matter. I want everything with you."

"Hold me tight, big guy. I gotta catch up on some sleep."

And with the only woman my heart had ever beaten for tucked safely against my chest, it became clear to me that no one-night stand could ever match the quiet peace I felt in that instant. With a cocky grin lingering on my lips, I buried my face in the mass of her hair and drifted off in no time.

I woke up to an empty bed. A quick perusal of the room was all it took to confirm that Addison wasn't here. The sun lingered low on the horizon, pink and orange brushstrokes decorating the sky. I put a pair of boxer briefs on and made my way downstairs.

My feet refused to move forward when I entered the kitchen, the vision in front of me stealing my breath away. Dressed only in lacy panties, Addison swayed her hips to the rhythm of a country song while she busied herself prepping food. Her hair was piled at the top of her head—the way I liked—and her left shoulder bore love marks. Her skin, lightly tanned, glowed in the low light. Every delicious curve of her body, the ones I'd memorized by heart and could recognize in the dark, tempted me.

Seconds later, I had her back to my front, my arms wrapped around her waist, my chin resting on her shoulder. "Is this what married life with you will be like? You cooking topless. Because if it is, we're flying to Vegas tonight, ditching any other plans we may have."

She spun to face me, her round breasts pressing into my bare chest while my hands descended to her ass, molding to its flesh. She yelped, and I swallowed it as my mouth feasted on hers.

"You still wanna go through with this insane idea?" she asked, leaning back to catch her breath.

"Yeah. Don't you?"

She shrugged. "I do, but it's big. And rushed. How do we know we're ready?"

I took a step back to study her face. "How did I become the one looking for commitment, and you the one having doubts?"

She brushed loose strands of hair away from her eyes. "Marriage is sacred to me, Tuck. It's important. It means something. In my mind, you don't do it twice. Unless your husband dies one night and leaves you pregnant and alone. Then, until then, you're allowed a do-over. I already told you I've been burned in the past. A baby, a wedding, don't you think it's too much, too soon?" Moisture welled up in her eyes. "See? I'm an emotional ticking bomb once again. When will this stop?" She hid her face in her palms, her shoulders heaving.

The sight broke me, and I tightened my arms around her, reminding her she wasn't alone. Not anymore.

"Don't cry. I don't know what to do when you do. It fucks with my heart. It breaks me." Silent tears streaked her cheeks, and I clung to her tighter. "I know it's a lot to process, but we won't do anything you're not ready for, okay? If you're pregnant, it's important to me that our baby has a family. A strong foundation. I told you about my parents. When I'm in, Wilde, I'm all in. I never do things halfway. You can't just have parts of me. Only the whole package deal, nothing less."

"Thank you. For...for being understanding. And supportive. I promise I'm not always a weepy mess. For what it's worth, I like your package. I love it."

I kissed her forehead. "I know, babe. Whatever it is, we'll figure it out. And by the way, my package loves you too."

"It doesn't show right now," she pointed to her tear-stricken face, "but I'm happy and grateful that if we're having a baby, you're the daddy."

We finished prepping dinner together, the remnants of our last conversation permeating the air around us.

"Tomorrow we'll go to the doctor," I said after a long stretch of silence.

Addison nodded, her eyes still red-rimmed, a thankful, tight-lipped smile playing on her lips. She was now dressed in one of my T-shirts, the one I gave her when she visited me in Chicago a month ago, bringing my undivided attention to her long legs.

Later, wrapped in a blanket on the couch, we watched a movie, her head resting onto my lap while I twirled the strands of her hair around my fingers.

"Thank you," she said, "for not thinking I'm a nutcase."

"I'm actually a big fan of your brand of crazy. Just so you know."

She poked her tongue at me and chuckled, and it eased the tension that had been surrounding us for the last few hours. That sound… If only I could listen to her laughter on repeat—forever.

With a long intake of breath, I summoned my courage. "Addison Wilde, would you be my girlfriend? I know it sounds juvenile, but I've never said those words to anyone before."

She nodded and moved to her knees, straddling me, her arms loose around my neck. "I'd love to be." She grinned. "I really do. I check *Yes*. And for what it's worth, being your first is kinda exciting." She smirked. "You know you proposed before we officially started dating, right?"

I mirrored the tilt of her lips. "It's us. Better get used to it."

———

The next morning, I woke up first. Little by little, I eased my body away from Addison's embrace, my heart heavy at the idea of leaving the bed, and got dressed in the dark. All my clothes were still at the hotel, so I did a walk of shame in the suit I wore for Dahlia and Nick's wedding two days prior. Real nice. On my tiptoes, I exited the bedroom and made my way downstairs.

Forty minutes later, I was back with breakfast, all my stuff, and two pregnancy tests, plus an appointment with a doctor Nick recommended for later that day. The lady at the drugstore gave me detailed instructions for the pregnancy tests to make sure we would do it right this time after I asked her over a dozen questions.

The house was silent when I entered through the kitchen door.

In the hallway upstairs, I undressed, ready to slip under the covers again and let my body mold to Addison's until she woke up.

In the bedroom doorway, I stopped in my tracks. My eyes took her in—hair disheveled, shoulders slumped—sitting on the edge of the mattress.

"Hey, you're awake. I had this plan to come back to bed for an hour or two. With you." I traipsed closer. "How are you feeling?" I studied her features closely. "What's going on?" I sat beside her and draped an arm around her shoulders.

The scent of her shampoo filled my nostrils, and I didn't find it as overwhelming as the day we met. In all honesty, I missed it every time we were apart.

"Tuck, I…I'm not pregnant."

"What do you mean, you're not pregnant?"

She dried her teary eyes with the sleeve of the hoodie she'd put on. "False alarm. My…my period started. I've been right all…I've been right all along."

"You sure?" I winced. "Sorry. Stupid question. Are you okay?"

She nodded. "It's for the best. We're not even a couple, and we're not ready for this. Baby, married life. It-it's better this way."

I swallowed, avoiding her eyes. Why were her words sounding like a death sentence right now?

Did she mean any of it? Sure, I had no clue what it meant to be in a steady relationship, to be a husband or a dad, but when my thoughts drifted to Addison, I always figured we could do this. Together.

"You must be relieved?" she asked, her head buried in my chest as my fingers combed her hair back.

"No." My tone sounded harsher than I meant it to be.

"Well, I am."

I tried to argue, but the words got stuck in my throat. Were emotions making her say those things? Didn't she hear a word I said yesterday? I remained silent, unsure of how to approach the new turn of events. The temperature of the bedroom seared. The gears of my brain worked overtime, about to catch fire. A chill skated up my back. Before I could overreact or panic, I pressed a kiss to her temple, untangled myself from her grip, and jumped to my feet.

"Gimme a minute, would you?" I said, locking myself in the en-suite bathroom.

I ran a hand over my hair. Splashed water over my face. Paced the room.

As if someone had turned off the lights of my heart, I slumped on the edge of the bathtub, curving my back and resting my elbows on my knees.

The lining of my throat itched. My heart tumbled down my chest. My stomach felt as if it'd been filled with lead.

After a while, a soft knock on the door brought me out of my daze.

"Tuck, are you all right? You've been in there for over thirty minutes. Can…can we talk?"

I cleared my throat and pushed my emotions down. "Yeah. Coming."

I met her on the other side of the door and wound my arms around her small frame.

"Don't be mad, okay? I changed my plans," Addison said, her voice trembling as she glanced down.

Something was wrong. I could tell. My heart pumped ice instead of warm blood. "Wh-what do you mean, you changed your plans?" I asked, my fingers digging into her hipbones, fearing she'd vanish if I didn't hold on to her. All I yearned for was her warmth. Her love. And her affection. Anything she could give me.

"My bus is leaving at the end of the afternoon."

I jerked away and ran both hands through my hair. This was a mistake. A freaking joke. Did I hear her right? Was this entire weekend even real, or was my imagination playing tricks on me?"Whoa. Pause for a sec. You're leaving? Yesterday we were making wedding plans and believing we might have a baby together, and now you're ditching me? What about us? How do you see our relationship evolving? Are we doing the long distance thing for a while? Do you expect me to move soon? Tell me what's the plan now because you lost me. I'm confused. Whatever we choose, I'll do my best to be available and make you a priority. But if you go now, I have no idea when we'll be able to see each other again. Or have this conversation. It's not something I wanna discuss over the phone. We've barely spent enough time together this weekend. After all that's happened in the last two days, I'm not ready to let you walk away. Now that our friends know about us, we don't have to hide anymore."

Addison traced lines over my shirt with her fingernails, avoiding my eyes.

I frowned, unable to look away.

Was she kidding right now?

My heart cracked and crashed on the floor.

I scratched my temple, trying to make sense of her rejection.

Yesterday seemed like a lifetime away.

"Can we talk about it?" I pleaded.

"Sure. The last thing I want is to break your heart."

"You have a funny way of showing it."

She reached for my hand. "Let's have breakfast. I'll explain everything."

Chapter 4

Addison

"Tuck, we're rushing into things. Every time in the past I've jumped into something that wasn't meant to be, it backfired. You're too important to me for us to go down that road and risk compromising what we have. I don't want you to feel like you have to force things on your end or become someone you're not just because you think it's your duty or what I expect."

We faced each other on the couch, eating bagels Tucker bought earlier and sipping tea. "Because caffeine isn't good for you," he had said earlier.

"I agree I don't have any dating experience, but let me ask you something. How can you tell our timing isn't right if we don't give our relationship a chance?" He slid his jaw back and forth. "I usually aim for what I want in life. Never backing down but always going all in. This is how I work."

"The thing is…we shouldn't have to try. It should come

naturally. Not by rushing into things and getting married on a whim."

My words echoed the conversation I'd had with Carter the night we all had dinner on that rooftop in Nashville six weeks ago. *Don't push it. Be yourself. Let them come to you.* Right now, I couldn't agree more.

Tucker rested his palm on my cheek. "Wilde, you are the queen of impulsiveness. You make rash decisions and always rationalize them like they make sense. I know because I've been on the receiving end many times already. I've never told a woman I love her before. It's all new to me, but deep down, I know it's right. I wanna give it a shot. Be together. See where it takes us."

I shook my head.

"Why not? I've heard what you said, but it doesn't mean I have to agree."

"Tuck, I've played men, and I've been played. With my exes…I went all in, never thinking twice. See where it got me."

"To me," he said, a tremolo in his voice.

For the third time, I was presented with a vulnerable version of Tucker Philips. Placing my mug down on the coffee table, I squeezed his hands between mine. "Tuck, you're a player…a womanizer." He growled. "Okay, a reformed one. But you proclaimed yourself as one for the longest time since we've known each other. You never shied away from who you are, and I love that about you. Your authenticity. Your no-bullshit attitude. As much as we get along and I like you, I'm fearful of risking my heart. I've been burned too many times. My dating record isn't great. My last two boyfriends were liars and cheaters. One was married, and I had no clue. Yep, I was the other woman, and the last one was a serial polygamist. Not my proudest moments."

"First, I'm nothing like those creeps. Second, I'm done with this shit. Already told you." He inhaled. "I want an *us*. We're great together. Wilde, you can't deny the chemistry we share. You're the one complicating things right now. Not me."

Pain masked his face. My heart leaked. So did my eyes.

I ran the back of my hand under my nose. "Maybe we should step back and give each other some space. Figure things out. Take the time apart to assess where we stand and where we're headed. Not under the pressure of a surprise baby or a shotgun wedding."

Tucker pushed away, and the distance he put between us sent a fresh batch of tears to my eyes.

He swallowed before speaking, his words drenched in emotions. "So, that's it? After everything that has happened this weekend and all we've shared, you're ready to move on and forget all about it? All about us?"

I tried to keep my calm as tsunamis and storms battled inside me.

I inched closer, but Tucker turned around, avoiding my gaze. Hurt seemed to pour from every inch of him, and it shattered another layer of my heart.

I spoke around the lump growing inside my throat. "That's not what I said. Impulsive decisions don't always turn out in my favor. This time, I'm done playing things by ear and forcing what isn't meant to be. If we're supposed to be together, life will make it happen."

"Sometimes, life needs a kick in the ass to get into motion. Destiny too."

Tears blurred my vision, but a smile still broke free across my face. "Tuck—"

I clamped my fingers around his upper arm. He resisted for a moment, then let go and turned back to face me. His glossy eyes tugged at the strings of my heart. I felt so much for him. The last thing I wanted was to make it more difficult than it already was.

He rubbed the heels of his hands over his eyes.

"Wilde, I'll show you that you're wrong. I'll prove it to you. No way am I exposing my heart and having you slam the door into my face. I'm not that guy. The one who runs when things aren't perfect or get complicated. I love you. Whether or not you wanna hear it, it doesn't change the fact, you're the one for me. Baby or not. Wedding or not."

"Tuck—"

He raised a hand between us. "Don't. Don't say anything you can't take back. *Truth always*. I'm only alive when you're with me, and I'm not willing to take the chance of losing what we might have…what we already have."

Startling me, he gripped my waist and leaned in to kiss me. His tongue proclaimed his love, and his lips promised me we'd be all right. Nestled against him, I truly believed we could do this.

I circled his neck with my arms, fusing our bodies together.

He traced my spine with one hand. The other descended to grab a handful of my ass. I purred against his lips. Tucker groaned into my mouth. Together, we were fireworks. But fireworks could be dangerous if not handled carefully.

"I'll drive you." It wasn't a question, but a statement.

"For what it's worth, I'm sorry," I whispered against his chest.

Strong arms wrapped around me, protecting me. Shielding me from the outside world.

"Don't be. It'll work out. You'll see. I won't lose you, sweetheart. Told you yesterday, I have your back. I'll make sure you find your way back to me and agree to let me care of your heart."

Emotions stirred inside me. Tucker spoke every word I'd ever wished a man would, but still, I couldn't bring myself to let the walls around my heart come down.

"I'm scared," I admitted after a long minute.

"Me too. But you don't have to be."

"I wish we could have more time."

"Stay with me. Until tomorrow."

I sniffled. "It's better if I don't. It's already hard enough. Our friendship is important, and I'll never risk it." I closed my eyes. "Thanks to my hormones, I'm a full-time crier this weekend. I can't think clearly. The space will do me good. To assess my complicated feelings."

Deep down, I prayed walking away was the right thing to do.

"Let's take a bath. Together. And enjoy the hours we have left before you gotta go." He quirked a brow, silently asking for my approval, and I bowed my head. "Come with me, Wilde. Let me hold you for a bit longer."

Chapter 5

"Wilde, I'm addicted to your kind of crazy. You could even say I need it in my life. Like a powerful drug that makes my body hum." Addison and I stood facing each other in the packed bus station. My eyes were on her, only her, as if the buzzing crowd around us didn't exist in our world. "You're everything I never knew I wanted. You're even crazier than I am, and I never imagined this could be possible. You've branded me to you, and now I'll never want anyone else for the rest of my life. You stole my heart. Why can't you see it? You can either cherish it or crush it—your choice—but I'll never take it back. I can't believe I'm saying this out loud, but I'm gone for you. I love you, Addison Wilde. Everything I've said since yesterday is true. Have me. Love me. Torture me. Because I feel alive when you do. Don't go. Please. No matter what, I still want you to be my wife. Let's figure it out. Here. Together. You're the only unpredictable variable in my life. The surprise of my days. The reason I've been smiling so damn much lately. The oxygen my body requires to function properly."

"Tuck, we already talked about it."

"I don't care. I've replayed everything you said this morning multiple times in my head, and I still don't agree with you. What if we never find our way back to each other? Are you willing to risk it? You're the one for me, sweetheart. Fuck, I sound like my worst nightmare. Who cares, right? You're happier when you're with me. I can tell. Those clouds in your eyes clear up when we're together."

"Okay, stop. My life is in Atlanta, and yours is in Chicago. Except for our best friends and maybe a common habit to do stupid shit, we—"

"We what?"

"What happened to 'no strings attached'? Now we go on with our lives. No harm done. And we see how it goes." She paused, drawing a breath through her mouth while rubbing her hands together. "Let's trust life and see how it unfolds, okay? I need time. As much as I'm desperate for love, I can't abandon myself completely to that emotion. I need to learn to be by myself and be my own person, without anyone else entering the equation. Even though I love love and everything it stands for, I have to do this. For me." She shut her eyes for a long second, catching her quivering bottom lip between her teeth to keep it from trembling. She opened her eyes, glistening with unshed tears, and met my gaze. "Oh God, this is so much harder than I thought it'd be."

I stood there, immobile, unable to form words or add anything. I wasn't used to laying my heart bare to someone else, and right then, I felt completely out of my element. I had no idea what to say to make her change her mind.

What she said made sense—in a way—but I couldn't see how it would be good for us. For our future together.

Addison moved to her tiptoes and kissed me. Hard and soft. Offering me a new window to her soul. It confirmed what I was aware of, that we belonged together. Now my sole mission was to show her just how much.

"There's nothing I want more than to surrender myself to you, big guy. It's not that I don't love you or care about you, it's just that I can't jump into this...us...the way you're asking me to. I shouldn't have said *yes* yesterday. I'm sorry if I led you on." Her lips claimed mine once more, and I lost myself in the kiss.

All my doubts melted away, and life felt ten times brighter every time we kissed.

"Wilde, I feel more alive gravitating in your orbit than I have in years of being on my own. We'll be happy. I promise you."

She pinched her lips together, fidgeting with her hands. "It's not that I don't believe you. I'm much happier when you're around too. My days are brighter when they involve you. I-I like us together. A lot. By now, I'm also aware you're a man of your word. Once I go...once I go home, I'll miss you like crazy. It's just... Tuck, it's all going too fast. I need time. To assess everything. To take a breath of fresh air on my own. The ride is scary, and I'm not sure I'm strong or brave enough to risk it all... Or that I'm ready to go all in blindly, without thinking it through."

"I know you're afraid, but I won't let anything bad happen to you or your heart."

"Gimme some time, okay? To sort out my feelings." With that, she stepped back, gathering her suitcase and bag.

I sighed. "Go. For now. But don't run away."

She twirled on the balls of her feet, and I grabbed her elbow before she could get too far.

"I'll give you time, but soon you'll realize I was right. I know because I came to the same conclusion. Believe me, it was a shock at first. That I could fall so hard for someone else. Mark my words. I'll come get you, Addison. Call me, and I'll stop everything and fly to be with you—anytime, day or night. I'll sweep you off your feet and never let you go."

I kissed her one last time, my heart in my throat as a flood of emotion hit me. My feelings ached as I tried to hide my helplessness from her. I was trying to be brave—look brave—but inside, I was a mess.

"Can…can we still talk at night?" I ventured, fearing she'd refuse and unsure how I'd react if she did.

She shook her head, and I choked on my own breath. "We…we better not. For a while at least." She swallowed, and I followed the ripples of her throat with my gaze. "Clean break. No communication until we're both ready to have that talk."

Her refusal sat heavy on my chest, shattering more pieces of my heart. "But—"

"Tuck, let's not complicate everything. Let's just take some time apart." She nodded once, as if to give weight to her argument. "Goodbye."

"No, no goodbye, Wilde. See you soon. It's way less dramatic."

"But being dramatic is my trademark."

Her eyes brimmed with tears, and the same dampness filled mine.

"See you around, Wilde."

She spoke again, but her words got drowned out as she disappeared further into the noisy station. All I heard was "Big guy," and it drew a sad curve on my lips.

I watched her leave, and I felt as if something died inside me.

My world turned a dull shade of gray, all its colors stolen away.

How long would it take for her to come back to me? To realize she'd made a mistake? She had to come to her senses, because the other option—the one where we went our separate ways—didn't sit well with me.

I kept my eyes trained on my heart walking away from me until it vanished, disappearing in the crowd without another look in my direction.

Shoulders hunched and back slouched, I dropped to the nearest bench, my legs stretched before me, my insides turning into a pile of rock.

Unshed tears burned the back of my eyes. It felt as if I'd been skinned raw, my heart left out to dry—bruised and weak—for everyone to see. A muffled cry escaped from the rim of my lips. How could being heartbroken hurt so fucking bad?

With the back of my hand, I chased my tears away.

Yesterday, Addison had agreed to be my girlfriend.

And today, she quit on us.

"Mommy," I screamed. "Don't go. Stay." With all my strength, I pulled at the strap of the bag she carried. Sobs drowned out my words. "Mommmmy."

Could she hear me?

Why wasn't she saying anything?

I tugged harder.

After a long moment, she knelt before me, pausing just short of the front door's threshold. "Tucker, real men don't cry."

"Will you come back? Where are you going?" I asked through hot tears, struggling to hold them back, to be a man like she asked me to.

My mother shook her head. "Your father and I have decided it would be better if I move out. He'll need you, Tucker."

"Where are you going?"

"Ron and I are moving out of town. It's for the best." She avoided my gaze, her fingers nervously playing with the strap of her bag. "You'll come visit us… Later."

"When?"

"I'll let you know when I'm ready. It's hard for me to leave, but this is what's best for you." She kissed my cheek. "Goodbye, Tucker."

"No. No goodbye."

The door slammed behind her as she made her exit.

The memory of my mother walking out on me resurfaced. I hadn't thought about that day in such a long time.

Addison was all wrong. I loved her. And never again would I let a woman I loved walk away without a fight.

I shut my eyes, fighting the grief playing behind my lids.

My body shuddered, as if I were in the throes of withdrawal from the drug I was most addicted to.

Time ticked by.

I had no idea how long I'd been sitting on the bus station bench, and I had no inclination to move either.

All my thoughts collided inside my head. I replayed every scene since arriving in Green Mountain. Every word, look, or kiss Addison and I exchanged.

Her words made sense. That was what upset me the most. Deep down, I was aware it was her fear talking—the result of past experiences trusting other men with her heart. Not the woman I loved. Not the wild temptress who had seduced me.

A thought popped up and nagged at me. Did she seduce me because she thought her heart would be safe, that she wouldn't fall for me? Doubts swirled inside me. Had I tried hard enough? What else should I have done—or said? Should I have run after her or locked her in the house until she gave in? Why was I questioning everything?

My cracked organ dangled freely in my chest. Addison left. With a tiny flame of hope still burning, I watched people entering and leaving the station. No. She wouldn't come back. If she were going to, she would already be wrapped in my arms.

Devise a plan. That was my new goal: win her back. That and win her complete love and trust. I would map something out. Not today, though. But soon. I couldn't let our story end like that.

A fresh wave of sadness swept through me, pooling in my aching chest.

I was right the day I met her and said she would be the end of me. Addison Wilde entered my life and tipped over everything I thought I knew. Like a hurricane. She left me to deal with the aftermath on my own while she figured things out for herself.

Through it all, she made me see things from a different angle. Made me realize things about myself I'd been ignoring. The truth was, I liked that vision. I liked how she believed I could do things I'd be proud of. That meant something.

With my hands pressed over my burning eyes, I prayed for her to return, knowing with absolute certainty that it was like wishing for rain during a drought. Hopeful but not realistic.

Someone sat beside me, offering me a flask. I cocked my head to the side to meet my best friend's worried gaze.

"What are you doing here, man?" he asked, perusing the train station.

"Reflecting on my life. How did you find me?"

Nick gave my thigh two quick pats as the burning liquid lined my throat. "Addison called Dahlia and told her everything. When you didn't answer your phone, I knew I'd find you here."

"Why? How?"

"Under your tough exterior, I've always known you are a softy at heart. Tell me the truth. Do you really love her?"

I shrugged. "Yeah. I do. But she's not here, is she? She left with my fucking heart in tow, leaving me bleeding."

"I'm sorry, man. Addison sounded sad when she called."

"Why do I bother with love? Is it really worth it? She never said it back, you know. The L-word. She acted like she loves me, but the confession never left her mouth. Occasional fucks are much safer and much less complicated."

Nick took the flask from me and brought it to his lips. "But they don't fulfill you anymore, right?"

I shrugged, brushing it off. "How do you know?"

"We've been friends for over two decades. I've noticed the differences in you. Even when I visited you last month, I could tell something had happened to you. Your heart was less guarded. Your smile looked genuine. You had a spark I hadn't seen in years. I just had no idea at the time what had set it off." He paused. "Or who."

"Look at me now. Why bother? She's not here to take ownership of any of it. She fucking left after I opened my heart to her."

"Give her time to miss you. To work on her confidence. To see the big picture. For what it's worth, love isn't all black or white."

We stayed silent for a long while.

"Both of you have worked on yourselves. Grown. For the best. She's a good one, and I stand behind what I've already said. You guys are perfect for each other. At first, I believed one of you would end up hurting. Next time, I'll listen to my wife when she makes predictions. You and Addi have issues, but I saw the way you watched over her on our wedding day and how she brightened up when you were around. Those things don't lie."

"Can you call Addison and tell her just that?"

Nick bumped my shoulder with his. "Don't be cynical. She'll come around."

"Man, the attraction was strong….nah, *is* strong. I can't explain it. My senses heighten every time she nears me. At your bachelor party, I tried to stay away…I really did, but she was all I could see. All I could smell. All I craved. I would have spent my life inside her, just because it felt like home. Because I know for sure that's where I'm supposed to be."

Nick ran a hand through his tousled locks. "I-I didn't know. No wonder you're hurting so bad. I'm sorry, man. I never thought I'd hear you say those words out loud, not in this lifetime. This updated version of you suits you much better. Welcome to adulthood." He rose to his feet. "C'mon. Let's go home. You are not spending the only vacation you've taken since you graduated in a bus station in Green Mountain, Tennessee."

My friend held out his hand, and I grabbed it, requiring his help more than ever to go through the rest of my day.

"Did you really ask her to marry you?" he asked with a sideways glance.

A loud laugh whizzed out from deep within me. "At this point, would you really be surprised if I did?"

He shrugged. "Nah, nothing can floor me anymore."

"You really believe she'll be back?"

"Yeah, I do."

Chapter 6

Addison

I exited the bus, ready to go home, my stubbornness and fears weighing heavily on my shoulders, the suitcase rolling behind me like a dead weight in my hand. It carried not only my personal belongings, but my sorrows, my broken heart, and my fucking ego. Amongst other things. Things I wasn't ready to dig into or assess. Things that scared me instead of bringing me peace.

My eyes, raw from all the tears I'd shed, stung. Three and a half hours was far too much time to replay my last conversation with Tucker—the pleas lacing his voice, the hurt shining in his eyes—and come up with a million reasons why I should turn around and gift him my heart the way it begged me to. The way *he* begged me to. Because that was all I wished for—but my head had the final say. It urged me to protect my weakest organ. How did we end up here? Tucker Philips was supposed to be a safe choice. A risk-free rebound.

He'd never been a commitment kind of guy. Until now…until me. Or at least, that's what he hinted at… No, he processed his love for me. That was not supposed to happen.

Looking at my track record, I'd always fallen for the wrong men. The ones unavailable, or the ones burdened with emotional baggage and childhood scars. I always dove into love with no safety net. Quickly and without questioning the validity of the feelings of the other party involved. Bad habit. Now I knew better. My heart would thank me one day. It would thank me for protecting it during a moment of weakness.

The pregnancy-scare precipitated engagements we weren't ready for. That *I* wasn't ready for. As long as I stayed away, maybe the hurt could be contained. Tucker's confessions caught me off-guard. They exposed my feelings. We made promises we had no idea we could keep, and now we were condemned to live with the aftermath.

How could I miss someone I'd known for just a little over a month? How could I feel like my heart had been ripped open when I boarded that bus?

Distance would do me good, to bring order to my tangled feelings. It would help me see things clearly, free from any outside distractions.

My pulse calmed—sorta—and I straightened my back and upped my chin. I had to convince myself that I was okay.

Sitting on the curb, I texted my best friend.

ME

Home safe. Well, not home per se, but almost there. Leaving the station right now. I'll talk to you later.

Love you

She replied within a minute.

DAHLIA

Thanks for keeping me updated. How are
you doing?

ME

Same. Confused.

Sad.

Broken.

DAHLIA

Can I tell Tuck you're all right? The guys got
wasted. We had a barbecue, and he didn't
say it, but he was clearly hurt. Talked about
you the entire time. Back in my old house
now. Sleeping it off. I'll keep an eye on him.

ME

Again, I'm so sorry. You should be living in
wedded bliss and having amazing married
sex. Not dealing with my fuck-ups.

DAHLIA

Don't worry about me. I'm getting all that.
And more *winking emoji* When Jack is
asleep. Anyway, you've always been there
for me. When I was shattered and thought
I'd die from a broken heart. I'll always
support and love you, girlfriend.

My gaze stayed glued to the little bouncing dots at the
bottom of the screen.

DAHLIA

But I'll say this because Tucker is my
friend too.

> I understand why you left. And I'm glad
> you're not jumping into something you're
> not ready for and taking the time to make
> sure you're doing the right thing. But don't
> lead him on, okay? If he's not the one you
> can see yourself with, be honest. He's a
> good guy. And he's proven himself over the
> weekend. For what it's worth, you guys
> looked good together. Sexy. Happy.

> I know you've been hurt before. But I can
> tell you like him. A lot. And from what I've
> seen and heard, he really likes you too. He
> wasn't faking it. Take some time, decide if
> going for what you wish for is worth it this
> time.

Emotions bubbled up in my throat. I typed a reply, then started erasing it. I had no idea what I should say. My best friend said it all.

DAHLIA

> Fine. Don't reply. I'm glad you made it
> home. I'll call you in the morning. Sleep on
> it. Our conversation isn't over. I love you xx

With the tip of my forefinger, I jabbed the screen until I erased all traces of my previous reply and wrote a simple *Thank you. Me too* instead.

As if my feet had been stuffed with lead, I staggered to the nearest public transportation station to catch the train that would drop me closer to home. Once on the sidewalk, I slowed my steps, not in a hurry to find myself all alone in my apartment. Rebecca was at Ben's. I knew because I'd checked earlier. She had no idea the shitshow my few last days had been, and I had mixed feelings about her not being home tonight. I usually told her everything about my life, but this time, I feared her opinion about the whole pregnancy-scare slash *Tucker asked me to marry him* followed by *for the first time I took a step back to analyze the situation* episode. Tonight, the company of my favorite movie and a tub of mint and chocolate chip ice cream would do. Not ready for another emotional breakdown fueled by alcohol, I ditched the wine. No, thank you. Sugar would have to be enough to up my spirits.

Tucker's proposal had been spinning around in my head since the moment the words had left his mouth.

"Let's get married. You and me. Make it official."

"But I may not be pregnant, Tuck."

"See, I don't care. I want you. All of you. Now. No matter what the test says. Let's not get influenced by the result. I love you."

"And I thought I was the impulsive one?"

"I have my moments."

"You're still in shock about the pregnancy scare. Let's not rush things, okay?"

There. My reasoning had made an appearance. The little voice in my head was onto something. I should've listened to it at that exact moment.

"Nick once told me, when you know, you know, when he was talking about Dahlia. This is the first time I understand what he meant that day. Because what we share is real...and rare. Wilde, you're the only person who can tame my ways, who makes me yearn for more."

But then he'd said just the right words to make me believe my feelings were reciprocated. After all his celibate talks, could he really do relationships? Could he leave his playboy ways behind for good? For me? For the chance at an *us*?

When he'd said... Gosh. Tears welled up in my eyes just thinking about it all.

That man... I hiccupped, clamping my hand over my mouth, trying to keep it all in.

He bared himself to me... His heart. His soul.

Time apart would tell me if being together was a spur-of-the-moment commitment or something worth exploring and nurturing. It had to, right? I'd made the right call by walking away. Distance would do us good. To reassess things, to step back from the emotions, and to avoid rushing it all.

"Addison Wilde, would you be my girlfriend? I know it sounds juvenile, but I've never said those words to anyone before."

"I do," I said out loud to myself, wiping my teary face with my sleeve. "But I'm afraid this can't be real. That it won't last. How do I prevent myself from getting hurt if it isn't? How do we do this, big guy? How can we be sure it's meant to be?" I closed my eyes, straightened my back, and breathed deeply. "Universe, life, or destiny, whoever hears me first. Please, if Tucker and I are supposed to be together, don't wait years to put us back on the same journey. Show me a sign I won't be able to deny or misinterpret. Please, be on my side this time. Thank you for listening to me."

I opened my eyes and exhaled the last traces of my doubts.

This would have to do. For now.

Wrapped in the blanket Tucker had gifted me—the one he sprayed with his mouth-watering cologne—I fell asleep, hopeful my love life would sort itself out.

———

The next two weeks bled into each other, and I just went through the motions. My heart was still aching, but more than anything, I missed my friend. I had gotten so used to talking to Tucker every night, sending a dozen texts a day —sharing small details about my life, asking whether I should buy the blue or purple dress, or indulge in tacos or pasta, yeah, super important stuff—that the void of his absence felt far bigger than I had first anticipated. I liked hearing his input on every subject, as if it truly mattered to him, and he seemed to take pleasure in advising me and listening to me.

Rebecca knocked on the slightly ajar door of my bedroom. "Addi, are you ready? We gotta leave in ten minutes." She moved closer. "How are you feeling?"

"Better. Still weak, but less dizzy."

"You've been spreading yourself too thin lately, trying to put Tucker in your rearview mirror. Is it working?" She folded her arms over her chest so as to say, "Don't bullshit me."

"Huh…not really."

"See? I agree with Dahlia. Fainting at the office yesterday is the unmistakable sign you gotta start taking care of yourself. No more taking on too many projects, even if Joseph insists. It's not healthy. You're lucky you came back to your senses before I called 9-1-1, or I would've dragged your ass to the hospital myself, forcing them to inject you with some common sense."

"Who's dramatic now?" I teased, grabbing her hand. "Thank you for driving me, though. And I'm sorry I scared you. I'm looking forward to getting my blood work results. My mama says it could be low iron levels…or stress."

"I hope it's nothing serious. Listen, I'm being your friend here, offering unsolicited advice. Just hear me out, okay?"

I nodded.

"Call him. You're miserable. So far, how's convincing yourself you're better off without him working for you?"

I looked away, biting my lower lip.

"You two have unfinished business. Maybe he's the

one. Maybe he's not… But unless you try, how will you ever know?" I parted my lips, ready to argue, but she continued. "If he's still in love with you, give him a chance to show you how things could be between you two. What do you have to lose?"

What she said added up. It didn't mean I was ready, or in the right state of mind, to listen or agree. "My heart. The one every man I've dated in the past stomped on and rolled in the dirt. When I'm with Tuck, it feels real. More real than anything I've ever felt before. What if…what if he decides he prefers his old ways? I'll be the one left heartbroken. Again. And I'm done… Done being that girl. The one who falls in love first. Who trusts without a second thought, who devotes herself to a relationship that has no future."

"Addi—" Rebecca said, pulling me into her arms.

"Love is messy, but it's not supposed to hurt me so bad. I don't deserve to be taken advantage of another time."

"I know. I know." She brushed my hair back with her fingers. "Let's go. You don't wanna be late."

An hour later, I exited the doctor's office in a stupor. My head and heart were blank, not processing the truth. Except for one thing.

That sign. I was the one who asked for it. Now destiny, life, or the universe had just slapped it right in front of my face so I couldn't miss it. Or rather, the doctor did. Guess the joke was on me now. How long could I pretend he was wrong before my friend called me out on my bullshit?

"What is it?" Rebecca asked, rising to her feet as I joined her. She had been waiting while I met with the doctor to go over my blood test results.

I neared her, stumbling on unsteady feet, sight hazy, pulse ricocheting to an offbeat rhythm, wondering if my thorax could even contain my wild heart.

"Addi, are you gonna pass out again? You're as white as a ghost. Do you wanna sit down? What did the doctor say? I should've gone in with you." She gripped my upper arm and guided me to a chair. "Addison Wilde, talk to me. I'm freaking out if you can't already tell. Are you dying? Is it serious? Are you sick?"

The spinning thoughts in my head interwove. My lungs struggled to inflate on their own.

Tremors shook my fingers, and I pushed my hands under my thighs. My tongue darted out to moisten my lips, but it failed. My mouth felt dry, as if I'd swallowed sawdust.

"Becca, it's my blood pressure. It's serious, but not terminal."

She sighed, relief evident in her features as I kept talking.

"Huh…the thing is… I-I fainted because it's too low and I gotta rest more, eat better, get up more slowly. Take vitamins."

"Oh, so you *are* iron deficient. Your mama was right. Mothers know best."

I shook my head and caught her gaze. "No. Becca, it's not my iron levels."

"No? What is it then?"

"I'm…pregnant."

The ground opened beneath me as the words left my mouth for the first time. I'd spent weeks bawling at the sight of puppies, and now, as reality hit, I had no tears left to cry.

My friend brought a hand over her mouth. "Oh. Shit."

"Yep. Oh shit. Oh fuck. Or any other expression that you deem fine."

She neared me and wound her arms around my shoulders, bringing me the comfort I had no clue I required, but appreciated.

"Whoa. This is…this is… What are you gonna do?"

I offered her a pointed look.

"You gotta tell him, Addi. Everything I said earlier carries a million times more meaning now."

"Yep. Let's just say that's not how I imagined our reunion." I paused, trying to clear my head. "I heard what you said, by the way. The thing is… Somewhere deep down, I had this plan to seduce him all over again, to start fresh. I wanted to take my time, date him, savor us, until the only options left were being all in or all out. It…it just sounds silly now. We haven't talked in two weeks, and now I'm just supposed to announce he's gonna be a father? Way to kill the mood. Dahlia says he's not angry with me, but what if he's changed his mind?"

"Girl, I'm aware you have a flair for drama, but this isn't a conversation you should have over the phone. Go to him. Meet him in person. You gotta decide if you wanna be *with* him. Live *with* him in every way that matter. It's not just about you anymore. You two will be a family, whether it's conventional or not, for the rest of your lives."

I dropped a kiss on my friend's cheek. The racing thoughts in my head were popping all over the place, spinning faster and faster. I was not prepared for such news, or for how much I would have to rethink everything I thought I knew.

I blew out a long breath, trying to wrap my mind around this new reality.

"Becca, even if I hate to admit it, you are right. See? I can recognize it." My voice broke as more emotions battled inside me, and I couldn't shake the image of Tucker's hurt face. "The irony is that I told him I didn't expect him to change for me. Now he'll have to because of circumstances out of our control. I'll talk to him, but don't rush me. Please. I might need a few days to process the news first, okay?"

"Sure. Whoa. You're going to have a baby. Can I be in shock too for a second?"

"Yeah. As long as you give me a moment to let the news sink in first." I let out a sarcastic chuckle. "It's all my fault. I...I asked for a sign..."

"What sign?"

I flicked my wrist. "Never mind. Let's just tell the universe I got the message. Loud and clear."

I pressed my hand over my abdomen and swallowed the barbs prickling my airways. I couldn't define how I felt. I had a fetus growing inside me. It all seemed so surreal. So right. And so wrong.

Rebecca nodded, her hand squeezing mine. "I'll help you. But then you'll put your grown-woman's pants on and face Tucker with the truth. Based on what you've told me, I know he'll do the right thing. By you and the baby. Wow, you're going to be a mama." Her eyes glazed over. "I'm gonna be an auntie."

I inhaled a shaky breath. "The thing is, I...I don't want him to feel obligated to move here or to marry me because I'm carrying his child. One day, he'll resent me if he's forced into this life. Or if it means he has to give up all his dreams and accomplishments because we're in this situation together."

"Addi, you're not asking for anything. If he changes his lifestyle, it'll be his decision. Tucker thought you weren't pregnant and still begged you to stay. He still wanted to marry you." I gave her stinky eyes. "Okay, that was a bit precipitated, but still. Girl, he showed dedication."

"Or craziness. Oh God, I'm pregnant. There's a

human being growing inside me. How crazier than that can it get?"

"No overthinking. And about Tucker, don't push him away because you're afraid. What if he's the one you've been looking for all along? What if life has decided to give you both a push forward in the right direction? It's not the scenario you had in mind, and it didn't happen the way you thought it would, but you're here now and must deal with it. Who knows, maybe that's exactly what Tucker needs to move on from his old ways once and for all. To free himself from chains and ties he's already disenchanted with. Have you ever thought about that?"

"Don't be right. 'Cause it unnerves me when you figure my stuff out before I do." I poked my tongue out at her, and Rebecca hugged me.

"Yeah, yeah. Keep talking. For the record, I love you too. And if you love him, give him a chance to prove he meant everything he said."

That night, I watched my phone screen for hours, hoping it could ring and the one person I had to talk to would be on the other end of the line—like he used to be. As if my brain could summon some kind of magic if I really poured all my psychic energy into it."

Sitting on the deck curled in the blanket Tucker had gifted me—in a way it was like he was there with me—I contemplated my options, writing the pros and cons on a piece of paper. At last, the tears that had refused to come until now streamed down my face, the shock slowly fading. It was a rush of every emotion I'd been holding inside. Rebecca's words of wisdom replayed in my head. After a moment, I came to the same conclusion.

For two days, I paced the apartment like a lioness in a cage. My body grew tired, but my mind remained restless.

I was all over the place. At home. At work. At night. Knowing that most of my symptoms were due to the pregnancy—and not because I was going insane without reason —eased my mind. At least a little.

On Friday morning, I was a bundle of nerves, desperate to know how Tucker was doing. I grabbed my phone and did the same thing I did every few days.

ME

Hey, it's me. How are you?

DAHLIA

Hey, girlfriend.

Awesome.

ME

Married life still good on you?

DAHLIA

It's the best *winking emoji*

I could picture her big smile in my head.

ME

Ready for your honeymoon?

DAHLIA

Counting the days.

Are you feeling better? What did the doctor say?

ME

Yes. No. Long story. We'll have to talk about it. Can I call you over the weekend?

DAHLIA

I'm free in fifteen minutes if you are too.

ME

Nah, I have a full day.

And I can't tell anyone before I tell Tucker, even though I wish more than anything that I could ask for your advice right now. Having my best friend in my corner would be a relief. She went through this all by herself. She had more insight than I did.

ME

How is he? Is he still in Green Mountain?

DAHLIA

Left last night. Said he had things to deal with that couldn't wait anymore. Have you talked to him?

ME

Not yet. I will. I'm done avoiding him. Gotta go. Love you xx

DAHLIA

Love you too. I'm so happy you're giving you guys a chance. He's a keeper. Be safe and call me as soon as you can.

Tucker was back home. For my plan to unfold, he had to be. No way would I have this conversation in front of our friends.

Five days later, after putting my plan into action and making the necessary arrangements, I packed a suitcase and booked the first flight to Chicago.

Doing the right thing began with telling the man I knew, deep down, I loved and prayed still loved me back that we were having a baby together.

I wasn't ready to jump into a relationship just yet, but I was dedicated to spending time with him and seeing where it'd take us.

Baby steps.

All pun intended.

"Oh, Tucker. You're in for the surprise of your life. You just have no idea."

Chapter 7
Tucker

I packed my belongings, zipped my suitcase, and surveyed the room after I made the bed, the odor of fresh laundry permeating my nostrils. Addison's scent infusing the sheets was gone now. The thought of it sent a weird zing to my heart. It had been about two weeks since she boarded that bus and left me to deal with many questions I had no answers to, all on my own. Sure, her heart had been skinned alive by jerks before me, and I could understand her resistance to a new relationship. I had many flaws, but I had never treated a woman badly. I'd always been honest with my intentions, never leading anyone on for no reason. No, my style was upfront and respectful.

Addison and I had been apart for two weeks—two weeks, for Christ's sake—yet I still lacked the words to explain how being away from her made me feel. How empty and colorless everything around me seemed when she wasn't there to add her own colors to my universe.

My phone rang before I could exit the bedroom. *Nick.*

"Hey, man. Still in town?"

"Yeah. I was about to stop by your place to kiss your wife goodbye. Hug your little boy. And maybe see you too while I'm at it."

"Yeah, yeah. I know you'll miss me too."

I let out a loud chuckle. God, I forgot how good it felt to laugh.

After Addison left, I cursed the world and drowned my sorrows in whiskey for a day or two—until I decided to do some introspection and think about what I really wanted and where my life should go from there.

After my whiskey blitz, I realized two things, beyond the fact that she had a point about us jumping on that *us*-wagon too fast without thinking it through

First, I spoke the truth when I told her my player days were behind me. Doing the same shit I'd done for a decade no longer satisfied me—living the same days over and over, no surprises, except for a different woman in my bed. I craved more.

Second, what I felt for Addison Wilde was called love. It hadn't faltered during our weeks apart. Since losing sight of her at the bus station, when she blended into the crowd, I'd been searching for her every minute, hoping she would appear and tell me she was done being afraid, that she would trust life and give us a chance. I lost count of how many times I checked my phone for a message from her. Even in the middle of the night, waking up with a start, convinced she was lying beside me or had whispered to me in my sleep.

My father used to say actions spoke louder than words…louder than any promises. And so, my stay in

Green Mountain had jumpstarted my plan—the promise I made—to prove to her that I had changed, that my bachelor antics were behind me.

Dahlia was on my team, and every few days, she updated me on her friend's whereabouts, and I was thankful. Without her updates, I would have been beside myself with worry, wondering if Addison was okay.

"I know you love me," Nick said, bringing my attention back to him. "You'll never leave town without a proper hug. No shame in saying so, man. I love you too."

"Oh Jesus. Married life is taking its toll on you. You've become a clingy motherfucker."

"Look who's talking," he added with a laugh. "You're in love, and you don't even hide from it. Times are changing. Tucker Philips is evolving. Finally being true to himself. I never thought I'd see this day. Still going forward with your plan?"

"Can't wait to start redefining my life and my priorities. Tucker 2.0 is coming to a town near you, my friend."

"Bring your ass over here. We're having brunch. Dahlia saved you a place at the table. Jack can't wait to see you too. What else will you do, anyway? Your plane is only leaving at three."

I breathed out my relief. Yeah, this new version of me was growing on me. "I'll be there in twenty. Tell Jack-Man, Uncle Tuck will be right there. He'd better line up his toy trucks. I'm ready for a rematch."

I finished cleaning up the house, and once I put my suitcase in the trunk of my rental car, I slid behind the wheel.

Addison's and my song started playing on the radio. My pulse quickened. For some reason, even destiny was on my side on this one. I relaxed my posture. Yeah, I was going to win her heart back. Every fragment of it.

And then I'd claim those chunks as mine. Yes, I felt confident. Addison Wilde would be mine. Soon.

———

After spending all this time in Green Mountain, where life was as laidback as it came, surrounded by people I cared about and who enjoyed my sorry ass too, my apartment seemed blah. The overpriced decor missed the cozy vibe of Dahlia's old house. The neighborhood missed the charm of Main Street. And my bedroom missed the presence of the woman I hoped I'd share it with.

The place I'd been living in for the last three years felt strange and, somehow, foreign. As if I'd walked into someone else's bachelor pad. It lacked personal touches. And warmth.

A tiny smile played on my lips. The updated version of me was blooming, and I was ready. Excited even.

In the bathroom, I watched my reflection in the mirror after I exited the shower and wiped the steam off the glass.

"Tuck, today is the day. One action every day toward your goal. You can do this. You'll win the girl back. I believe in you. Stick to the four-step plan. It might look scary, but it will all turn out fine. You've got this."

I fist-bumped my reflection. Like a fighter about to enter the ring, I stretched my neck on both sides, jumped up and down, rolled my shoulders back, increasing my confidence and pumping myself up in my head.

Stepping into the high-rise where I worked, wearing a suit—something I hadn't worn since the wedding—I was met by Zion, the security guard, who greeted me with a friendly nod as he checked IDs.

"Look who the cat brought back. How was the vacation, Tuck?"

I handed him the two-milk-one-sugar coffee I got him on my way here.

"I've missed this while you were gone," he said, lifting his cup to thank me.

"Vacation was great. I feel like a new man." This wasn't far from the truth. Now I had concrete objectives and goals. I was focused on my newfound mission, and the thought filled me with a sense of hope. Gone were the fears and anxieties that the idea of settling down used to bring me.

"It's been a long time since I saw a genuine smile on your face, son. It suits you."

I returned his grin. "Thanks. I feel much better. Alive."

I stepped into the elevator, and just before the doors closed, a small hand slipped between them.

A girl who worked for an accounting firm in the same building, whom I'd encountered a few times before, gave me a wide smile and moved closer. "Tucker Philips." She purred my name, tracing the length of my arm with her fingernails. "I've missed you."

A chill ran through me. In the past, I would have relished the attention. Now it made me feel weird. I took a step back to escape her proximity, but instead of giving me some space, she moved forward.

"A while back, you promised me a date," she said with a suggestive wink. "How about tomorrow night? Your reputation precedes itself. I can't wait to test the merchandise." Her eyes flicked to my crotch, and a crooked smile tugged at the corner of her lips.

I swallowed and shut my eyes.

How did the old version of me live for nothing but this? Everything about this woman touching and seducing me felt wrong. My blood cooled down in my veins, the opposite of what it used to do when a good-looking woman entered my peripheral vision in the past.

The air in the elevator felt thick, so I loosened the tie around my neck to draw fresh oxygen into my lungs.

Had the thirty-seventh floor gotten higher while I was gone? And why hadn't anyone else entered the damn elevator, forcing her to step back?

Jerking my arm free from her grip, I stepped aside. "I'm sorry. This ship has sailed."

Her eyes crinkled as she watched me, stunned, her collagen-filled lips drawn into a pout. "Huh. What do you mean?"

"There's someone in my life. I'm not doing this," I gestured with a finger between us, "anymore. I'm done. Retired from the game."

She blinked. "You what? I must have heard you wrong. Sasha told me you weren't the type to settle. Unless it's me. Aren't you attracted to me?"

I turned to face her. "It has nothing to do with you. I swear. I met someone. She stole my heart and we're meant to be. End of the story."

Anyone who knew me would think I was talking nonsense. And yet, it brought me peace to say the truth out loud, even to an almost-stranger.

Jace would roast my ass if he could hear me right now. He had no idea how much my life had changed in the last two months.

The doors finally opened on the thirty-third level. The woman offered me one last puzzled look before stepping out. "If you ever change your mind—"

"I won't."

And I wouldn't. No matter how this thing between Addison and me turned out, I was done with my old ways. For good.

"See you around, Tucker."

I nodded, stuffing my hands into my pockets. "Sure."

I let out a long exhale as the doors closed again. The tension I hadn't realized had built up along my back melted away. In that moment, I knew I was doing the right thing. There wasn't a trace of doubt in my mind.

"Whoa, I didn't see this one coming," Steven, my boss, said after I revealed my new career choices to him half an hour later. "You sure about all of this?"

"Yes. I am. I've been mulling it over for weeks. This is what I must do."

He bobbed his head twice. "Can you give me a week to transfer your smaller accounts to simplify your workload? I think the transition would be smoother if you handled it yourself. Your clients trust you. You're one of the best in this profession."

"Sure. I'll give you five days at the office and after that, I'll work remotely." I ran a hand over the side of my jaw, still smooth from my morning shave. "Steven, I wanted to thank you. For this opportunity... For believing in me, right from the start. It meant a lot. I wouldn't be here without you, and I appreciate everything you did for me. I couldn't have found a better mentor. You kept me out of trouble and jumpstarted my professional life."

He rounded his desk and stood before me. I held my hand out to shake his, but he pulled me into a hug instead. "Tucker, you've always been like a son to me. I saw the potential in you, even when you were still in college. I'll miss having you around, but I also understand your desire to follow your heart. Mindy and I have been married for twenty-one years. I get the feeling. Remember, my doors will always be open if you change your mind along the way or if you miss me so much that you have to visit."

"Thanks."

"And that woman of yours is a lucky gal. I hope things work out." He shook his head. "I'm like a proud papa bird watching his offspring fly off the nest."

He let out a warm laugh, and I joined him.

"I'll keep in touch." He gripped my upper arms and nodded as I added, "I'm around for five more days. Maybe you'll be happy to get rid of me by then."

"Never."

I waved and made my way to my office and closed the door and the blinds, requesting a little privacy to get on with my day. Even if it were the right decision, I still required some time to process the idea my life was about to change.

Work remotely. *Check.*

———

Elisa had agreed to meet me in the pub that used to be our Friday night watering hole during our college years. I waited for her in a corner booth with a bottle of red and a basket of chicken wings and taquitos. She was a fundamental part of my plan to put the next step into action.

"Gosh, I'm having a date with the famous Tucker Philips. Women are going to throw daggers at me now. How are you doing?" she asked after I moved to my feet to greet her and kiss her cheek.

"Great. You look beautiful. I swear you look younger than me now. What's your secret?" I waggled my eyebrows. "Hamilton?"

She slapped my forearm and laughed, tilting her head back. She resembled her brother so much right now.

"Why does it feel like I'm right?" I teased.

Her laughter died, and she shook her head. "Tuck, you

have a special talent. It's like you can always tell what I'm up to. Seriously, how do you do it?"

"No real talent, only a keen eye. I spent the evening with Barry last month after a playoff game, and the entire time, he couldn't stop gushing about you. I just put two and two together." I shrugged, and she failed to hide her smile, seated before me with her chin resting on her closed fist, a love-struck expression in her eyes.

Barry Hamilton, the star and captain of the Chicago Busters, was Elisa's long-time friend from college.

"Fine, Barry asked me out on a date. We've been spending more time together in the last year. I'm just not sure what to make out of it. We've been best friends for a long time…and he's friends with Jace too. I'm not sure if getting together is the right thing to do. For all parties involved."

"What is it that *you* want?"

"I wish it were a simple question," she said with a sigh.

"It is. Or it should be." I paused. "In his defense, you won't know unless you give it a shot."

Yeah, I was rocking my new Tucker 2.0 *I'm fluent in relationship drama* persona.

She took a sip of her wine and leaned back in her seat. "I guess you're right. When did you grow up? Become reasonable? So full of wisdom? Where's the guy only looking for a quick romp in the sheets and a fun time?"

I pasted a cocky smirk on my lips. "I have my moments," I teased.

"Fine. You got me. I had feelings for Barry back in the day. I know for a fact he did too. But then he got recruited into the league and said there was no room for love in his life. Timing wasn't on our side back then."

picked at a chicken wing, nibbling at the crispy edges. "Things change. People change. Life goes on."

"The rejection was hard, even if it made sense at the time. I got burned. My heart got crushed. It was hard after that…being just friends with him."

Her confession reminded me of Addison's. Elisa poured more wine into my glass, and my attention snapped back to her.

"I knew a guy just like that. Afraid to commit. Actually, that's part of the reason why I wanted us to meet."

She offered me a pointed look and folded her arms over her chest. "Tell me more, Tuck. I'm curious now. You were mysterious over the phone. Talk. The last time you asked for my help was at the fundraiser when you were being stalked by that unhinged woman and we pretended to be madly in love for a few hours."

"Oh, that was an epic night." I shook my head, unable to get rid of my stupid smile at the memory. "Jace wanted to kill me when he thought you and I had slept together. Came to my place, challenging me to a fistfight."

Elisa cupped her mouth. "Oh God, I didn't know about that. My brother can be a tad protective sometimes."

"Like I said, epic." I sipped my wine. "Be honest, though. We had fun."

"Yes, being with you is never boring. That's why you've always been my favorite. Shhh. Don't tell Nick," she added with a wink.

I drew a cross over my heart. "I won't. Your secret is safe with me as long as you don't tell Jace I love you more than I love him."

Elisa chuckled and held out her hand. We shook on it. "Tucker Philips, we have a deal. Now tell me why I'm here."

"Nothing bad, I promise. You won't have to save my ass this time. Or pretend anything. You'll actually be proud of me."

"Shoot."

"I met a girl. And, well…I fell in love."

My smirk doubled in size while Elisa spat out her wine and covered her mouth with a napkin, her eyes big and inquisitive. "Okay, say it again, and don't mess with me this time."

In between catching up, I told her all about Addison.

"That's the woman Barry told me about. Said you two looked cozy together and that she could hand you your ass without even blinking. She made an impression on the team."

"Hamilton has such a big mouth." A heartfelt chuckle crossed my lips.

"We've been telling each other almost everything for as long as I can remember. It's a gift and a sin all at once."

I cleared my throat. "Yeah, I've become accustomed to the feeling."

"Tuck, will you take me to your place?" she teased with a quirked brow when we exited the pub three hours later.

With my palm resting on her lower back, I walked her forward. "You bet."

"Can't wait to see how huge it is. I've heard great things about it. I hope the rumors are true. I would hate to be deceived if it doesn't meet my expectations. Or the ideas I've formed in my head about you…and your place."

I winked. "Woman, be prepared to be astonished. Tucker Philips never does anything half-assed. He always gives his best shot."

Elisa's contagious chuckle warmed my insides. I loved being able to joke around with my friend.

"Lead the way." She snaked her arm through mine, and side by side, walked toward my condo building, just four blocks away.

Chapter 8

My heart lurched into my throat as I stood on the sidewalk, my suitcase at my feet and my eyes brimming with hot tears. I should've known better. And the worse was that I couldn't be mad at him. I knew who Tucker was when we started this thing between us. He never shied away from it. He'd always been honest and upfront with me about all of it, even though, at some point, my stupid heart imagined we could be more. Somehow.

Shame on me, because it didn't take him much time to replace me. For a guy who wanted us to get married, raise a baby together, and have a happily ever after, it certainly didn't take long for him to mend his broken heart.

It began to drizzle, and I tilted my head back, enjoying the rain as it mixed with the moisture filling my eyes.

I lowered a protective hand to cover my belly as the rain picked up, watching the man I loved tuck a strand of dark brown hair behind the woman's ear. They exchanged a knowing smile, and she lifted to her tiptoes to kiss his cheek. He shook his head, one palm cupping her face. Her hands pressed into his chest, and for an instant, they shared a moment. One I wasn't supposed to witness.

My heart died right there, and I only had myself to blame. "I'm sorry, baby. I promise your daddy is a great guy. He really is."

The downpour intensified, and chills traveled through me. I rubbed my arms, trying to inject myself with some warmth, unable to avert my eyes from the train wreck happening in front of me.

My breath lodged in my throat when Tucker's head pivoted in my direction. As if he could sense me standing here in the rain, watching him through the wide glass of his building lobby.

Our gazes locked for half a second. His lips pursed. He blinked, as if wondering whether I was real or just an illusion. Oh God, he looked so handsome in a pair of dark jeans and a simple long-sleeved black shirt. More like the Tucker I'd grown to know. No suit to conceal the vulnerable side of him—the one I had the chance to witness on multiple occasions.

He dropped his arms at his sides, said something to the woman, and I used the distraction to stalk away, my suitcase in tow. I pushed through the few people on the sidewalk, glancing over my shoulder at him every now and then to make sure he wasn't following. I couldn't deal with him right now. I needed time. A lot of it.

Rushing outside, his eyes searched the night, he tugged at his hair—a bit longer than what it used to be—and screamed something I couldn't hear from where I stood.

Tucker stopped and kicked a puddle of water, splashing

around him, and seconds later, my phone chimed. I pulled it from my back pocket, trying to shield it from the rain.

TUCKER

Wilde, tell me I didn't dream you're here.
Fuck, tell me I'm not going insane.

My heart leaped. The image of him with that woman flashed through my mind.

Ping. Ping. Ping.

More messages came in, but I ignored them all.

Opening an app on my phone, I booked a cab, ready to get away from the man who'd just crushed my heart.

My phone rang, but I declined the call. It rang again, and I declined a second time.

Exhaustion weighed heavily on my shoulders. The day had been long, and nothing had gone as planned.

Ping. Ping. Ping.

Unable to stay indifferent, I read the feed.

TUCKER

I know it was you. Don't deny it. I can feel
you. I always know when you're around.

Stop running away. Let's talk.

I'll search every hotel, every restaurant,
camp at the airport if I must, but you're not
leaving before we have a real discussion.

Again, why are you here?

Don't you think it's a bit childish to avoid
my calls?

I saw you. You saw me too.

Pick up.

Fuck, Wilde. What are you so scared of?
Why come all the way here just to
avoid me?

Fine. We'll talk when you're ready. You
know my number. You know where I live.

Night.

I hope you're somewhere safe.

Don't do anything stupid, okay?

Chapter 9
Tucker

If Addison thought she could outrun me, she had no clue who she was dealing with. The rain intensified, and the moment I secured my phone in my pocket, I spotted her by the side of the road, looking for an escape. Anger filtered through me, but decreased as I took her in, my steps carrying me in her direction. She was wearing a see-through white shirt thanks to the downpour, and I was grateful for the early darkness the gray clouds provided. Her drenched blonde hair clung to her scalp.

When my eyes had found her through the window a minute ago, a surge of happiness had waltzed through me at the realization that she had come back. For me. To me. But just as quickly, she pulled her little disappearing act, and the sparks of joy I had first felt were now turning into wrath.

This woman.

She was driving me nuts.

How could she infuriate me so much and yet call to my heart like nobody else had ever done before?

I sighed.

Before she could climb into the cab that had halted before her, I padded closer and circled her waist with my arm. "Not so fast, sweetheart," I whispered into her ear, relishing the shivers that worked through her body. *Fuck, I've missed you too.*

My pulse quieted.

My entire body relaxed.

Yes, we were both still in sync with each other.

She cocked her head until we faced each other. "Let me go."

After sliding a twenty-dollar bill into the half-cracked window, I urged the driver to keep going. "The lady doesn't need transportation."

Addison tried arguing, but the driver sped away after I tapped the rooftop twice.

"Wilde, where did you think you were going, huh?"

"Home," she said, trying to wriggle out of my hold.

"Home? Not a chance. Why are you here?"

She closed her fists at her sides, fury illuminating her blue eyes.

I huffed my annoyance before releasing her. "Fine, you're free." I lifted both hands in surrender. "Better?"

She adjusted her now-fully-transparent shirt, her eyes throwing flames at me, singeing me down to ashes.

Heat, wild and untamable, rushed through me.

I softened my tone. If it were just up to me, I'd have been already balls-deep into her. "Can you please explain why you're in Chicago right now? I don't recall you telling me you were coming."

She clenched her hands tighter, raised her chin, ready to launch an attack on me. "Oh, so you'd have had time to hide your side-piece? Nah. I prefer to learn I've been replaced sooner rather than later."

I raked my fingers through my hair, unable to reel in my laughter. Addison Wilde had a jealous side, and for a reason I couldn't explain, it boosted my ego. And my desire to get her naked.

"Geez, you think it's funny?" Her irises turned into missiles. "Many promises said, few kept. The guy I fell for said he'd find his way back to me. You sure were convincing. You got me hooked, and I almost believed you for a while. Enjoy the destruction, big guy."

"Are you done?" I asked.

The entire time her rant lasted, Addison had claimed every inch of space between us. Yep, our connection hadn't faded. Whatever she was feeding her mind, her body knew better.

A groan left her mouth, and she swiveled to leave, but I clutched her wrist. Her pulse hastened, and I felt every thump under the pads of my fingers.

"Wilde, you said you fell for me? Care to tell me more?"

She cursed under her breath. "No, I never said such a thing."

"Pretty sure you did. Want me to play it back to you?"

Her eyes widened, full of anger. "A replay? Are you high? Stop with the nonsense."

I mimicked her stance and rested my fists on my hips. "Am I? Talking nonsense?"

She wrapped her arms around herself. "Enough. I'm not having this discussion with you. I didn't fall for you, Tuck. Now move. I'm outta here."

"Where are you going? You know no one else in the city except me."

"Wrong again. I have friends….huh, many friends. Anyway, as I said, I'm going home so it doesn't matter."

"Jesus, you can't fly back tonight. Not in this state," I said, gesturing to the length of her drenched self. "Names?"

"Names of what?"

"No. Who. People you know in town."

"None of your business. Go back to your lady friend."

I raised one brow. "Lady friend?"

"Would you prefer *fuck of the day*?"

"*Fuck of the day*? Wow, I'd like to see how Jace's sister would react to be called that. Go ahead and ask her boyfriend if you wanna know if she's worth it."

Addison blinked, confusion clear on her expression.

"Ask him. You two already know each other, anyway."

"Stop sidetracking. I saw you two together."

"Nah, you think you saw something. It's an imagined deduction. Your personal spin on a situation you're not privy to. For your personal knowledge, Elisa is Barry Hamilton's girl."

"Oh."

"Yep. *Oh*. Never assume things about me, sweetheart. That's not how I pictured our reunion to be. You've said your piece. Ready to come home with me now?"

"This conversation is over. I'm out of here. Already told you."

She tried to escape again, darting to my left. We were both drenched, and I longed for a hot shower and dry clothes. Before she could get too far, I scooped her onto my shoulder, balancing her suitcase in my free hand.

"Tuck, put me down." She kicked the air, and I only tightened my grip around her.

"Houdini, you're done acting-out tonight."

"Tuck," she growled. "Let me go."

"No."

Minutes later, we entered my building, Addison still cursing down my back, punching my lower back.

"Go ahead, sweetheart, get that angst out. The way I see the next few minutes looks a lot like you spread naked on my bed with my face buried between your thighs. If that's your definition of foreplay…I can work with that. Next, we should try roleplay, no?"

Leo, the concierge, held the door open for us. "Welcome back, Mr. Philips. Hi, Ms. Wilde. I'm happy to see you again. I wish you two a great night."

"I'm not staying," she barked.

"Well, we'll see," I said, pressing the button to my floor after we entered the elevator car.

It wasn't until the elevator started moving and the doors closed that I lowered my furious woman to her feet.

"Happy?" she asked, her face flushed and her drenched hair clung in tousled strands all around her gorgeous face.

I grinned. And my dick stirred in my pants. He also agreed that, even looking messy, she was a sight for sore eyes. "Absolutely."

She punched my chest, but I caught her wrists on the second attempt. "You can't do that," she screamed. "You can't take me hostage."

"I beg to differ. I know how much you enjoy the chase. And the game." Her dilated pupils gave me all the confirmation I needed. "Stop pretending this fight isn't turning you on as much as it's turning me on." I pointed a finger at her chest. "Tell me. Why are your breathing so fast, Wilde? Do I bother you that much?"

She groaned. "I gotta go."

The elevator door opened to my floor, and baiting Addison with her baggage in my arms, I got her to follow me inside my condo.

Puddles of water pooled at our feet.

"Gimme a sec."

Moments later, I returned with towels and handed her one. "With or without?" I asked.

She frowned.

I explained. "Shower. With or without my company? There's this trick I've mastered that always helps to put a smile on your face. Also, my dick has tricks of its own you can't seem to resist."

She rolled her eyes. *What's with the attitude?*

"Fine. Tonight, you do you. Just tonight, though. You get one free pass."

Before she could protest, I carried her suitcase to my bedroom.

"I'm not staying," she repeated.

"Wherever you think you're going, you can't—not like that, soaked in a see-through shirt."

She gasped, taking in the sight of her red bra through the fabric for the first time. With her arms folded over her chest, she spun until her back was facing me.

Stepping behind her, I locked my arms around her waist and kissed the back of her neck. Addison went rigid before relaxing against me.

"Whatever the reason you're here, I'm glad you came." Chills skated along her back as my lips met her nape once more. "Go shower. I'll make some tea to warm you up, and we'll talk."

The fight in her left upon hearing my words. She nodded, murmuring a quiet, "Thank you."

I led her to my bedroom and dug a sweater out of my closet. "Here. Wear this."

She rummaged through her suitcase for a pair of shorts. "I brought clothes."

"I know. Wear this," I repeated, my tone not open for discussion.

Addison closed the bathroom door behind her without another word. Hurrying to the guest room, I showered in the en-suite in record time and returned to the kitchen.

A flood of questions raced through my mind. Why was Addison in Chicago? Who were her mysterious friends? In the hundreds of hours we spent talking and opening up to each other, she never mentioned anyone.

Dressed in a pair of cotton shorts and my sweater, Addison joined me. Every bit of my ire melted away when I laid eyes on her. She looked both beautiful and vulnerable. Her hands remained tucked inside the sleeves of the sweater. She avoided my eyes and moved to stand in front of the floor-to-ceiling windows, gazing out at the city. The rain had eased, and we could make out the lights of the bustling streets below.

Taking the spot next to her, I breathed easier in her presence.

We stood there for a long while, both of us looking at the dark body of Lake Michigan in the distance.

After a moment, I cleared my throat. "Her name is Elisa. We've known each other forever. As I said, she is Jace's sister. We had dinner together."

Addison said nothing, glancing away, sipping her tea.

"We met because I asked for her help. Not because I was looking for my dick to get sucked. Already told you my words are important to me. Don't picture me as the villain in our story because I'm not." I heard her sharp intake of breath as I explained, "She's a realtor."

Addison remained silent, her face stoic.

I sidestepped until I stood in front of her, cutting off her view and forcing her to meet my gaze. "Wilde, you are truly something." I exhaled my annoyance. "Jesus, I'm moving. Selling this place."

"You are?"

"Yes. Because I have plans. For the future. Let's talk about you first. Why are you here? You never said." For the first time, I noticed dark flecks of gold in her eyes. "Or perhaps you missed me too?"

She closed her eyes, pushing me away and keeping me from reading the expectations in them, or from glimpsing her thoughts.

She scrunched up her face and finally spoke, keeping her eyes shut. "Just know I'll be okay with whatever you choose to do. No pressure. We can discuss it. Don't go overboard or make promises you can't keep."

I erased the gap between us and tipped her chin up with a finger. "Open your eyes, sweetheart. Look at me when you tell me why you flew here. I gotta know, Wilde."

Her lips hovered a hair's breadth from mine. One tiny move forward, and I could capture them.

Heat spiraled around me as we shared the same air.

I drew in a deep, cleansing breath meant to calm the excitement thrumming inside me, but it did nothing. I couldn't ignore her proximity. As always, it was doing strange, thrilling things to my body.

One by one, her eyes opened, a bright smile illuminating her face as she delivered the words that would forever alter the course of our lives. "Congratulations, you're going to be a daddy."

Chapter 10

Tucker

My heart stopped.

It literally stopped.

My knees wobbled.

Then reality—and Addison's words hit, and I regained control of my body. Without thinking, once my brain had processed her words, I lifted her in my arms and spun her around, nuzzling her neck and breathing her in. *Congratulations, you're going to be a daddy.* That was really what she'd said. We were having a baby. I lacked words to capture the whirlwind of questions and emotions swirling inside me.

When I lowered her to her feet, Addison watched me with a stunned expression. "Wait. You're not upset? Wow, I had no idea how you'd react to the news."

"Upset? Me?" I pointed to my chest.

"Huh, who else?"

"Sweetheart, why would you think that?"

I rubbed her forearm, but she pulled away from my touch.

"Stop. Now. Don't sweetheart me. We gotta talk."

My fingers itched to brush the contours of her face. To stop myself, I clamped a hand around the back of my neck. "Wanna sit?"

She nodded, her features strained and impossible to read. At that instant, all I wanted was for her to let me in and not keep anything from me.

On the couch, I maintained a safe distance, angling my tall self toward her, silently showing I was there without crowding her.

"Do I ask questions, or do I let you talk?"

Addison closed her eyes, inhaled, and met my gaze, her pupils drifting in my direction. "Questions. But let me just say this first." She paused. "I'm keeping it. Whether we're together down the road or you've changed your mind or whatever, this baby is already a part of me…of…of us. I've moved here so we can prepare together. If…huh…that's still what you wish for."

I lifted a hand. "You moved here?"

"Yeah. Can we talk about it later? I'm tired. These hormones are still tampering with my sleeping schedule."

I scratched the column of my throat, my emotions twisted into chains, tangled together and impossible to separate. "Fine. Let's see. I'm not a pregnancy expert, but I'll try. How far along are you?"

"Eleven weeks."

"Eleven? Our little Nashville bet was like nine weeks ago. I might not be a hormone genius, but I'm a math nerd."

"That's how they calculate it. From the last period. Back in Green Mountain, the bleeding…it's called spotting… The doctor says it can happen in the first few months, and I shouldn't worry."

"Oh. It was my next question. What about that pill you took?"

"It failed. Big time," she said, pointing to her abdomen.

"Oh." I regrouped my thoughts.

She lifted a finger, then rose to rummage through her purse for a piece of paper before handing it to me.

I unfolded it. A dark square fell, but I ignored it as I read the results of her blood work. One word stood out. *Pregnant.*

Sensations foreign to me invaded my body. Pride? Anxiety? Fear? Contentment? How could I define the cocktail of emotions simmering inside me? Tingles transformed into goose bumps. Now I had the written confirmation I'd be a daddy.

I'm going to be a daddy. That sounded so surreal.

Whoa, I'd have to rehearse saying it when I was alone. Until my mind came to terms with the fact that it was real.

Addison wrapped herself in the blanket I kept at the end of the couch, and seeing her at ease in my home sent my heart into a frenzy. How could she have no idea how perfect we were for each other?

Our stares fused, and something powerful and raw passed between us. Foreign emotions welled up in my eyes. I blinked them away as my throat constricted, crushing my vocal cords.

Addison gestured to the square of paper that had landed on the rug, and I picked it up.

If I thought seeing the word *pregnant* would shatter me, nothing had prepared me for the black-and-white picture of a tiny bean that I guessed to be my baby. *Our baby.*

My heart beat fast, leaping in all directions inside my chest.

I rubbed the column of my throat and tried to swallow. "Wow," I mumbled, my eyes fixated on the colorless form. "Why didn't you tell me sooner?" Hurt seared in me at the idea she'd kept me in the dark about something that concerned both of us. "By now, I thought I'd proved you could trust me and that I'd have your back."

"Listen…I'm sorry for all the back and forth. I really thought I wasn't pregnant. Until I lost consciousness at work… At first, I-I blamed long hours, lack of sleep, and low mineral levels. The doctor told me it could happen. Now I know better, though."

"You fainted?"

"Yeah. Due to low blood pressure." She fidgeted with her hands. "Just so you know, bleeding instead of a period at the beginning isn't uncommon…and it can be misleading, as you can tell. It's also a side effect of the morning-after pill. Unless I'd taken the test you got, I wouldn't have known. I-I'm sorry." She twisted a strand of blonde hair around her forefinger, her gaze barely meeting mine.

"How are you doing? For real? Aside from the fainting and the exhaustion?"

"Under the circumstances, I'm doing okay. I'm still a bit shocked, so it's hard to tell. I'm not sure I've fully realized it yet. On the other hand, I'm already attached to this little peanut. It's a part of me. It's hard to explain… And a bit confusing."

I scooted closer to her and grabbed her hand, squeezing it in between mine. Using a fingertip, I traced the lines of her palm. "Where do we go from here? What are we to each other? How will this work?"

Addison pinched her lips together and said nothing for a long beat. "No idea. As I've already told you, I want to be with you…just without the pressure. Can we take our time?

Learn to be with each other without officially being a couple? See how we work together? Learn each other's habits, what drives us crazy, who we are in this relationship, and decide if we can still stay together when we get on each other's nerves or fight. If we're better as lovers…or friends."

"What you say speaks to me. It doesn't mean I'm overjoyed with the idea of being only friends with you, Wilde, but we can give it a try…if that's what you wish. Be warned, though. I'll be here. Every step of the way. No matter what we are to each other."

By now, I had a permanent, stupid grin etched on my face. I could tell by the stretch of my lips and the tautness of my cheeks.

Without being aware, Addison and I had come up with very much alike plans, and it confirmed the validity of mine. It all had a purpose now—greater than just getting the girl back. I'd just have to adapt the moving-to-Atlanta part.

"What about your apartment?" I asked.

"Becca's He agreed to move in at the end of the month if I decide that staying here is what's best for me…for us." She locked her eyes on mine. "They were already talking about moving in together, so it makes sense. For now, I'm working remotely, but I've been offered a position at a marketing firm in town starting next month. If I stay here. Let's just say it's a lot to deal with. Also, I have my first scheduled sonogram in a few days, and I thought you might like to join me. My OB-GYN back in Atlanta referred me to a great doctor here in Chicago. He said we'd be in good hands."

More sparks of joy packed my chest, and I nodded, lacking the words to express how I really felt.

"So…you agree…huh, with everything?" Addison

looked at me with a lopsided smile, her gaze filling with what could be defined as hope. Or expectation.

"Sweetheart, I wanna do it all with you. I haven't changed my mind. We'll go slow, help you find your pace, but I'll be by your side through all of it."

I leaned in to claim her lips, but she cocked her head, and my mouth connected with her cheek instead. I blinked, unsure what it meant.

"Sorry. Too much too soon. Can we wait and see how it goes? Please."

My throat worked, and I barely contained the flecks of annoyance rising inside me. Nothing was going according to my plan, and I had to adapt. Still, I hadn't expected us to be just friends. Not in a million years. "Platonic relationship. Sure. Understood."

Addison flicked a hand between us, her smile fading. "No. Yes. Friends with no benefits…only for now, okay? I know it's not what you want. Don't be mad. Please. Give us a little more time to adjust. Gimme a little more time because it's a lot to take in. A few days ago, I was still freaking out."

I let out a chuckle, and she stared at me with an arched brow. The curve of her lips did wild things to my dick. I had to focus and not listen to the bastard for once. But God, it felt good to know he was still well and alive around her, that he too recognized her as ours.

I cleared my throat, silently begging my hormones to calm down. "How long have you known?"

"A week. Telling you in person was the right thing to do. I-I couldn't have dumped the news on you over the phone, but it felt wrong. And I couldn't tell you right away because I had a few things to deal with first and also…well, I had to wrap my head around it. To be able to have this discussion with you."

"Thanks. I really appreciate that you came here to tell me." My voice sounded calm, though inside I was still reeling from the news she'd delivered.

"Are you all right?" she asked. "I unloaded all this on you. I wanna make sure you're okay."

I nodded. "I will be. Are you moving in? You should have told me, I would have... I don't know, but I would have made room for you. Clear half of my closet or something."

"I'm not. We need our own space to make sure that if we jump into this, we do it right. For our baby's sake."

My breathing quickened. Knots tightened in my stomach. A million questions circled in my head. I had to know. "How do we see us being an *us*?"

Addison pushed loose strands of her hair away from her face. "Like I said, I wanna be with you. I really do. But I'm not willing to rush it. If we do this, we gotta do it right. Take our time. Learn to be together."

"Why do you wanna live anywhere else then? Stay here." The next words burned the tip of my tongue. "In... in the guest room. You can make it yours...for now. Or whichever room you choose...mine included. I'll never kick you out or ask you to leave."

"I already have a place. Trust me, it's better this way." Her eyes rounded with curiosity. "Wait. Didn't you say you were selling this place? Where would you go?"

I huffed. "Atlanta."

She blinked.

"To pursue you. To show you I'm serious about us."

"You were? For me?" A lone tear flowed down her cheek, and I caught it with my thumb.

I nodded. "Always for you. The last three weeks without you have shown me just how much I enjoy your presence in my life. I've missed you, Wilde. That's the ugly truth."

Scooting even closer, I pressed my forehead to hers.

"I've missed you too. I'm sorry for making things complicated, but for once, I just wanna do it right. Because you're precious to me."

"We'll be okay. We'll find our normal..."—I slid my hand under her sweater, letting it rest over her belly, feeling the warmth beneath my palm—"before Mini-Wilde is born." The small gesture encompassed all that I was feeling, like being the protector of the two most important people in my life.

"Thanks for understanding. For being you."

"You sure you don't wanna stay here? With me? I just got you back. I have two of you now to watch over, and I'm not sure I can sleep peacefully, knowing you're somewhere out there and I have no say about it."

Addison's laughter warmed my heart. "Don't get all possessive, big guy. I'm living like ten minutes away from you. We'll make it work." Her lips stretched into a yawn. "I gotta go. Some of my stuff is being delivered in two days. I want to make the place mine. Set it up. And today has been the longest day ever."

I moved to my feet and shoved my hands into my pockets. "Sure. I'll drive you."

"Tuck, you don't have to—"

"I do. You're the woman I love and the mother of my unborn child. Jesus, saying that out loud makes it seem even more real."

She poked my shoulder with a fingertip. "Get used to it. It's happening."

Twenty minutes later, we were in my SUV as I followed her instructions to her new place. The rain had stopped, and the dark cab of my truck felt more intimate as I blanketed her hand with mine, resting it in her lap.

"Next light, on your right," she said.

"You picked nice. It's a wealthy neighborhood. I thought you'd have rented an apartment. I'm feeling a bit better knowing you'll be here rather than in a two-room shithole in a sketchy neighborhood."

"A shithole was all I could afford in this economy, but a friend of mine offered me his pool house for as long as I would need it. It's way better than living with some roommate I've never met."

"I prefer you somewhere safe. Funny, though, Rory Dupont lives here. You may run into him."

I turned right. Then left. Then stopped in front of a massive red-bricked house behind a black-iron gate.

My eyes zoomed in on the address plate twice. Then I looked around, making sure we were at the right place.

"Thank you for driving me," Addison said, fetching her purse from the backseat. "We'll talk later. Find time to be together. Date, like couples do. Get to know each other better. Like we used to do."

None of her words registered. Specks of anger lodged in my throat. With a strained voice, I studied her features and barked, "Are you staying at Dupont's? Is this a joke?"

With a stiffened back and tightly pressed lips, her demeanor told me she knew I'd be pissed. "It's not what you think. Listen, I was talking with Ted the other day and—"

"Duffy? The goalie? Why were you talking to my friend?"

"As I was saying before you interrupted, I was talking with Ted about a second custom shirt he had ordered and told him I was moving here."

I harrumphed despite myself.

"Don't act all jealous and stuff. Anyway, Ted said Rory has a pool house on his property that nobody uses, and since he's barely ever here, I could live in it rent-free and house-sit for him when he's away. Don't be a jerk about it. I'm not technically staying *with* him."

"Semantics."

She flung her arms into the air. "Oh, c'mon now. Are you serious? Let's leave it at this for tonight. We'll talk about my living arrangements later."

She motioned to open the door when I pushed the lock button—twice for good measure.

"Tuck—"

"Fuck no. No way. You're not staying at Dupont's when I'm in town. No. Not happening. My woman. My baby. Never."

She balled her small fists. "Tuck—" My name sounded like a warning on her lips.

"I know my friend. Forget it. The answer is still no."

I put the car in reverse and pulled away from the driveway before I could say something I might regret—and before Addison had time to escape my truck. She crossed her arms over her chest, a pouty expression taking over her face. One I wished I could kiss away and turn into a smile. Aimed at me. Not fucking Dupont.

Once I calmed down a little, I gave it a try. "How in hell did you think I'd be okay with you living at another guy's house, pregnant with my child? Tell me, Wilde. I'm confused right now. Even though he's my friend, he's still a guy."

"Tuck—"

"Both of you are staying at my place. End of discussion. Sleep in the guest room. In my bed. On the couch. As long as it's not at another man's house, I'll be reasonable and give you all the space you're asking for."

She sighed. "Geez, I had everything planned."

"Well, I did too. I had a four-step plan. To win you back. But you showed up here unannounced before I could make it to step three."

After a long moment, Addison asked in a softer tone, "What's step three? And what were steps one and two?"

My wrath dissolved. Bit by bit. "Sell the condo. Work remotely. Move to Atlanta."

The ripple of her swallow was all I could hear. "And step four?" she asked, her voice barely above a whisper, her eyes glinting with suppressed happiness.

"Get the girl."

I turned my head to gauge her reaction, but before I could, her focus switched to the busy city streets through the passenger window.

My heart lodged in my throat. Did my confession scare her, or was it exactly what she hoped I'd say? Silence fell upon us. Thick and intense.

Addison Wilde usually had a ready comeback or a fight in her, but this time... nothing. Not a word. I dragged a hand over my face. All I wanted to do was to kiss her senseless, fuck her till the morning, make her mine, and never let go of her. Because, through her craziness, she brought me peace. And it still made no sense to me most of the time that I craved a relationship, but we hadn't seen each other in almost a month, and my thirst for her hadn't decreased—it had just multiplied. Now I was condemned to sit on the sidelines until she decided she was ready to give us a chance, and it fucked with all my instincts.

I could push her, but I doubted Addison Wilde would react positively to being pushed, and the last thing I wanted was for her to backtrack and leave town because she felt pressured into a relationship she wasn't ready for.

So, I'd be patient. And wait. Prevent anger or disappointment from getting between us.

"Hungry?" I asked after a beat.

She cleared her throat. "Yeah. I haven't had dinner yet."

I stopped at a red light and rotated my upper body in her direction. "I'm no doctor, but not eating while you're pregnant isn't the way to go."

"I'm well-aware. I wanted to ask you out on a date when I first got here. I had this idea in my head. Then I was going to set up my new place. Make it mine. You made sure this wouldn't happen." Her words sounded more exhausted, and sad, than angry. "You had your way. Twice so far. Now I can't even throw myself a moving-in celebration."

"Wilde—"

"It's fine." Tremors filled her words.

"Pizza. What about the deep-dish you like?"

"Sure."

"You can still celebrate moving into your new place. In my condo. Until further notice, it's your new address, and I hope you'll make it yours."

She sent a lopsided smile my way but added nothing.

It bothered not only my heart but also my soul that I'd ruined her plans.

———

Sitting by the window overlooking Lake Michigan, just as we had been the first time Addison surprised me with a visit, we indulged in pizza on paper plates. Neither of us said anything, a heavy silence echoing between the walls.

"What about your needs?" I asked once I flushed down the last bite with a sip of water. "How do you take care of yourself? I'm aware of the intensity of your libido, woman. Let's just say it's explosive. And insatiable. So, I'm curious."

I hated the distance that had fallen upon us. Perhaps a lighter subject could lift the heaviness in the air, easing the tension in the room.

Addison rolled her eyes at me. Yep, she did. Again. "FYI, I can relieve myself just fine."

I responded with a noncommittal, one-shoulder shrug. "The offer still stands if you ever need help." My lips curved into a mischievous smile I knew she couldn't resist.

It worked. Her cheeks tinted red, and I winked in reply. The air around us instantly crackled with explosive heat, every glance and half-smile loaded with unspoken desire.

Addison tried to hide the hunger in her eyes as they roamed over me, but failed. Flames of desire ignited when she gave me a slow once-over, biting her bottom lip while desperately avoiding my gaze.

"Nope. All fine. I just filled my spank bank with brand new images. Thank you very much."

"If you ever change your mind, just say the word."

Her cheeks flushed darker. Yes, I still had a lot of effect on her.

"Our story is skipping chapters, and we gotta figure out how to write the missing parts together. Stop trying to fuck my brain out."

A brand-new smirk formed on my lips. "It's not your brain I wanna fuck, but sure, if you're offering."

Addison backhanded my upper arm. "Tuck. Not funny. Keep your dirty scenarios to yourself. I'm trying to act like the grown-up here, and you're trying to pervert my train of thoughts." She shook her head. "*Clear head. Not drenched panties.* That's my new motto when it comes to you."

Jesus, I'd missed her so damn much.

"Drenched panties? Wanna tell me more?"

"Tuck." My name, dripping from her lips, sounded like a warning, but she was unable to hide the amusement playing on her face.

I raised my palms between us. "Fine. No more sexual innuendos. I forgot you were a prude, Wilde. My bad."

She threw up her hands. "This isn't funny. I'm confused right now. Sex is usually my go-to therapy. Always has been… Not this time, though. In case you didn't know, you're supposed to be supportive, and right now, you're not helping. At all."

I cupped her face. "I can't wait to see how long you last."

She closed her eyes, did some meditation thingy with her fingers, and breathed in and out a few times.

"Is it working?" I asked.

She opened her eyelids one at a time. "Shhh. Zip it." She closed her eyes once more, yet that teasing curve of her lips remained. "By the way, I'm still mad at you. Kidnapping is a felony in the state of Illinois. And everywhere else in the country."

"From what I remember, you're the one who handcuffed yourself the last time we were together. It's fair to say you're a willing participant in a kidnapping scheme. You just lack a way of expressing your gratitude."

While I cleaned up after dinner, Addison moved to stand by the panoramic window. I stepped behind her while she watched the city lights below.

"Won't you miss this view?" she asked.

Her gaze caught mine in the glass, and this time, it was I who looked away.

"Maybe. But I stand behind the decision to sell this place. I love it here, but I've overextended my stay in this bachelor pad. Thanks to you, who opened my eyes, I wish for more from this life than a career and expensive shit. Chicago isn't the place where I wanna raise our baby." I wrapped my arms around her waist, resting my palm over her flat stomach. After a beat, she leaned back against me as I whispered, "No matter what, we'll be all right. I promise."

With a cock of her head, Addison's eyes found mine over her shoulder, trying to read my intentions—and my soul. No one guarded the door when it came to her. She had full access and held the only VIP key that existed.

"Wh-what if we can't be together?" she mumbled after a minute.

"Time will tell. For now, I'm more than happy that my best friend is back because I freaking missed her while we were apart. I had no one to send random text messages to or to call late at night when I was home alone."

She snorted. "Glad to know I'm so useful. Were you really moving to Atlanta if I hadn't come here?"

I nodded. "Yes. There's nowhere else I'd rather be than with you." And as I'd been dying to do for weeks, I pulled her against my heart, my lips resting on the crown of her head.

Calmness washed over me, and my heart resumed its beating, at peace for the first time since the day after Nick and Dahlia's wedding.

———

"Do you maybe wanna share a bed?" I asked Addison after I showered and met her in the kitchen. She was having a late-night craving, eating peanut butter toast. I studied her face, wondering if I'd pushed my luck with my offer.

"Sure you don't want one?" she asked with a mouthful, a square of toast in her hand.

I shook my head, smiling.

She looked so damn cute, dressed down, her hair braided over her shoulder, pregnant with my child—not that she showed yet, but I knew it, so it was just as fucking hot. I couldn't wait for her to get bigger, to feel the baby kicking.

"It may blur the lines even more than they already are."

I shrugged and got closer. "I've missed you. We'll just cuddle. That's our thing. I wanna hold you. Have you two with me. Protect you. And make sure you being here isn't a dream. Just for a few hours. Before you freak out and start running again."

We exchanged grins. The friction in the air from earlier had faded. We were back to being our usual selves, the fight forgotten.

"For your information, I won't. Soon I'll be too fat to run, anyway."

"No, you'll be perfect. To me, you already are."

The smile she aimed at me settled every inch of me. It lodged in my chest.

She chuckled. "No wonder you played the scene. You always have the best replies."

I propped my elbows on the kitchen island until our faces were inches apart. "Yeah, but this time I mean every word. It's not a ruse to seduce you. You're already under my charm, Wilde."

Addison pushed my chest with a hand. "That's a hell of an ego you've got, big guy."

I took a step back and pumped my fist. "Ladies and gentlemen, Addison Wilde is back."

I winked and saw her squirming on the bar stool.

One day, she'd be brave enough to tell me she loved me. Because I could tell she did. All the signs were there.

The way she watched me and grinned when she thought I didn't notice. The tilt of her lips, her dilated pupils, her flushed cheeks. How she always found a reason to touch my hand or hug me a little longer than required. Nonetheless, and most importantly, she'd moved across the country to be with me. It had to count for something.

After not many arguments from me, we both climbed into bed, and before we positioned ourselves, I pushed the covers back. "Can I touch you?"

Her eyes flared and her breathing accelerated.

"Your belly, I mean. Let him or her know I'm here."

She combed my hair with her fingers, the tingling in my scalp addictive and playing with my weakened composure. "Tucker Philips, you're an amazing man. You see, that's the problem. You're too good, and I'm not ready for you. At least, not fully yet."

Staring into my eyes, she lifted her shirt, exposing her bare stomach, and in that moment, all I wished for was to make her mine. In every sense imaginable. My body pulsed. My breathing picked up. Everything about Addison Wilde enticed me. Her beauty. Her vulnerability. Her energy.

She continued brushing my hair back with her fingers, and right then, I realized something as if it had been carved into my soul: I would love this woman forever. She had rescued me from the prison my life had been for so long, freed my heart, added colors to my black and white existence, and glitter to my days in the way she shone. No matter what had brought her back into my life, she was here. That was all that mattered. She had come to me.

Dipping my head, I peppered kisses all over her flesh. "Hey, baby. It's the first time we're really meeting. I'm Tucker, and I'm your daddy." Swallowing became harder. All those feelings flooded my chest. I closed my eyes for a fraction of a second. Never before had I felt the way I did at the moment. And somehow, it was impossible to define it with words. The corners of my eyes leaked, but I kept going. "I have no clue if you can hear me or not or how this works, but from now on, you'll hear my voice every day…" My voice cracked on the last word.

"Tuck—" Addison's voice sounded rough, laced with emotions.

I inhaled through my nose to be able to deliver the rest of my message to my unborn child. "Baby, I promise you here and now, in front of your mama, to do my best. Even when I mess up, remember that I love you. That…that I'll always be there for you. Can you do that? I-I'll never make you feel like you don't belong or you are in the way or not important to me. We'll make it work. Trust me. From now on, your mama and you…you two will forever be the center of my universe."

Addison's hand froze above my head, and when my gaze drifted to hers, I saw her drying the silent tears cascading down her cheeks with her other hand.

"Oh, and one more thing. 'Cause I don't want you to ever believe otherwise. I love your mama. Very *very* much. We may have to remind her frequently because she isn't ready, but I'll prove to her I'm worthy of her love too. And that I'll step up. Be there. Support her and her devious plans, cheer her on when she has had a bad day, or rock her to sleep when the insomnia kicks in. She's the most amazing woman I've ever met, so be gentle with her. She has the wildest spirit and biggest heart I know. She's funny and crazy at times, but in the best ways. You're lucky to have her. I am too. And, to be honest, I didn't believe in love before her."

I kissed Addison's belly once again, not ready to move away.

"Tuck? Did you mean everything you just said?"

Addison's voice, soft and strained, drew my gaze back to her face. "Yep. And it's just the beginning." I adjusted her shirt back over her stomach, pulled the covers up, and rolled to my side untilI could hold her the way I'd been aching to. "Now sleep. I'm watching over you two." I kissed her nape, imprinting the fruity scent of her shampoo on my senses, and closed my eyes, relishing this moment and knowing I would for the rest of my life.

In the middle of the night, I woke up to the glow of my phone, telling me it was almost three in the morning. I patted the bed around me and wondered for a few seconds if I had dreamed the entire night. Addison. The baby. Our entangled bodies sharing my bed.

With my fists, I chased sleep from my eyes.

Tingles prickled along my nape. I could still feel her energy clinging to the space around me. Her presence here was real, not a figment of my imagination.

If it wasn't a dream, then where was she?

A clamp tightened around my heart as a thought crept in. No. She wouldn't leave…right? I jumped to my feet, slid my limbs into a pair of cotton pants, and padded through my apartment in search of her.

My pulse thundered as I looked around and found no trace of her. I dragged a hand over my face as I reached the guest room where I'd put her stuff in earlier.

I huffed a long breath and relaxed my shoulders when I spotted her unzipped suitcase on the bed. Yet, no sign of her either. In the doorway, I scanned the room, waiting for my heart to settle.

"Wilde?" I called out as I returned to the living room.

No answer.

I tried again. And again.

It was like she had vanished into the night.

I pressed my fingers to my temples, dread coursing through my veins. Spinning on my heels, I went back to my bedroom and grabbed my phone to call her number.

It rang, and I found her device lying discarded on the kitchen counter.

Where was she?

That was when I noticed the blanket and pillow missing from the couch. It hit me then, a hunch telling me exactly where to find her.

The rooftop.

Two by two, I climbed the stairs until I reached the door leading outside.

There she was, lying on her back, one arm resting protectively across her abdomen, the other tucked beneath her head. I moved closer, the steady sound of her snoring curling my lips.

Careful not to wake her up, I slid under the blanket next to her and circled her waist with one arm, nuzzling her neck.

Addison wriggled beside me. "Hey you," she said after a moment, settling between my arms. "How did you find me?"

"I looked everywhere for you. My bed is empty when you're not in it. Thought for a second you'd disappeared on me."

She kissed my cheek, and I could've died right there. "Tuck, we're linked for life now. I'll never leave without telling you first. I swear."

Her words brought heat to my core.

"Truth? I'm scared."

I brushed the side of her face with my knuckles. "I know. I am too."

"But you said—"

I gave her a small shrug. "It doesn't change the fact I have no clue how to be a father. You didn't plan for this… and I…huh…didn't either. With anyone else, I would've freaked out by now, but somehow, with you, it's different. *You're* different. You bring me peace. Also, I believe together we can achieve anything. We can achieve greatness."

"Why do you have so much faith in me? In us?"

"With you, it goes over simple attraction. It's much bigger than that. I can't explain it, so I trust my instincts. The same way I trust you."

"But—"

I framed her face with both hands. "No but. Lean on me when it gets too much, and we'll be just fine."

"Thank you."

We stayed in each other's embrace for a little while, all the words we spoke enveloping us. Linking us for life. And healing more layers of my previously bruised and thick-walled heart.

"Just so you know, when I joined you, you were snoring. I heard you. Loud and clear."

Addison's laughter resonated in the inky night, and she pushed my chest with a hand. "No, I was not."

"Ask this baby of ours, and you'll see it'll team up with me on this one."

"Shut up, big guy."

"Never." I paused and sucked in a breath as our eyes, in the dim light of the rooftop, promised things we hadn't discussed yet. Things only our souls could recognize. Yeah, something had switched between us. "Come to bed. It's late."

She nodded and gripped the hand I offered after I moved to my feet. My eyes widened when I noticed she was wearing the hoodie and pants I'd worn earlier. The realization shot me with so much pride—and a smidge of possessiveness. Addison Wilde would be mine. Someday.

"I see you're wearing my clothes," I teased as she made no move to remove her hand from my grip.

"You told me once that your clothes looked good on me, so…" She shrugged, as if that explained everything.

I stepped closer, and the air soared between us. Time stopped. My heart banged against its cage. Addison's breathing picked up. She licked the length of her bottom lip with her tongue, and I followed the motion with my eyes, entranced by everything that she was. Vibrant and mesmerizing, her eyes darted to mine. They traveled to my mouth as she moved closer.

In that instant, I just lost it. Tilting my head, I kissed her lips. Slow and torturous at first. Starving and hungry afterward. Addison melted against me when I molded my hands to her hip crests. Our tongues touched, and she gasped, and gravity left me. I tangled my fingers into her mane, devouring her sweet lips, wishing to keep her as close to me as possible for the rest of the night—and the rest of my life.

"Tuck. We shouldn't," she said between breaths, the air surrounding us catching fire. "But for some reason, I can't seem to stop. I-I lied to you earlier… Thinking about you when I come is not nearly enough… It never is. Now that you're here…next to me…I want you so bad. I always do."

"I know, sweetheart, and I don't want to stop either. I've missed you so damn much."

Our bodies engaged in a conversation that required no words.

We kissed for what felt like hours. Taking our time. Playful. Both of us, teasing and starving.

"The truth is, I'm sex-deprived. Can we have sex and still learn to be with each other without actually being together, or will it complicate everything?" she asked, detaching her mouth from mine, breathless.

"Right now, I'll do whatever you ask of me, but please, don't take this away from our relationship. Our connection is more than physical, and considering we're both sexual people, it feels wrong to remove this perk from our friendship agreement. I believe it's important for the baby to sense his parents enjoy being with each other. Making each other feel good is the root of it."

Addison smiled against my lips. "Oh, you didn't just go there. You can't use the baby to convince me. It's called emotional blackmail."

"I did," I said in the cockiest way I could muster. "My sidekick and I will be an unstoppable force. And right now, I'll take one for the team."

My tongue tasted the flesh of her neck, the length of her collarbones, the lobe of her ear.

She ground her hips against mine in an erotic tempo. "Oh...keep going...okay," she said in a throaty voice that powered up my entire body. "Only to relieve the tension and calm my crazy pregnancy hormones. For now."

I nodded because, at the moment, I would've agreed to anything to bury myself in the woman I loved and who was the mother of my unborn child.

Somehow, through the daze of kissing, we made it back to my place and tumbled onto the bed, panting. My greedy self longed to touch Addison everywhere. Every delicate inch of her. The ones I memorized. Those I knew by heart. The ones I'd been deprived of cherishing for weeks now.

Hungry for her breasts, I peeled the hoodie over her head and dropped forward. Her puckered nipples looked darker than I remembered. I sucked one hard tip, trying to tame some of the thirst for her searing at my core.

Her back arched, and she let out a loud cry. "Sorry. My body is hypersensitive. I should've warned you."

I kneaded her other breast under my palm, the fullness heavy in my hand. "Want me to stop?"

"Nah, never. Don't ever mention this silly idea again, you hear me? I don't care how painful it gets. You offered to be the man for the job, so just put those fingers inside me now because I'm throbbing down there, and I'll throw a fit if you don't draw an orgasm out of me soon."

"Jesus, Wilde, you kill me with your words alone. Your suffering ends now."

On my knees, I yanked the pants down her legs and licked that moist junction between her thighs, while clutching her ass cheeks with my hands. She trembled when my tongue entered her and glided in and out of her tight channel in slow thrust.

"Tuck...I-I... Oh God. *Yesss*." She jerked her head back. "More. So much more."

"It's just the beginning, sweetheart. Now relax and enjoy the ride." I plunged two fingers inside her and sucked on her clit. Sliding my digits back and forth, I dragged the pleasure out of her. Addison rolled her hips, increasing the friction, moaning as her walls clenched around my fingers. I pressed my tongue harder against her bundle of nerves as I enjoyed her sweetness and increased the tempo. She was close. I could feel it. My hand reached inside my pants, and I fisted my dick, trying to relieve some of the painful tension straining it. Addison's thighs pressed on either side of my head, preventing me from moving. I kept the rhythm of my tongue and fingers until she exploded in a climactic bliss. We both breathed hard, staring into each other's eyes.

"Wilde, you taste too fucking good. I missed this. I missed you."

She surfed the wave of pleasure while I got rid of all my clothes, ready to rip them to shreds in my hurry. Soon, I had her pinned under me on the mattress, her legs spread.

She brushed my skin with her hands, sending flutters through me. Jesus, this felt as good as it was torturous after all this time.

She moved one hand lower, and I held my breath as she curled it around my painful erection. Squeezing and pumping me, her grip unrelenting, she became its sole owner. My cock and I made a pact right there. To surrender ourselves to this woman, no matter the cost. Because, against all odds, she possessed advanced expertise in my body. Everything else melted away as she played me like I was her favorite instrument, every movement igniting me from the inside out. In one swift motion of her hips, she positioned me at her entrance. Spellbound, I watched her engulfing each throbbing inch of me in one long, slow thrust, her slick wetness now both my undoing and salvation.

Her eyes flared as I filled her up completely.

She shivered, and the look of pure lust radiating from her, illuminating every line of her face, broke me in the most animalistic way.

She smiled, and there was no going back.

Using my tongue, lips, and teeth, I devoured the flesh of her throat, marking her as she cried out her satisfaction. Once I sampled every inch of her, I pounded into her, my hips like pistons against her flesh, delivering on the promise I'd made to rock her world and satisfy all the need and hunger inside her. And brand her as mine.

"Fuck, you're so hot."

Addison watched me, sweat beading along her hairline, her pupils wide, and all hell broke loose.

I rammed into her until neither of us could suck a full breath in, and we both went over the edge, crying each other's name.

I slid down her sinful body and trailed kisses from the sensitive flesh between her thighs to the valley of her breasts.

"Wilde, I'm taking the job. I'll be your sex slave, no matter the time of day or night. Just say the code word and I'll take care of all your needs."

"And what's the code word?" Her husky voice had some amazing effect on my dick, bringing it back to life all over again.

"Pineapple."

Addison burst out laughing, the sound resonating through each cell of my body. "Pineapple?"

I nodded. "Yeah. You're both nectar and spikes."

We washed ourselves and fell back under the covers, where I fastened my arms around her. I had no idea what we were, but I would take whatever she was willing to give me. For now. Until all her fears melted away. Until we became each other's entire world.

"Night."

She buried her face into my chest. "Good night, Tuck."

Chapter 11

Addison

"**A**re you gonna sit down and eat with me?" Tucker asked, stepping closer. "We've been living together for over two months, and you barely ever make it to the table, always perched on the countertop or eating while you walk around." He kissed my cheek. "Were you always this restless growing up?"

I spoke with my mouth full. "Pretty much. Now that the tiredness from the first trimester is something of the past, I've got all my energy back. And more in bank. Sitting down is a waste of my time. I much prefer doing anything else. Want me to redecorate your place?"

"What's wrong with the decor?"

"Nothing. I'm just looking for a new project to tackle."

"Wilde, you work full time for that marketing firm, work over twenty hours on your own business, and find time to house-sit for Dupont. And on top of that, you're pregnant."

I rolled my eyes. "Stop being dramatic."

"I'm serious. Don't you think you're already burning the candle at both ends? Sooner or later, it's going to bite you in the ass."

"I just possess all this pent-up energy. Meditation helps, and I don't want to start running around the block or going to the gym. Not my style. I much prefer keeping myself busy."

"Fine, but if I think you're overdoing it, we'll revisit this conversation."

Placing my empty bowl on the counter next to me, I jumped down.

Tucker eyed me. "Where are you going?"

A big part of me loved the caring version of him. It always spoke to my heart whenever he worried about me or got protective in the sweetest ways.

"Hilary, from next door, invited me to her book club meeting."

"When did you find time to read a book?"

"Saw the movie." I shrugged. "And Dah told me about the missing parts, so I'll be fine. I can pretend and talk my way through it. Don't worry about me. I don't have girlfriends here because all your hockey player friends are single and never in town, and you still haven't introduced me to Pam."

"Forget it. I won't. She's the devil. Don't want her around my child."

"But he or she is not even born yet."

"Still. Not up for discussion." His hands found my waist, and he pulled me to him. "Will you join me for that barbecue on Saturday? It's an off-work event. A family gathering. You'll meet people."

"Sure, I'm free. I have a yoga class in the morning, but other than that, my schedule is empty."

A frown etched Tucker's forehead. "Yoga? Since when?"

"Last week. Trying to be zen. For the baby's sake." I searched his face. "Since you're not moving out of town, are you going back to the office, or continuing with remote work?"

"For now, I love working from home. I've even cut back my hours to focus on that side project."

I gave him my best puppy dog eyes, but he didn't relent.

"Nope. Not telling you. Not until it's ready. Forget it."

I sighed.

"Anyway, until we decide what we'll do with us, the baby, and where we'll move, I prefer handling my schedule on my own terms." He crossed his arms over his chest, as if to add weight to his words.

Tucker and I looked like a couple. We acted like a couple. We bantered like a couple. But we were just friends for now. Anyway, that was our official title to describe our relationship. We slept in the same bed at night, and we cuddled for hours, but we were taking things slowly.

"Anyway, I always have to pick up after you," he said with a shake of his head. "I can't believe how sloppy you get. Exhausted Addison had an excuse to be lazy. Energetic Addison doesn't have any."

"Life is already stressful, so don't add another layer. I'll do the dishes later. When I return. Nothing says it can't be done in a few hours. There's no rush. I'll get it done when I'm in the right state of mind to tackle it. Don't worry."

"I hate it when the place isn't clean. Cleanness eases my mind."

"Coming from the guy who orders his ties by color, I understand the frustration. Let go, big guy. It's good for you to learn to relax."

His lips connected with mine. "That's not how I relax." His hard body pressed against mine. Air charged around us. All my cells vibrated at the promise in his voice. "Got other ways… You sure you wanna go to a boring book club meeting?"

I nodded and spoke against his mouth. "Mm-hmm. It will be fun."

He took a step back and raised his hands between us. "Fun?"

"Yeah. Fun. That's what I said."

"Suit yourself then. I'll go back to my dinner."

My body froze at the withdrawal. What Tucker and I shared couldn't be explained, but it was real. More real than anything I'd ever had before.

As if he sensed the broken connection too, he spun me around, his front pressing against my back. With a skillful gesture, he lifted my shirt so it billowed around my waist and yanked my panties down. The sound of his zipper being drawn down sent a thrill through me. I shivered when he traced my lower back with his thick erection and embedded it between my ass cheeks, thrusting up and down at a slow pace.

"I've changed my mind. Dinner can wait. You sure you wanna go?" His husky tone sent all my hair standing on end. He leaned forward, sucking the flesh between my shoulder blades with hungry lips.

"Y…yes."

He caressed my belly before lowering his fingers between my legs. The slightest pressure of his hand's heel against my clit was electrifying and enough to send my head spinning.

"You want me to fuck you, Wilde? To brand myself on you, so you'd remember the feel of me all night?"

I bobbed my head fast, half-cries tumbling from my lips as he increased the pace of his fondling. "*Pleassse.*"

Pushing me forward with a hand until my upper body lay sprawled across the countertop, Tucker asked in my ear, his voice pure lust that electrified every one of my cells, "You want me inside you, sweetheart?"

"*Yesss,*" I croaked out, my voice barely sounding like mine.

With purpose and skillful fingers, he spread the lips of my sex apart. "You're so wet."

He inserted himself inside me to the brim with no hesitation until a soft yelp broke the silence of our combined, rushed breathing.

He gripped my hipbones, and I disconnected from the present. My world had narrowed down to the flesh pounding into me and the waves of pleasure surfing inside me.

Tucker rammed hard, and I saw stars. A full galaxy. The sound of his flesh slapping against mine increased the arousal dripping from me.

I pushed away from the countertop with my hands, trying to keep my body from dissolving against his.

Keeping one arm around my shoulder, Tucker drew closer, increasing the contact of our bodies, his thrusts harder and faster. "Want me to punish you for going to that stupid book club?"

"Do it," I screamed. "Fuck me like you hate me."

Gliding out of me and lifting me in his arms, he spread me on my back on the kitchen table. The cold surface sent chills through me, heightening every sensation. I enjoyed the contrast beneath my heated skin, Tucker burning hot as he resumed his steady rhythm inside me.

The taut expression on his face reminded me of the

guy who fucked me for endless hours in my hotel suite back in Nashville the weekend we first met.

Animalistic. Unapologetic.

He rubbed lazy, delicious circles over my clit with the pad of his thumb.

I detonated against his fingers, but he never reduced his pace. Instead, he drove into me with more conviction, never giving me time to surf the climax working through me.

"Want more, Wilde? Want me to fuck you so you're late and all flustered and everyone knows I got my way with you?"

I nodded.

He leaned over me, pinned my hands above my head with one of his, as his gaze turned darker. Growls sliced through his throat. He attacked my mouth with bruising kisses. My tongue darted out to battle with his, and I bit his lips. He nipped my tongue. I hollered as more pleasure traveled through me.

"You're lucky you're pregnant, Wilde, or I would have spread you on your front."

A twinkle passed through his eyes. Directed at me.

He stepped back, and lowering to his knees, assaulted the flesh he'd just speared into with his tongue. His licks weren't gentle. They were meant to rob me of my common sense, of everything in that moment that wasn't him.

I linked my ankles behind his neck and squeezed his head between my thighs, forcing him to continue his ravishing of my center.

Tucker pushed a digit in and out of me, and a second orgasm tore through me, leaving me breathless. I relaxed my grip around his neck. Wiping his mouth with the back of his hand, he resumed his standing position and entered me, and chasing his own release, he pounded into me ruthlessly.

His body went rigid, and I sensed him coming inside me. A split second later, he slid out and pumped his cock a few times. With his free hand, he pushed my top up just in time to shoot his load in the valley between my breasts. The warmth of his semen soaked my bra and heated my skin.

Tucker watched me, panting, a satisfied smirk grazing his lips. "Mine," he muttered before leaving me there, barely able to land back from the rush.

He returned a minute later and washed my chest with a warm cloth. He traced my skin with his lips and tongue, licking where his cum had just been erased off me."Have fun tonight," he said with a wink.

I tried to pull his mouth to mine, still hungry for him, but he stepped back. *Tease.*

The realization I was almost ten minutes late hit me. Hurrying to my feet, still dizzy and living in a world far away from here, I put my panties back on, trying to smooth my wrinkled clothes with my fingers the best I could.

Tucker was right earlier. I'd be flushed all night and would never be able to conceal the pleasure coursing through my bloodstream from anybody. When my eyes met my reflection in the entryway mirror, I relished the image staring back at me. I looked high on sex. High on love. The realization ignited a blaze of euphoria deep within me. For once in my life, could I be on the right path?

"Hey, Wilde," Tucker called out before I could leave. I spun to face him as he walked up to me, his expression relaxed but serious, and his lips drawn upward. "I was thinking… Would you marry me? I haven't asked you yet this week."

His cockiness made him so attractive. His confidence. That smirk. He knew exactly how to toy with my mind. Even more after what we'd just done.

I mirrored his smile. "Let's not rush it. We're not there yet." I winked. Because that was what he'd do if the roles were reversed.

Every week—or two—Tucker Philips asked me to marry him. It started as a game, but the more time we spent together, the less a game it had become. Deep down, we both knew it.

Every time I gave him the same answer, and he held my gaze and murmured, "One day, you'll say yes. Because we both know I'll call you Mrs. Philips before our baby is even born."

"Perhaps I wanna call you Mr. Wilde."

"Fair enough. I'll take your name anytime, sweetheart."

He pressed a kiss to my lips, and I made my exit.

"Come back to me." His words bore more weight than anyone could ever tell. But I knew better.

"Always. I'm yours. You made sure of it, and you're stuck with me for a long time, big guy."

"I wouldn't want it any other way."

***

"What's wrong?" I asked, pushing an arm inside the refrigerator to grab a bottle of water, forcing Tucker to sidestep to the right.

He was cursing, his back tense, looking agitated.

"Anything I can do to help? You've been cleaning this fridge for the last hour."

He spun away from me. Anger radiated from him.

In the three months we'd been living together, I recognized that cleaning-obsessed Tucker usually had something on his mind, something gnawing at him.

"Hey, talk to me. What happened?" I rested my hand on the middle of his back, but he recoiled from my touch.

"Nothing," he finally said in a harsh tone.

"Liar. I call bullshit."

He turned around, and specks of hurt swam in his eyes.

I grabbed his hands in mine. "Talk to me." He averted his eyes, and I raised a hand to brush my palm across his cheek. "Be honest with me. Truth, remember?"

"It's you," he said, not meeting my gaze for a long second.

A surge of annoyance washed through me. "Me?" I asked, pointing to my chest. "Why?"

He stuffed his hands into his pockets, looking unsure for the first time ever. "We've been living together for a while. And…and I still don't know where we stand. I'm not the kind of guy who likes labels, and to be honest, I always thought I didn't need them. But with you…with you it's different. Call me alpha or whatever, I don't care. I wanna stake a claim on you and be able to tell people we're together. That you're mine. A third guy from work asked me earlier when I went in for a meeting if you and I were still *friends*." He quoted the word with his fingers. "Presenting you as my friend at that barbecue that day was wrong. I told you. They all think we're just roommates having a baby together. Like…like it's no big deal. Collin asked if I could give him your contact info. The guy wanted to ask you out, Wilde. Who's bold enough to… Whatever. Forget it. Never mind."

"Tuck, you should've told me. We gotta talk about this."

"You keep saying you're not ready for a relationship,

yet we spend all our time together. We have sex almost every day. We sleep in each other's arms, but as soon as we're outside the bedroom, we're more like roommates. It…it doesn't sit well with me anymore. I thought it would be okay because everything you said when you first moved in made sense, but maybe it's because I've never been in a relationship before, but… Anyway, forget it."

"No," I almost screamed. "We'll talk about it. I understand, and I agree. That's why we shouldn't have added sex to the equation. It complicates everything. Tuck, I truly believe we'll find our way. I swear. Gimme a little more time, okay?"

"Yeah. Sorry. I shouldn't have dumped all this on you. Not now. You're trying to meditate and stay put for more than five minutes, and I've added stress to your day. Not my intention." He gave me a tiny lopsided smile.

"Anything I can do right now to make it all better?" I offered.

"Yeah." He locked his hands around my waist. I stared at the ripple of his Adam's apple, the lust shining in his irises, the darkness of his gaze. I almost lost it right there, ready to put all the voices in my head to rest and give myself to him, heart, body, and soul, without restraint. "Turn that meditation music down. It drives me nuts. The bowl thing you hit with that wooden wand, I fucking hate it."

Okay, that was not what I thought he had in mind.

"And stop shuffling around the contents of the fridge. Please make an effort to return things to their rightful places."

I let out a loud chuckle. "Where's the fun in that? Rotation is better. You get to see the food at the back that you'd otherwise forget about."

Tucker shook his head. "No. Not convincing enough."

"Please," I begged, pressing my palms together under my chin in a prayer.

"Sorry. The answer is still no. You're, without a doubt, the messiest person I know."

"But it's a part of my charm, right?"

He wound his arms around me. "I guess."

"If it annoys you too much, I'm sure Rory will take me back into his pool house."

"Not a chance. You're mine. Whether you know it or not. Now come here." He pulled me to him, the beating of his heart strong against mine, his chin resting on the top of my head, and my round belly caged between us.

We stayed in each other's embrace for a while.

"Sorry if I'm too much sometimes."

"Nah. I love how you turn my life upside down. It's refreshing. Occasionally, it's hard for me to adapt, but I will. Except for Nick, back in college, never before have I lived with another human being. But unlike you, he cleans after himself."

I punched his chest, and his arms tightened around me as we shared a laugh.

"You really hate my singing bowl?"

"Hate it."

"Fine, I won't use it anymore when you're around."

"Oh, and another thing I hate."

I tipped my head back to look at him.

"When you put on clothes to do your yoga. If you were my girlfriend—or my wife—I'd want you to do that downward facing dog pose fully naked."

"Good thing I'm not your girlfriend then."

Tucker's loud chuckle resonated through the room. "Yep. You get a free pass."

We stayed like this for a bit longer, just enjoying the comfort we always brought each other.

"Wilde, will you marry me?"

"Let's not rush it. We're not there yet. Let's enjoy our time together for now."

"One day, you'll say yes. Because we both know we can't escape our destiny and you'll walk down the aisle before our baby is born." His lips grazed my forehead. "I'm not taking no for an answer, so I'll ask you again later."

"And I hope you will." I paused, just to be certain I wasn't imagining it. No, this was it. Now I was sure. It had happened several times in the past two days. "Tuck," I said, putting some distance between us. "I agree I'm untidy. That I can be hard to keep up with. And that the meditation music sucks. But still, I have a surprise for you."

"You do? You didn't have to. All that I care for is in this room right now."

"Believe me, big guy, you'll thank me later for this one. It's something even money can't buy." With my fingers laced through his, I led him to the bedroom.

"A new kinky trick? Or head? I'm down for both," he teased. "I've changed my mind. If it's your lips servicing me, bring on that surprise."

Peeling my shirt up over my breasts, I lay on my side and beckoned him with my finger. "Get over here." When he positioned himself behind me, I pressed his open palm gently against my burgeoning belly, glancing at him over my shoulder. "He or she moved. I-I felt it. At first, I thought I was dreaming, but no. If we're lucky, the baby will do it again. I don't want you to miss it. It's subtle, but… Feel that? I swear, our little one is kicking in there."

Tucker blinked, his eyes filling with a layer of moisture. "Are you serious?" I nodded, and positioning me on my back, he leaned forward, his mouth inches away from my stomach. "Hey, baby. It's me. Daddy. Your mommy says you're kicking in there. If you could do it once more, I'd love to feel you too. It would make me so happy."

We spent the next hour in bed, waiting for our little peanut to flutter in my belly. He or she did. Just a tiny, barely perceptible movement under Tucker's palm.

"Was that—?" he asked, his voice congested with emotion.

"Yes."

"Wilde… Wow. We created this. Together."

He fused his mouth with mine, and every word our hearts bore bled into that kiss. Our lips and tongues found solace together. Our hearts beat to the same melody. Yes, our baby was in there, growing every day, turning us into a family even when we still hadn't figured out our own definition of it.

Tucker slid one hand under the cup of my bra, enveloping my sensitive breast, and a purr left my mouth as his soft flesh massaged mine. "I'm so gone for you," he said, breaking our kiss just long enough to draw in a shaky breath, then claiming my mouth again with a hunger I could feel in every inch of him. Before I even realized it, we were both naked, hungry for each other.

Tucker moved his palms to cradled my face. "Thank you. This was amazing."

I agreed with a nod, my eyes clouding.

I curled my fist around his manhood, working him, rubbing the moist tip with my thumb and relishing the way he jerked his hips in response.

"Wilde, I don't wanna play. I just wanna be buried deep inside you…and feel you all around me."

Hovering over me, our hands linked together, Tucker settled himself between my thighs and pushed inside me. I gasped at the contact, loving the way he filled me and how the first waves of pleasure electrified my core.

After a beat, he halted, watching me, his smoldering gaze turning me into molten clay beneath him. Somehow, in that instant, Tucker and I connected on a brand-new level. That was the moment I knew that no matter what I did or wherever I went, I was his, and he was mine. No matter how hard I was trying to fight this, our bond was stronger than anything we could define with words.

The three words he was dying to hear burned at the tip of my tongue. Before I could utter them, he rocked his hips, pushing deeper, and I lost all sense of gravity.

Tucker pumped inside me, and my legs wrapped around him, keeping his body as close to mine as possible, the friction driving me insane. I looped my arms around his neck, tugging him closer, and I wished my mouth could translate the words I hadn't spoken out loud yet but felt for him. The ones I couldn't escape or hide from anymore.

I kissed him with all the passion living in my heart.

We were branding each other.

With quick jerks of his hips, he rammed into me with abandonment, and I met him thrust for thrust.

He brushed my hair away from my face with his fingers, his eyes lancing into mine, carrying promises to never let me go. To love me with everything he was. To cherish me for eternity.

Sobs clogged my throat.

It was beautiful, life-shattering, wonderful, and scary all at once.

With my knuckles, I skimmed the side of his face and tipped my head back, hoping he could read my me—down to my soul. That he could understand I was ready to give myself to him. Entirely. That I wanted to be his. And to love him. And let myself go, knowing he would be there to catch me on the other side.

We moved together in a slow tango, our mouths never breaking apart.

His lips devoured mine. I treasured his.

We had become this unstoppable force.

Our movements turned more frantic, both of us chasing our release.

Tucker pounded into me faster, hard enough that he had to hold me to keep me from flying upward. He anchored me to him. My legs fastened around his waist, and I dug my fingernails into the skin of his nape.

My soft whimpers mixed with his animalistic groans.

Both of us could detonate at any moment.

He molded one hand to the back of my head, holding me so our mouths wouldn't part. I felt that kiss in every cell of my body.

"Wilde, I'll—"

"Come," I said. "I'll… Just let go."

His body stiffened. Scorching heat spiraled inside me. He rolled his hips faster. His tongue swept mine with shorter strokes. He tugged on my bottom lip with his teeth while I cried out my climax, my head tilting back and my vision blurring.

"Tuck, I'm—"

He pressed a finger against my sensitive lips. "I know, sweetheart. Not tonight. Let's just enjoy this moment."

As if he hadn't kissed me in years, his mouth returned to mine, possessive and demanding. I lost myself in the comfort of him. In his love.

Without a word, once he softened inside me, Tucker led me to his glass-paneled shower. Neither of us said anything as if words could burst the bubble of bliss we found ourselves in.

A serene expression painted his face, but the gleam in

his eyes broadcasted how much happiness waltzed inside him. I bet it mirrored mine.

He took his time to lather each curve of my body and to lave me with his tongue, imprinting himself onto me. Spinning me until I faced the wall, he positioned my hands on each side of my head. His digits ventured between my legs, sliding back and forth in lazy strokes, building pleasure deep in my core. I could barely stay upright, my legs wobbly and knees weak.

From behind, Tucker held me up with one arm wrapped around my waist, his torso pressing against my back, the firm tiled wall holding me still.

I turned my head, searching for his lips, unable to resist him any longer, our bond tightening with every heartbeat. A series of moans parted my lips, their echoes bouncing against the wall of the shower. The hot stream enveloped us as his fingers continued to play my body. His every movement stole my breath away.

My pulse raced.

Adoration filled my chest.

Pushing my forehead against the wall to steady myself, I slipped my arm behind me and grabbed his throbbing length.

Tucker pushed my hand away.

We needed no words to understand each other.

He pressed his forehead to my back between my shoulder blades, hastening the gliding of his fingers inside me.

I couldn't breathe. Or think. Or process anything else other than his body taking mine hostage.

His thumb rubbed against my clit.

I closed my eyes, helpless against the sensations that consumed me.

Unable to fuck me with his fingers the way he craved

to, Tucker squeezed himself between the wall and me and kissed the length of my body until he sat on the floor. Clutching my ass cheeks, he maneuvered me until I sat on his face, his mouth sucking on my clit. He returned one hand between my legs, his fingers resuming their motions inside me. My body shook with tremors. It was too much. And too little. Too hard. And too soft. Too fast. And too slow. I lowered myself until there was no space left between us. The friction sent black dots dancing in my vision. I was riding his face, about to collapse at any moment. He replaced his fingers with his tongue, but after a few strokes, I writhed against him, wanting more.

Understanding my silent plea, his fingers found their way back inside me. With my hands pushing against the shower wall, I let go, unable to resist any longer.

I had no time to come back from the rush when he moved back to his feet, standing behind me. I heard him pump himself, but I was too dazzled by the orgasm that had torn through me to do anything about it.

Without a warning, Tucker entered me in one push and emptied himself with a thrust of his hips. I gasped, and he released a guttural, low groan that drove me over the edge for a second time.

Chapter 12

My phone went off, and I accepted the call, unable to hide my happiness at the face lighting up my screen.

"Hey, girlfriend," I greeted Dahlia.

"How are you? Is Tucker taking good care of you?"

"Yes. Always," I said with a clear laugh.

"He better." She sighed. "I'm sorry it took me two hours to call you back. Jack was having a tantrum. And Nick is away for two days. Some construction project in Nashville. He went to check on his guys to make sure they were on schedule. Jack is reacting to him not being home. It's just that, except for Cart, Jack and I have been on our own for so long that now, with Nick fully a part of our lives, my baby can't get enough of him. Their bond is strong, and it's all I've ever wished for. It's beautiful… Truly. I know Jack is missing him right now, but instead of using his words, he has decided to go evil on me."

"Sorry, Dah. I know it's a lot."

"Also…huh…he has started to call Nick *daddy*. Not sure how Carter will react to this one."

"Oh," I exclaimed, lacking a better word.

"Yep. Oh," she echoed. "He'll be in town in a few days, so we'll see. Jack will stay with him three days a week for a full month."

"I think it's cool. How the three of you make it work. My nephew is the luckiest kid on Earth."

"We do our best." She blew out a breath. "Anyway, it's all good now. He's busy drawing a picture for me, so I'm all yours."

"Listen, I wanted to talk to you about something…" I breathed some courage from deep inside me. "Did you… well…hmm…did you have like any body insecurities while you were pregnant with him? It's just... I'm not usually shy about my body and everything, but I've gained so much weight that I can't see my toes anymore. And…huh…this pregnancy is far from over."

I swallowed, not sure if I should open up about what had been eating me up lately but needed another mother's opinion.

"I did at the beginning. The worst was people asking my age whenever they crossed my path. Like it was illegal to be pregnant at twenty. As if I did something wrong. Anyway, after Jeff died—in my grief, I could barely eat—I started losing weight. The doctor worried. I had to get extra checkups to ensure both I was healthy and the baby was okay despite my lack of appetite. What I realized, though, is that it's all temporary. Your body bounces back. The truth is, you'll never be exactly the same, but you'll be amazed at what your body can go through. It's creating life. Don't be too hard on yourself."

"It's difficult to look at myself. Today, I-I had two ladies asking me if I were pregnant with twins. And yesterday, a stranger in line at the grocery store congratulated me on the triplets. Twins run in my family. Do you…do you think they could have missed a baby on the sonogram?" My sarcastic laugh turned into sadness. I used my fingertips to dry my cheeks. "I…I'm sorry for breaking down. My emotions are a tangled web these days."

"Hey, it's okay to have doubts…and to need time to accept all those changes. We never know how pregnancy will affect us, mind and body, so it's a day-to-day acceptance. I'm here whenever you question everything, okay? Or whenever you're unsure if you'll be able to get through it. You need to know that these insecurities are happening now…and that they will probably come again after the baby is born."

"Thanks," I croaked out, my voice weak, sobs now rocking through me.

A loud bang resonated on the other end of the line. "Oh no, Jack just broke something. Baby, don't move." Her attention returned to me. "Can I call you back? I'm sorry. The timing is all wrong today."

I sniffled. "Yeah, sure. Go take care of it."

"I love you, Addi. I'll call you later. Don't be too harsh on yourself, okay?"

"I'll try."

Sitting on my bed, cross-legged, I caressed my belly, lost in my mind.

"This is all new to me," I said to my unborn child. "I'm happy you'll be tall and strong like your daddy. It's just hard on me right now. Just know that none of it is your fault. It's I who is having a hard time getting accustomed to my changing body. I just wanted to be honest in case you hear me panicking or if I'm sad and you can't comprehend what's going on with me."

The tears resumed as I caught my reflection in the full-length mirror next to the door. All my insecurities bubbled up to the surface once again.

"Hey, what's going on?" Tucker asked when he entered the room sometime later.

I tried to hide my meltdown. In vain. I couldn't fake it around him.

He sat next to me and draped an arm around my shoulders. "What happened to you? You missed me too much?" he asked in a teasing tone. "You knew I was at the gym downstairs. You could've come to join me. I would've loved the vision of you in spandex."

"Do you think I'm too fat and I should go to the gym?"

His eyes snapped in my direction. "What? Why? How? Wilde, what is this all about?"

"It's this," I said, pointing to my stomach. "And what people have said... And how I look when I glance at myself in a mirror... It's just... Forget it. It's silly."

"It's not silly. If it were, you wouldn't be crying about it. Talk to me."

"My emotions are ruling my life nowadays. When I was a little girl, my daddy—"

Right there, I almost confided about my father's struggles, but for some reason, I feared it would affect the way Tucker perceived me, so I changed the subject.

"I don't fit in any of my clothes. This belly is ginormous. Today, it all seems like a big deal." The little bent of his lips sent warmth through my bloodstream. "Don't look at me like that," I said, backhanding his chest.

"Like how? Like I'm in love with you? Or I wanna eat you up. Yeah, you're right, it's so wrong." He tugged me to him. "I'm here, Wilde. Whenever you need a pep talk. Or a hug. You can come to me. Always. Okay?"

I bobbed my head, and he dried my teary cheeks. "Yes."

"Come on, let's go take a walk. Clear your mind. Fresh air will do you good. It's Saturday, and there's a craft expo not too far from here. You love those. Gimme time to shower first, and I'll go with you."

I hugged him close to me. "Thank you." My lips met his, and my heart flipped in my ribcage. Tucker Philips was the one for me. I just had to draw the courage within me to be honest about my feelings once and for all.

We strolled around town, and the sunlight bettered my mood. Sitting on the deck of a small eatery, we ordered lunch. The waitress flirted with Tucker. A wink here, a touch on his shoulder there. It grated on my nerves. Every time he addressed her, she fake-laughed like he said something funny. He ignored her for the most part and only offered polite smiles, yet she was relentless, complimenting him on anything and everything. From his eyes to his food choice.

In the past, I would have sucked my date's tongue for everyone to witness or sharpened my claws and staked my claim. This pregnant version of me, moody and lacking confidence, felt insecure instead. Throwing my napkin across the table, I stood and hurried away, pushing the server as I stalked toward the exit. I heard Tucker say something and seconds later, he had cornered me on the sidewalk.

"Wilde, stop."

"Don't Wilde me," I said, through gritted teeth.

"Hey, hey, hey. Come here," he said, enveloping me in his arms. "It's okay. I'm with you. No one else. She is not even a blip on my radar."

I jerked away from his touch, requiring some space to

breathe. "Your old self would have gotten her naked within the hour. You would've fucked her."

His lack of immediate answer confirmed my apprehensions.

"See? You can't even deny it."

He grabbed my hand. "I'm not that guy anymore. That version of me was hiding from his feelings. He didn't thrive…or love. It was just a front. This version right here, with you, does all these things."

I shook my head. "She acted like I didn't exist. How can I be invisible when I am this big? It was rude. Hitting on some other woman's date. I can't believe she flirted with you in front of me. I'm pregnant, for God's sake. With your child."

"You're not invisible. Not to me. And it has nothing to do with your pregnancy. I saw how she scrutinized you when we took our seats before she even laid eyes on me. She was rude because she was jealous of you. That much was evident."

He kissed my lips, and I relaxed in his embrace.

"Where's the Addison Wilde who would have given that woman a run for her money? That Addison is fearless and can kick some asses."

"I'm still here….I think… Somewhere. Buried behind Mini-Tucker." His lips drew into the one smile that was intended only for me. One that tipped my heart. "Fine, I should get her back. You're right." I sighed. "She's a badass. Thanks for reminding me I'm not lost."

"I prefer you feisty. Come on. Let's enjoy the rest of our day."

———

"I'll be back in two hours tops," Tucker said the next day, leaning in to press a kiss to my forehead. "Do you think we'll know the sex of the baby?"

"At this stage, we're supposed to. Do you wanna know?" I twisted a strand of my hair around my finger and winced. "See, I'm not sure if I want to.."

"You don't?"

"Nah. I love the mystery of not knowing."

Tucker huffed. "I think I'd prefer it to be a surprise too. Like everything has been from the start."

"That's what I had in mind. Glad we agree."

He held me against him, his arms keeping me prisoner. "I love it when we think alike. Can we still look at the monitor, or will it be too obvious?" he asked.

"Pretty sure we'll be safe. It's all black and white and blurry lines. Except for the head, arms and legs. I'm not a pro sonogram reader. Neither are you. Unless you have special powers I wasn't aware of."

"Except for being able to extract multiple orgasms from you, I possess no other superpower. The appointment is at three thirty. I'll be home by three. Wait for me here. I'll pick you up, and we'll go for a celebratory dinner after."

"What are we celebrating?"

He shrugged. "Us. This," he pointed to my belly, "all of it."

"Awesome. Be on time, big guy."

"Always."

He left, a grin spreading across his handsome face, his pupils brighter than usual. Flutters invaded me. Yes, having Tucker in my life made more sense every single day. He fit into a slot in my heart as if he were born to rest there, and I reveled in sharing my days, and my life, with him more than I ever imagined.

"Where is he?" I asked out loud, talking to my baby while pacing the kitchen floor.

Tucker was never late. It was three-fifteen, and I still hadn't heard from him. I'd called his phone and his office, and both went unanswered. I'd texted him a dozen times. Nothing. I bit the tip of my thumb, unable to stay still. One breath in. I refused to go into panic mode and imagine the worst. One breath out. Did he say we'd meet at the doctor's office, or was he supposed to drive me? No, he said he'd come get me. Where was he?

Three-twenty.

Voicemail. And no answer to my five additional text messages.

I hauled my pregnant self into a cab, unable to wait any longer for the man I shared my life with.

Around five, I left the doctor's waiting room where I'd been camping for the last hour, praying Tucker would show up. With a hand splayed across my baby belly, as if that could protect it from whatever else was going on in my life, I walked back home, using the exercise to quiet the voices in my head. Jitters now assaulted my stomach. I still hadn't heard from Tucker. His office phone line was still busy, and his phone went straight to voicemail each time I called. Dread spread through me. Something was wrong. I could feel it in my bones.

Back at the condo, I removed my makeup and changed into pajama pants and one of Tucker's shirts that fit my new form much better than my own clothes and called my best friend.

Silent tears slid down my face. Maybe it was my hormonal state, but the fact that Tucker was missing really got to me. It didn't help that that my mind conjured every worst-case scenario.

"Hey, Addi. How are you doing? How was your sono-gram appointment? Did you get a picture?"

My lips quivered. Tremors shook my hands. "Dah, he…he's…he's missing."

"Addi, who's missing?"

"Tuck. He…he was super excited about the baby appointment. He had been talking about it nonstop for days. This morning, he said he'd pick me up and never did. He had everything planned for tonight. I called his office, his phone, sent texts, all the things a perfectly clingy girlfriend would do, and I still haven't heard from him. It was like five hours ago. The guy is punctual to the dot. Dedicated. This is so unlike him. I'm sorry I'm dumping all my shit on you…again. I-I'm on the verge of a panic attack. Do you think that…huh…do you think Nick can help me? I'm helpless here. The city is too big… I can't search for him by myself. Anyway, I have no clue where to start. What if something happened? At what point do I call hospitals? Or the police? Ohmygod, my baby's father is MIA."

"Slow down. Breathe. Let me get Nick. We'll find him. He'll show up."

Her husband joined the conversation, and I explained everything that had happened since Tucker had left earlier today.

"Let me get back to you," he said. "I won't let you run around all over Chicago, alone and pregnant. I'll make a few calls and get back to you."

I nodded, even though he couldn't see me. "Thanks. Do you think he's…huh…okay?"

"Yeah. Usually, when Tucker goes missing, it's because he needs time to think."

"Oh…okay. Should I worry?"

"Nah. We'll find him. Trust me."

We hung up, and I continued my pacing of the condo,

halting in front of the giant window I liked so much and wishing the door would open and Tucker would walk back in. Back into my arms.

My heart knotted in my chest, unable to keep a steady rhythm as its other half was nowhere to be found.

My phone rang twice from an unknown number. Holding my breath, I answered. "Hello?"

Chapter 13

With my elbows resting on the sticky wooden top of the bar, I swirled my glass then downed my fourth whiskey—or was it the fifth? I couldn't tell for sure. I'd stopped counting after two. Drinking had been a rare occurrence over the past few months, or rather, since Addison had moved in. In fact, I hadn't numbed myself since the day she had left Green Mountain and broke my heart months ago.

These days, nothing in my life reflected a hint of my old habits. No more booty calls, late night drinking, or bar hopping on Saturday nights looking for my next fuck. I had become an updated version of myself, the complete antipode of the person I used to be.

I wasn't complaining. I was thriving. I spoke the truth when I told Addison I much preferred the life we were building together to my old bachelor existence. The only thing I was truly missing was the woman herself. I had her, but not the way I wanted. Still, she slept in my bed every night, my arms wrapped around her. No one else. That, in itself, felt incredibly rewarding—to be the one she shared her daily life with. I had hoped that, soon enough, we'd be more. Much more.

I flicked my hand to catch the bartender's attention and gestured for another drink.

A surge of all the thoughts I'd tried to drown in alcohol clawed its way back. My face sank into my open palms, and I rubbed my skull with my fingers.

A hand clapped my upper back from behind. In the past, I would've thought it was Nick out looking for me. But he wasn't in town. The only other person who could find me here was Jace.

"Hey man," I said, not even turning to acknowledge his presence. "What are you doing here?" I took a sip of the fresh drink set before me on the bar top.

"People are worried about you."

I let out a sarcastic laugh. "How did you end up mixed up in this? You've become the champion at being unavailable since you married that…that…huh…Pam," I said, choosing my battles.

My friend sat next to me and ordered himself a drink. "Stop blaming me for being happy in my personal life, Tuck. It's shitty. And juvenile. I love her… Pam. She gets me, and I don't care if you think she's a head case or if you two don't get along. Sure, I'd like for my friends and my wife to be on good terms, but I'll choose her over anyone else every single time. Hold your grudge if you want. It's fine. Because in the end, it's my life. Not yours. Have you heard me call your girlfriend nuts or give her attitude? No. Sure, my wife is flawed. Aren't we all? But hey, I'm happy. Just be happy for me. That's all I'm asking."

I lifted my hand and let it fall right away. "Ever since

you got together with her, you've been hurting your best friends, man. Guys like Nick and me, who've been by your side your entire life. It...it's not how brotherhood works."

He sipped his drink, taking his time to answer. "Tuck, you and Nick aren't less my friends because you can't stand my wife. I'm sorry I missed his bachelor party, okay? And his wedding. It wasn't what I had planned. Something came up. I'll make it up to him. You two are my brothers...for life. It's just not easy to always juggle my time between all of you without receiving complaints from either side. But I hear you, and I'll do better. Maybe not tomorrow, but I promise I'll make an effort to be more present."

"I've missed you, man," I said, pulling my friend into a hug. "I need you right now. My life is slipping through my fingers, and I feel fucking lost."

Jace hugged me back before he released me. "I thought everything was great. Last time, you said—"

"Earlier today, it...it all went to hell. It made me question every single thing. I don't think I'm... Let's just say, I'm not wired to be a father. I thought I'd be at least good at it—not perfect, just doing my best—but life proved me wrong. Now I'm not sure where I stand. It all went down so fast... Addison has been telling me for a while we should take things slow, and I...I didn't agree. But now? Now, I think she may have a point because I—"

A soft voice broke through my confessions. I'd recognize this voice amongst thousands. Even though I hadn't laid eyes on her yet, just sensing her presence behind me brought me peace. And peace. Addison Wilde had that effect on me. I chugged my drink, trying to shake off the overwhelming effect of her sudden appearance.

Jace moved to his feet. "I'll let you two discuss," he said, placing a bill on the counter next to his empty tumbler. "Call me if you need anything. I promise I'll do my best to make more time for our friendship. Gimme some time to adjust, okay? And for what it's worth, I have no doubt you'll be the best father to your baby. This new role suits you because you already care. Don't lose faith in yourself. You've got this, man. I can tell."

I nodded, my throat tight with knots that refused to unravel. "Thanks," I croaked before he walked out after exchanging a few words with my woman and making sure she was fine driving me back home later.

Addison took Jace's empty seat and ordered a glass of water. I glanced at her sideways. Her hair was piled up at the top of her head, her face bare, and she wore one of my hoodies over a pair of flamingo-patterned pajama-set. She looked adorable and so out of her element in our little corner bar.

The one where my friends and I always came when things got tough and we weren't in the mood to chat. The last time I was here was when Nick mourned Derek. Over a year and a half ago.

We drank in silence, both of us keeping our gazes trained forward.

"I was worried," she said after a while. "I've been trying to reach you for hours. You missed the doctor's appointment."

Reality hit me like a slap in the face. "Fuck, Wilde. I'm...I'm so sorry," I admitted through a booze-induced numbness. "Jesus, this day is a disaster. I screwed everything up."

She spun in her seat to watch me. "What do you mean?"

I shook my head and let out a loud sigh. "I'm not sure I can...I can do this...with you," I said, my stare darting to her abdomen and shame filling me. "Not sure I-I possess what it takes to be a daddy…or at least, a good one."

She blinked. "Whoa. Stop. And rewind. Can you explain yourself? Now. What made you change your mind? When you left earlier, you seemed so excited about all of this." She gestured to her belly with her hand. "A baby isn't something we can return to the store because things are not working the way we expected, Tuck. What do you mean when you say you're not sure you can do this? After you promised we'd get through this together, after you asked me to marry you, after you forced me to move in with you, now you're telling me you're not fucking sure?"

I shook my head, avoiding her piercing stare, her angry tone poking holes in my heart. "I-I've had the worst afternoon."

"I'm sure there's an explanation. A lot can happen in a short amount of time. We've already talked about this and agreed it's okay to be scared. Because I am, and I have no clue what I'm doing either. You said we'd figure it out together. I believed you."

"How can you have faith in me?"

"Because I see you. I see every day what you're made of…what you can achieve, your limitless dedication, and how selfless your heart is."

"Wilde, you've only witnessed the good side of me so far."

"Then show me the bad side, and let me decide if I can handle it," she said. All my feelings for her multiplied in that instant. "Let's go home, big guy. Then you can tell me all about your day."

I pushed my almost-empty tumbler aside and motioned to stand, feeling wobbly on my own legs.

"Where's your phone? I've been trying to call you for

hours?" Addison asked, urging me to lean on her for support as we stumbled out of the bar together.

I fished out the plastic bag containing rice and my ruined device out of my jacket pocket and waved it before her puzzled expression. "It's…it's a part of my shitty day. I'm sorry I missed the appointment. I was really…I was really looking forward to it." Dampness settled over my eyes, blurring my vision. "I-I wanted to be there. I'm sorry I let you down…"

Hauling myself into the passenger seat of my truck, I shut my eyes as Addison drove the ten blocks to my building. We made our way to our floor. By then, the liquor I'd drunk, my tangled emotions, and Addison's care had turned me into an emotional volcano on the brink of eruption. Everything I felt teetered at the edge, ready to explode into the open.

As soon as I kicked the front door shut, I fell on the floor in a puddle of limbs, exhausted and bearing more mixed feelings than ever before.

Addison made some tea and joined me, sitting beside me, her legs stretched before her, her baby belly impossible to conceal anymore."Drink this," she ordered in a gentle tone as I accepted the mug she placed between my hands.

We remained silent. The air thickened around us.

"What if I'm genetically programed to be like my mother? A lousy parent? How do I know I haven't inherited her selfish ways?"

"Tuck, you're nothing like her. You're good to me. To us." Her thumb indicated her burgeoning stomach. "Our story isn't your parents'. It's ours. And we can write it however we wish. There's no rules, no limits. Whatever happened before doesn't define us and has nothing to do with us."

"Today was a test, and I fucking failed. Even I would be afraid of my own parental abilities."

She wrapped her arms around my biceps and rested her cheek against my shoulder. "Tell me all about it. I'll judge for myself."

Moisture clung to my lower eyelashes, and this time, I didn't blink the tears away. "You'll throw my sorry ass away. That's how bad it got. I… Well… Huh, today, I got checkmated by a two-year-old."

She said nothing as I told her all about my afternoon.

"When I went to the office to drop off those documents, I needed to consult with Smith about a client, but he was on an important phone call. His wife came with their son, you know, Theo. You met them at the picnic." She nodded. "Well, Theo's nanny was sick, and Lacy was dropping him off at the office because she had a meeting. The three of us have known each other since college, so she didn't hesitate to entrust her son to me when I offered to watch him until his dad was free. Anyhow, Lacy handed me Theo and a diaper bag, telling me it would be good practice before our baby's birth, then hurried away— leaving me with no other instructions."

I scratched the top of my head. My memories were a bit blurry, considering the amount of alcohol I'd consumed.

"It started great. Really, I was confident in my abilities. I've watched Jack in the past, so I thought I knew what I was doing. We sat in an empty office with his toy cars. But Beverly, the secretary, walked in and didn't close the door after her. I was rummaging through my bag to find the document she was asking for when I spotted Theo running toward freedom through the opening. Let me tell you, two-year-olds are freaking fast. By the time I started chasing after him, he thought this was a game and ran straight into

Brittany's empty chair that bumped into her desk and sent her fresh extra-large mug of coffee flying all over her desk, soaking piles of documents and her keyboard. I caught the kid and gathered paper towels to wipe the damage the best I could, sitting him on that evil chair. Next thing I knew, he was unsteady on his feet, standing on that stupid piece of furniture and dropped my phone. Which, for the record, up to this moment, I still have no idea how he got. It landed in the turtle desktop pond Brittany keeps on her desk, splashing water all around and creating a second mess."

Addison gasped. "Oh, that explains the rice."

I grumbled and continued. "The tiny devil was driving me nuts, but I ended up taking control of the disastrous situation, and we were back in peaceful territories. Until I learned the coffee slash turtle-pond clusterfuck had short-circuited something under Brittany's desk and the entire office experienced an internet outage. It took down the presentation with the investors from Japan in the conference room, along with the entire phone system."

"Oh," Addison said, covering her mouth with a hand.

"Yep. Thirty minutes with a toddler, and that's how it turned out." I felt like a failure, and the idea that I'd be like my mother with my own child one day had been haunting me ever since, weighing heavy on my shoulders, gnawing at my conscience, and crashing my hopes about this whole paternity adventure I was about to jump into and never questioned until today.

""Explain to me how this is connected to what your mother did. I can't see how it's related."

"Addison, I...I gave up. This was too much. I saw red. The whole office went crazy and instead of helping out or making sure Theo was safe, I handed him to Brittany. Without a second thought. And I...I just walked away. I just left. Not a care in the world if the kid was okay or if Brittany could take care of him. Lacy entrusted me with her son. I failed her too. What if… Jesus… What if I fail you too? Or get overwhelmed and just hand our baby to the next available stranger because I can't deal with something?" There, I said it.

"Tuck, listen to me. It's just one day. One episode in your life. It doesn't define who you are and your abilities as a man and as a father. You should learn from today and not draw a definitive conclusion about your abilities as a father."

The tears I'd been holding back now flowed freely. "That's the thing, Wilde. I'm not sure I-I can do this. I'm not sure I'll be any great…or that I'm what our baby and you need. What if I'm such a failure I put his life in danger? Or I fail you both. If it happens…I…I would never forgive myself."

Doubts crawled along my spine.

"You're not alone. We're a team. You think you're the first parent to ask himself if he's good enough? To wonder if he'll get through this?That's why there are two of us. So, we can take the lead when the other is down or when we have no idea how to proceed."

Desperate for her proximity, her heat, and her love, I cupped the nape of her neck and pressed my forehead to hers. Nothing I did or said helped keep the tears I'd been holding back at bay. In a way, it felt liberating to just let them out, draining my sorrows and insecurities away.

"The first time I babysat Jack, I put his diaper all wrong. It made a…you can only understand if you were there. Little babies are cute and look innocent, but they can cause devastation, I'm telling you. Anyway, thinking it was just a mishap, I bathed him, changed him, and cleaned the mess. Only to start all over again later because I had no idea that his penis should be pointing south, and things got chaotic a second time. By that point, my clothes were ruined, and I smelled like baby pee. And last year, when Dahlia and Nick went to Carter's concert—the one you bought him tickets for—I babysat Jack again that evening. He fell and bumped his head. You should have seen the bruise on his forehead. Quite impressive. Almost traumatizing." She cupped her heart at the memory. "In the end, it was just a bump. Nothing serious. I could've decided right then that I wasn't fit to be a mother—or his aunt—or even his babysitter. But I didn't. Those things happen. With kids, they always do. Dahlia taught me that. One day, ask her about the stories when she was a single mom at twenty. Things weren't easy for her. Sure, she could afford a nanny and anything the baby needed, and yet it still turned out to be quite a challenge. No parent is immune to this."

I sighed. "I hear you." Silence stretched between us. "Wh-what if I'm the exception to the rule? Until now, I've only been taking care of myself. I've never been responsible for another human being's life."

Addison shook her head. "You won't be. We've been living together for months, and I've witnessed you interacting with Jack. The boy loves you. I'm his *Addidi*, but you're his Uncle Tuck. Children are perceptive. If you were bad news, he wouldn't want to be around you—or follow you everywhere. Or pretend to call you on the phone when you're not there. Your connection with him is real. It will be stronger with your own blood. It already is."

She brushed her lips against mine in a featherlight kiss.

"Let's get you to bed, big guy. Sleep on it. Tomorrow will be better, I swear. And I'll hold your hand, okay? Every step of the way."

My brain went blank as my woman took it upon

herself to undress me, removing my shoes and helping me out of my trousers. She peeled my shirt off after unbuttoning it, caressing my bare skin with her hands. Shivers ran through me, and a new layer of comfort descended upon us.

Once in bed, she positioned my head along the ridge between her breasts and her belly, combing my hair back with her fingers. "Don't shut me out again. We're in this together. I wanna be there for you when you have doubts. And I want you to be there for me when I'm the one who's unsure about everything."

The beating of her heart combined with her soft breaths acted like a lullaby, and I fell into a deep slumber.

———

The next morning, when I cracked my eyelids open, I watched Addison getting dressed for work. Fragments of last night's meltdown flashed before my eyes.

"Hey. How are you feeling this morning?" she asked.

"Fine. How bad was last night?"

Wearing only a bra and a pair of maternity jeans, she slid into my arms. "Nothing we can't overcome."

"Again, I'm sorry for missing the appointment. That's not like me. I'm the guy you can always count on."

She traced the contours of my chest muscles with her fingertip. "I'm aware. We're all allowed a slip-up here and there."

"Still."

"I never doubted you. Let's get you hydrated before I head out."

"Was my mind playing tricks on me, or did you actually pick me up at a bar yesterday dressed in flamingo pajamas?"

A heartwarming laugh crossed her lips. "I did. For you, I would do it again. And even go naked. You…huh…really scared me. I thought something had happened. An accident. Or—"

"I'm sorry… That kid… It just brought back bad memories. And doubts I've been trying to avoid dealing with."

"When something bothers you, promise me you'll come to me from now on. If it's that bad, I'll pour you the drinks myself. Deal?"

She looked at me with a mix of warmth and patience, and something potent I could get addicted to.

"Deal," I echoed, my lips tasting hers before I pushed back, figuring I probably had alcohol-tinged morning breath.

Addison found my eyes. "Tell me the truth. Are you okay?"

"I will be."

"Awesome, because I have a surprise, and I think you'll like it."

I arched one brow.

"I couldn't bring myself to have the sonogram yesterday. You weren't there, and it felt wrong to go through the experience on my own. If you're free during lunchtime, the doctor said he could squeeze us in. What do you say?"

I blinked. "For real? You did that? For me?"

"Yep. I'm a pretty amazing partner, no?"

I locked my arms around her waist. "You're an amazing woman, sweetheart. Thank you for rescuing my sorry ass last night. I'm sorry I worried you."

I kissed her again, but she was the one pushing me back this time. "Teeth. And a shower."

Laughter bubbled out of me. It felt really good to share my life with her and be happy without having to fake it.

"Wait for me, Wilde. I'll be right back. Don't go yet. I'll drive you to work."

"Hurry, big guy. For the record, I'm not going anywhere without you."

———

A couple of days later, I left early to run some errands while Addison was still asleep. On my way home, I picked a bouquet of white roses, Thai food, and a maternity C-shaped pillow. A co-worker had recommended it, and I figured Addison could use a little extra comfort, whether she was sleeping or just relaxing.

With excitement pouring out of me, I entered my condo, ready to surprise the woman I loved, but halted at the sounds coming from the bedroom. I swore they were sobs. Maybe Addison was watching some TV or was sleeping and those were snores.

Setting my purchases on the kitchen island, I tiptoed to the bedroom. Now there was no doubt—she was crying.

I knocked on the door. "Hey, sweetheart, it's me. Can I come in?"

She mumbled something I interpreted as a yes.

The scene playing before my eyes as I opened the door broke me apart. It fractured a slice of my heart.

Addison sat on the floor in one of my T-shirts that hugged all her pregnancy curves. She had mountains of discarded clothes and used tissues scattered around her.

I pulled her into my arms. "What happened? Did someone try to raid your side of the closet?" I asked, trying to infuse some humor into my words.

I handed her a tissue that looked clean, and she blew her nose before answering me. "Nothing fits anymore. I have nothing to wear except your clothes. How am I supposed to go to my book club meeting tonight if I can't get dressed?"

"Just so you know, pregnancy and all, you look stunning. You always do. And fucking hot wearing my shirts." She offered me a death stare, and I lifted my hands before me. "Just saying. How about that dress we bought last month?"

"Too small."

"And that new pair of jeans you like so much?"

"I don't fit into them anymore. I'm telling you, I got way bigger in the last twenty-four hours."

"Okay, let's be honest then. Living naked has its benefits." I jumped to my feet, undid my tie, and proceeded to remove every single piece of clothing from my body until I only had boxer briefs on.

Addison let out a warm chuckle as I sat back down next to her. "Tuck, don't be silly."

"I'm not. You go naked, I go naked. Unless we go shopping. Your call."

She shook her head, that fragile smile now fixed on her face. "You'd walk around in just your boxer briefs if I asked you to?"

"Always. We're in this together, remember?"

"Ohmygod, we're so weird."

I turned until I could cradle her face in my palms, wiping away the last drops of moisture from her eyes with my thumbs, then lowered my lips to hers. "You're stuck with me. So what will it be? Shopping spree, running around town naked, or wearing my stuff from now on?"

"Perhaps I'm being a bit overdramatic. Before we go buy a new wardrobe, I'm sure I can find something that still fits for tonight. I just really wanted to wear that dress… And I got upset." She motioned around the bedroom with one hand. "And then this happened."

"How long have you been in here, on the floor, in this state?" I asked.

"Over an hour…I think. I tried calling Dahlia, but she didn't answer. I-I got really sad. Like *really, really* sad."

"Wilde, next time you call *me*, okay? You're the one person I'd always answer the calls from, even if I were being tortured or drowning in the middle of the Pacific."

"You better save yourself first. Then answer my call."

I leaned in to kiss the tip of her nose, and she grimaced.

"Tuck, I'm serious."

"I know you are. Come on, let's sort this out. I'll help you. But first I got you something."

"Did I forget an anniversary or a birthday? I'm telling you, mommy brain is a real thing. Those women claiming they can't think clearly when they're pregnant aren't joking. My head is filled with jelly most days. My thoughts are enveloped with fog."

"You forgot nothing. Since you're the one pregnant, you deserve some pampering"—I shrugged—"and to get plenty of restful nights."

Holding her hand in mine, I led her to the kitchen.

Addison's eyes took in the pillow and flowers. "For me?"

"No one else."

She hugged the pillow to her heart. "I heard about this. It's supposed to be amazing."

"That's what I heard too."

"Tuck, you're the best." Her eyes filled with a fresh batch of tears.

"Hey, if you don't like the color, we can go to the store and exchange it."

Her crying resumed. "It…it's not that. Damn

hormones. I-I'm happy. I swear. See? I can't even be thankful without shedding tears anymore."

I pulled her into my arms and kissed her, threading my fingers through her hair. "I'm not scared by the hormonal version of you." I grabbed a handful of her ass cheek, and she ground her hips against mine. "Here. Being hormonal can be a big turn on too."

"Pervert," she whispered against my lips.

"Only with you. When is that book club meeting?"

"Seven tonight."

"Then let's go. We'll go for a walk and grab food on the go. Fresh air and sunshine will do both of you good."

"What about the food you brought over?"

I shrugged. "We'll put it in the refrigerator. It can wait."

"Tuck?"

"Yes," I said.

"Thank you. We're good together."

I pressed my lips to her forehead. "I know."

Addison got ready, and I studied her from a distance. I didn't like seeing her so distraught. It occurred more frequently these days. Her glossy eyes and the firmness of her lips were undeniable signs that whatever troubled her before wasn't quite resolved.

Our eyes met, and she mirrored my smile. We'd be okay.

Or I prayed we would.

Chapter 14

Addison

"Do you need anything before I go?" Tucker asked.

I watched him over the bowl of soup resting on my impressively round, five-month-pregnant belly—yes, our baby would have Tucker's stature, no doubt—the spoon halfway to my mouth.

"Want me to refill this?" he asked with an adorable cocky smile gracing his lips. He knew me too well at this point.

"Yes, please. And can you bring me a pillow? My back has been hurting today."

"Sweetheart, all you gotta do is ask when you're down for a massage or a bath. Or an orgasm."

"No, I'm good on all those counts. I've already come three times today. I should be able to survive until tomorrow. Any news about that secret business project you're working on? I still can't understand why you won't tell me anything about it."

He shook his head. "Nah. Nothing to announce just yet. Don't worry about me. I've got everything under control. I'll tell you when the time is right. Be patient, Wilde. It's a virtue."

"I consider myself super patient, big guy. Look at me, less than four months to go. It feels like I've been pregnant forever."

I'd had only a handful of meltdowns in the past few months. Some days, darkness coiled tightly around me, and everything looked bleak for a moment. Then it would dissipate, and I returned to my usual cheerful mood. Since the day Tucker caught me crying on the bedroom floor, surrounded by piles of clothes, I'd been careful to hide the emotional tumult of my off days from him. I could see how worried he got, even though he said nothing and tried to cheer me up. I didn't want him to be concerned about my occasional, temporary lack of enthusiasm.

"You're wonderful. Beautiful. And sexy." He filled my bowl and brought it along with a few crackers, which he set on the coffee table before locking his lips with mine. He was always showering me with attention and compliments, as if he could sense I needed his reassurance.

I'd been struggling with the weight gain so far—more than most women gain during their entire pregnancy. My insecurities about my body spiked on days I didn't feel at my best, or when I studied the stretch marks in the mirror after a shower. Except for that one time I broke down, I hadn't really mentioned them to Tucker, but he could tell. He complimented me every day and always made sure I felt pretty on my off days. He could read me so well that sometimes I avoided looking at him, just in case he could see what I didn't say out loud.

"Wanna see what I've been working on lately?" I asked, adjusting myself on the couch.

"Always." I pointed to my laptop, perched on the kitchen table. Tucker leaned over it and powered it on. He opened the file where I stored my work. A loud whistle left his mouth as he scrolled through my latest shirt designs. "Wow. You made these?" He scrolled down, his eyes trained on the screen.

I couldn't contain my pride. "What do you think? I got inspired….huh…to try something new. Mini-Tucker is triggering the creative side of me. Maybe I should wait until he or she turns eighteen and make them partner in my business."

Tucker angled himself until he faced me. "Wilde, these are amazing. I'm ordering them all as soon as they become available. In every size. Our little one will be the most fashionable and cute baby out there. I'm telling you."

I snickered as he turned the laptop off and joined me on the couch.

"You're very talented. When did you have time to work on those?"

"Every day when I have a few minutes to spare. I love designing clothes. I wish I could do it full time...or plan events. Honestly, I want to do both. I just… I don't know." I sighed. "I haven't planned anything since Dahlia and Nick's wedding, and I miss it. One day, I'll be my own boss, doing all the things I've always dreamed of, free from anyone's rules or restrictions."

"I know, and I'll be there to help you reach your full potential. Whatever it is you wanna do. Some time off when the baby arrives will do us good. I could also resign and be your handyman." He wiggled his brows. "I heard I'm quite skilled with my hands. And other body parts. Just sayin'. There's this girl I'm spending all my time with.

She could vouch for me. She'd be a great character reference."

I snickered.

Amusement left his features. "Seriously, you should catch on some sleep, though. Don't exhaust yourself. Please."

"I won't. Stop worrying about me."

"It's my job." Tucker rose to his feet. "Call me if you need me. I won't be long, okay?"

"I will."

He dropped another kiss on my forehead, and I melted inside. "I'll see you later."

"Sure. Any dinner plans tomorrow?" I asked. "I was thinking we could go out after I'm done with work."

He nodded. "Count me in."

He let himself out and closed the door behind him. I heard the lock click into place right after. And, just like every time we were apart, a heavy mass grew in my chest, crushing everything inside me.

So far, Tucker had proven himself to be the most dedicated father-to-be. He made himself available every minute of every day in case I required his help—or company. Initially, when we had regular sex, satisfying both our needs, our relationship had mostly stayed in the friend zone. But since we truly made love—the first time the baby moved inside me—everything had changed. I was waiting for the right moment to tell him how much I loved him, because now there were no doubts in my mind. I was done being scared and done ignoring my gut.

Dahlia called our living situation a modern arrangement.

Sure, it had suited me at first, but now I craved the real thing. I was done denying Tucker my love. I wouldn't waste any more of our precious time.

Yes. I would be honest with him about my feelings. Soon.

A shiver of excitement ran through me as I tucked the fluffy blanket around me on the couch.

Trepidation jolted my heart as my thoughts drifted to Tucker. Unable to restrain myself any longer from what I truly desired, I dialed him, hoping he hadn't left the building yet.

"Miss me already or can I help you with something?"

I snickered. This man. He'd evolved so much in the months I'd known him. He was still irresistible, cocky, and handsome—too much for his own sake—but he had a calmness about him that wasn't there before. A serenity. I bet barely anyone noticed, but I did. Because it mattered to me.

"You know I always miss you when you're not around. Even if it's just for an hour. This place feels too empty without you. I know soon I will pray for silent nights, but until then, it's better when you're here."

"Don't be shy. It's okay to think I'm irresistible. I agree with you."

"Oh God, that ego of yours." We both burst into a fit of laughter. "Where are you meeting Jace? You never told me."

"At the same pub we went to last month."

"Oh, I can still taste that burger. And now I'm hungry. Can you bring me one when you come back?"

"Yep. With the spicy mayo you like?"

"Double portion, please. On another note, I gotta tell you something. I'm sorry for always keeping you at a safe distance. It's not what my heart truly begs for. From the very beginning, we've been taking all the steps in a random order. One-night stand, make a baby, become friends, marriage proposal, break up, have a baby together, become friends again, sleep together, being together while not being together. It's hard to keep up. What I'm trying to say through my rambling is that I wanna try for more."

"Wilde, I don't wanna try. I'm certain you're it for me. The last few months have only confirmed it. You're either all in, or we keep doing what we've been doing—this dance—but at some point, it comes with an expiration date. And that's not fair to either of us, or to our baby, to be one foot in and one foot out."

I sighed and rubbed my eyes. "Maybe I didn't make it clear enough. I'm ready for more….with you." I swallowed the panic rising inside me as I spoke the words I'd been locking away for so long.

"As lovers or—?"

My belly tensed, the tautness stretching up to my back.

"Oh, fuck. Gimme a sec," I gasped, cutting him off, both hands tracing the tightening muscles of my abdomen.

I heard the door slam open but ignored it, too focused on my breathing, wishing the tension would ease.

Two muscular hands wrapped around me, and Tucker's gaze locked on mine. "Better?"

I bobbed my head as the contractions lessened. "How? I-I thought you'd left?"

He offered me a non-committal shrug. "Nah. Wasn't feeling like it. I texted Jace before you called. I didn't wanna be away from you guys. I was hoping you'd call and beg me to come back, so I sat by the door, playing silly games on my phone, trying to decide what to do. I was just about to get up and grab that burger for you."

I blinked. "You did?"

He nodded.

Tucker held my face between his muscular hands, kneeling between my legs. "So about what you were saying before our little peanut decided to interrupt… Were you serious?"

"I've been ready for a long time. I didn't want to admit it to myself…and to be honest, I tried once, but then I chickened out and missed the chance. We're already a couple. No matter what I tell myself. You are mine, Tucker Philips, and I wouldn't want it any other way."

He crashed his lips onto mine, curling a hand around the back of my head to tug me closer. "I'll make you the happiest woman on Earth."

"You better, because I wanna make you the most satisfied man in the universe."

"Wow, woman, it's a big commitment. Are you sure you're up for the challenge?"

"I was born ready. Also, I possess a few skills that make me irresistible, you'll see."

"I can't wait." He sat on the couch beside me and pulled me into his arms. "Later. Let's just watch a movie or something. I wanna hold you while you fall asleep. It's one of the best moments of my day. When you surrender in my arms, trusting me to watch over you. Unless you're really hungry."

"Nah, just an indulgence I can live without."

Tucker slid under the blanket and repositioned it over me, and with my head resting on his lap and his fingers toying with my hair, we simply enjoyed being together, no more *what-ifs* hovering over us.

"One thing though before I agree to date you."

"What is it?" I asked, tilting my head back.

"One. Stop using my towel to wrap your hair after your shower. I hate when it's damp. Two. Naked yoga and meditation as often as possible. So, I can enjoy the view."

"I thought you said one thing."

"Changed my mind. I make the rules," he said,

echoing the words I spoke when we first started having our night chats months ago.

Bile rose in the back of my throat as his words replayed in my head. How could I tell him that the idea of parading naked in front of him made me uncomfortable? That I wasn't at ease in my own skin these days and didn't feel confident showing off my pregnant curves?

Sparks shone in his eyes as he watched me, waiting for me to agree. One by one, they erased most of my doubts.

"Big guy, you got yourself a deal," I said before I changed my mind.

We kissed to make it official.

Now at peace, my head giving up its fight and letting my heart take the lead for once, tucking all my pregnancy doubts far away, a wave of contentment washed over me. I drifted off to sleep, feeling his steady, protective energy within me.

———

The next day, I woke up with strong arms wrapped around me, shielding me from the rest of the world. I took a moment to inhale, savoring the ease we'd slipped into last night.

"Morning, sweetheart," Tucker's husky voice said from behind as he peppered kisses all over my bare shoulder.

I squirmed against him, his short stubble tickling my flesh. "Stop. We gotta talk."

He busied himself with sprinkling kisses along my spine while gently caressing my belly.

The baby kicked, as if to agree with our new commitment.

"I don't wanna talk. We did that enough last night. For

now, I wanna love my girlfriend. Now that we're officially a couple, I wanna show her just how happy she makes me."

"Babe, I'm serious. I forgot to discuss something. It may change the way you feel about me," I said between laughter as his hands traveled all over my naked flesh and lodged between my thighs. I gasped as he inserted one finger inside me, my hips rocking of their own volition, unable to stay indifferent to his seductive touch.

"Call me babe again," he pleaded, positioning me on my back, tasting my breasts with slow, deliberate strokes of his tongue.

My hips moved faster. I panted, trying to infuse my brain with oxygen to recall the words that had deserted my mind seconds ago.

"Sweetheart." Tucker captured my mouth with his, hungry and insatiable. His lips covered mine, filled with lust and a million unspoken promises to make me feel good. I locked my arms around his neck, and he shifted his weight backward, positioning me over him until I straddled his thighs, and we moved together, our bodies in sync.

I was about to come undone when the words I'd been selfishly withholding emerged. "I love you, Tucker Philips."

He halted underneath me, his gaze taking mine hostage. He blinked, and his Adam's apple bobbed while he stared at me.

"I love you. I didn't tell you last night…or all the times before. But I do." I exhaled. "It feels good to finally put it out there. To let go of my fears."

He cleared his throat, and his eyes illuminated with something I'd never seen before. "She said she loves me," he screamed at the top of his lungs.

I nodded, now smiling like a fool.

"I've been waiting to hear those words for so long." Ache laced his voice.

I rested my fingers on either side of his face. "I'm sorry. It's not that I didn't feel it. It just scared the shit out of me to admit it. Every time I said those words before, things fell apart not long after. But I'm tired of being afraid. You're nothing like the men I dated before. I wanna be yours…all yours…only yours. I love *you*, and I'll tell you every minute of every day until you believe it. I'd climb Everest for you and shout it from the top if that's what you need to know I mean it."

Tucker watched me with a seriousness that sent my heart rate into a sprint. My hair stood on end over my arms. Knots tied my stomach. Did I say something wrong? Did I fuck up everything between us by voicing my feelings out loud?

I blinked, trying to keep at bay the tears that were now threatening to fall. When I tried to pull my arms from around his neck, he slid his hands upward, holding them firmly in place.

"Don't." He paused, averting his eyes for a long second that seemed infinite. "You know, other than Nick when he's feeling emotional, it's the first time in over a decade that anyone has spoken those words to me. I haven't heard *I love you* from a woman since I was twelve years old…I think. Before the shitshow hit my family." He swallowed hard, and I traced the undulation of his throat with my eyes before lifting my gaze back to his. "Do you know how happy I am right now? Do you realize what you just did?" He crashed his lips on mine, unapologetic and starving. "She loves me," he repeated when our mouths detached. "Finally, she said it."

My heart broke for the kid in him and for the man who never got close enough to somebody else to hear those words. The ones that mattered. The ones powerful enough to transform war into peace and tears into smiles.

"I love you, Tucker. You'll see. I'll say it enough you'll grow tired of hearing it."

He nuzzled my neck, kissing my skin. "Never. I'll never get tired of anything when it comes down to you. You're my best friend. You get me. You make me wild and tame me. Even when you drive me nuts, I can't resist you. And when you're black, I'm white. Together we're the perfect shade of gray. Every single time. And for your information, I knew…all along."

I slapped his chest as we shared a laugh. "How?"

"You're not as subtle as you think you are, sweetheart. Or I'm very good at reading you. But don't beat yourself up. I was waiting for you to realize it. Maybe I would've started dropping hints soon enough, though."

"How?"

"Anonymous text messages. Sticky notes. Here and there."

"What would they have said?"

"*Addison plus Tucker.* Or *I love Tucker*. What about, *Tucker is the one for me.* Or *Tell him you love him already. Why are you being so stubborn? L-O-V-E. I'm in love, and I'm the only one who doesn't know it…* Things like that."

I tilted my head back, laughing. "I prefer simpler declarations. Perhaps you should have tied a ribbon behind an airplane, or asked the diver in the shark tank at the aquarium to hold a sign. Oh…or done a lip dub. Those kinds of things."

He kissed me hard. "You crazy woman, I love you. Now let me make you come until we reach another galaxy together."

"I'd live in space with you anytime. And I'm calling in sick today. We're spending the day together. To celebrate."

Chapter 15

Tucker

Addison and I couldn't detach ourselves from each other. The idea of the two of us dating for real was a powerful aphrodisiac. We made love in bed, against the kitchen counter, in the shower—this one turned out to be a bit more complicated now, the space a tad small for both of us.

We were eating lunch, half-naked on the couch, her legs sprawled over me, when she moved to her feet with a wide grin.

"What is it?" I asked, flushing a bite of pasta down with a sip of water. "I haven't seen those devilish sparks since the night of the wedding." My body heated up just at the memory of her tied to the bed, wearing nothing but the red piece of lingerie I got for her. "Should I be worried? Or run for my life?"

Her contagious happiness bled on me, and I was now smiling like an fool too. I sprang upright to a ninety-degree angle, bracing myself for whatever craziness she might throw my way.

Tingles lined up my spine. Yes, Addison Wilde being wild excited me because I had no idea what to make of it all.

She paced the living room, dressed only in one of my T-shirts showcasing her burgeoning belly, and I zoned in on the swell of her ass as she walked back and forth. "My eyes are up here, big guy," she warned with an even larger smile.

I swallowed. "Yep. There's just something incredibly hot knowing you wear nothing else underneath that piece of cotton. Just trying to sneak a peek."

I felt my cheeks warming as if I'd been caught doing something bad.

Addison offered me a sharp stare. "You've had both hands, tongue, and dick deep in the candy jar earlier. Now focus if you wanna be granted another visit later."

I bobbed my head. "Yes, ma'am."

"See, I was thinking... It's the first time I feel one hundred percent like myself in so long... No more fears, secrets, or denying myself everything I crave. I wanna immortalize this day. We have very little time before Mini-Tucker arrives. Let's go shopping for the nursery, pick out paint swatches for the walls, and get matching tattoos."

I chuckled before joining her, resting my hands on her hipbones. "I love you. Nothing will change that. But I have to stop you from getting tattoos. Not that I'm against the idea, but you're five months pregnant, sweetheart. Nobody is going to poke a needle into you. Not right now. Not under my watch. We'll discuss it again in a few months."

Her lips curved into a pout, and I kissed them, unable to wipe the curl from my own.

"But I really wanted to do this. With you," she grumbled.

I framed her stomach with my hands. "Can't you do something else for now?" The baby kicked at that exact moment. "See? Mini-Wilde agrees with me. No ink and needles for you two."

As if another bright idea had just landed, she blinked, forgetting all about the tattoo. "I know. There's something I've been thinking about doing for a while now, but I didn't do it… No idea why, though."

"Does it involve alcohol, stunt, needles, raw fish, bungee jumping, car racing, or putting your life or the baby's at risk in any other way?"

She shook her head. "None of the above. Nothing dangerous or reckless involved. And it won't be permanent, so if we don't like it, it'll go away. At some point."

"Intriguing. Can I have hints?"

She shook her head again. "No. Maybe. Because you're cute. Makeover. That's all I'm gonna say. I'll need about two hours to put this together, and once I'm done, we'll go out on our date as planned."

I pulled her against me, our little bundle of unborn joy pressing between us. I claimed her lips in a slow sizzling kiss, to show her just how much she meant to me. "Are you shaving your eyebrows? I heard it's a thing."

Her warm laughter enveloped me. "Nah. I would never dare. Not sure it'd be a good look on me."

I let out a dramatic sigh. "At least we agree on that. Not that it would or wouldn't fit you, but I can't see the appeal. I prefer you with brows."

"Great, because I'm keeping them. Let's go. We have a lot on our to-do list for the rest of the day," she said, leaning back.

"We'll get you something new to wear tonight. After

all, it's our first date as a couple. And I want it to be perfect. I've been waiting for this day for a long time. I'll make a reservation."

"You'll see, big guy, it will be fabulous." She clapped her hands together. "Can't wait. This is so exciting."

My hand smacked her ass. "Go, get ready."

Addison strode toward the bedroom but pivoted to watch me. "Tuck? Thank you. For always having my back. And loving me." She paused. "Have you talked to Elisa lately? Did the couple who had been interested in your condo counter with another offer after you declined their first?"

"They're supposed to come back with a final figure within a day or two."

"If we can't stay here, we should discuss moving. You said Chicago isn't an option, and as much as I love you, I won't argue about it because damn, it's cold. And windy."

"Wanna go back to Atlanta?"

"Nah. Too big a city. Except for the weather, it's not much different from here. But it has great suburban neighborhoods."

"Green Mountain?" I proposed.

"Don't you think you and I would get bored in no time? Sure, it's peaceful and the scenery is to die for, but other than that, there's not much to do. Let's think about it for a little longer. Once the baby is born, we can decide. I can't wait to meet Mini-Tucker and be a family, the three of us."

Slivers of excitement spiraled through me. I inched closer, lifted her in my arms, and twirled her around. "Can we forfeit all our afternoon plans and spend the rest of the day in bed instead?"

Addison beamed, joy radiating from her. Jesus, she looked so perfect. And mine. I wouldn't joke about marrying her anymore—because the next time I asked, it would be the one.

"No," she said. "Not that it doesn't sound appealing, but remember, I have a makeover to tackle, and you said something about getting a new dress. I really love the idea. I'm looking forward to our first date."

If this place sells sooner rather than later, we should look for a townhouse in the meantime. Somewhere that doesn't require an elevator when we want to go for a stroll, and where the car is parked right in front instead of in a concrete underground garage. A place that isn't downtown. I'm still working remotely, and you'll be on maternity leave for quite some time, so neither of us will have to commute morning and night. What do you think?"

"I love the idea. Our own place. Starting afresh. We—the urban folks—living in the suburbs. If you had told me last year that I would do this, I would never have believed you. Look at us. Becoming so mature."

I lowered her down to her feet. "I'll ask Elisa if she can come up with a few listings. We could rent until we figure out our next step."

Addison lifted herself onto her tiptoes to kiss my lips. "I'm supposed to have lunch with her next week. You could join us, and we could go over our options."

"And gate-crash your girls' time? Nah."

"No big deal. Think about it."

Addison and Elisa had become close friends since she moved in with me. They worked a block away from each other and often met for lunch.

My woman disappeared into the bedroom, swaying her hips, aware of how crazy it made me. The night we met, later at that bar in Nashville, she kept doing it, and laughing every time she glanced at the erection that my trousers couldn't conceal. Addison Wilde was a temptress. My temptress.

———

Around six, I knocked on the door with a hint of nervousness and loads of exhilaration. First dates meant chivalry and excitement, and I relished the jitters fluttering in my stomach as I waited for the woman I loved to let me in. The dress we chose together earlier was royal blue, knee length, hugging all her pregnancy curves, and offering a glimpse at her cleavage. Perfect. Just like the woman wearing it.

The door opened, and I held my breath.

"Ta-da!"

"Wow. Wilde. Wow. I'm speechless." My gaze traced the length of her—black ballet flats, a delicate gold bracelet at her wrist, and that blue Otto & Newhouse dress that emphasized the ocean color of her eyes. The one I'd convinced her to try on as it reminded me of the night we toured Atlanta together on scooters and she wore a piece by my favorite designer. My eyes stopped their ascent when they reached her face. I blinked, momentarily unable to speak.

"Oh, you don't like it?" she asked, uncertainty taking over her features.

"You're kidding, right? I love it. A lot. You look fierce. You can't look this hot and expect me to keep my hands to myself all night. Unless torturing me was your plan all along. In that case, take me hostage right now and make me your prisoner."

Her clear laughter warmed my insides.

"Turn around. Let me see you," I ordered, my voice husky. Addison executed herself. "Fuck, how can we go out now? I want all of you to myself. All those fuckers are gonna check you out."

She smirked, pride and love pouring out of her.

"You're doing this on purpose because you enjoy the effect you have on me, Wilde. How can you be the only one who can always bring me to my knees?"

Her tongue swept her painted lips. That devilish-looking woman was a maneater, and I wished for nothing more than to be her first and last meal. "I might take extra pleasure in watching you lose your mind."

I stood there, admiring the woman about to become the mother of my child. "You did it yourself?"

"Yeah. Told you my mother owns a beauty salon. I've learned a few tricks over the years."

Unable to resist her any longer, I captured her mouth, one hand sliding into her shorter mane, and the other one taking a handful of her ass. Goodbye, long blonde locks. Addison now wore her hair in a mid-length bob with bangs. She looked gorgeous and sexy. I promised myself I'd tell her all night, and for the rest of my life.

"Where are we going?" she asked as I circled the SUV to open her door.

"Dynasty. Got us a backroom booth. There's a pianist playing tonight. Dark room. Dim lights. And a date looking like a queen."

All night, we ate, chatted, and laughed like we always did. Addison had had a new peacefulness about her since this morning. Nothing could express how thankful I was to have my best friend—and the woman I couldn't resist—in my life full-time. All of her. Plus the chance to be granted every delectable inch of her without restriction anymore.

We were almost done with our main course when her hands slithered up my thigh. Cupping my junk under the table, she leaned toward me, her lips millimeters away from my ear. "Listen, I know it's a first date and everything, but I'm pregnant and full of naughty hormones, so it gives me the right to put out tonight."

"Agreed," I whispered, breathing fast, her hand rubbing my pulsing hard-on, toying with my sanity as I focused on not coming in my pants.

She pressed her full breasts against my ribs, the siren in her not shying away, boldly taking charge. "And I was thinking, we could play a little game. You look so damn hot and smell divine, it would be a shame to see all that go to waste. Or to push away the unavoidable."

"Yes," I panted. "Anything for you, sweetheart."

"Remember that night when you made me come under the table in front of our friends? I kept my cool, trying to act unaffected, and it worked...for the most part."

Her hand turned greedy, and I tried breathing at a normal pace.

A traitorous smile peeked through my lips at the thought of Carter Hills calling us out that night. "I...I do."

"Lucky you, you have an advantage tonight. No one's sitting at the table with us. There's music playing, and it's dark. Let's see if you can come before the server takes our dessert orders, okay?"

I caught my breath when she unbuckled my belt and unbuttoned my trousers, slipping her hand inside my boxer briefs to fist my throbbing dick.

She worked me a little, and I closed my eyes, trying to force oxygen back into my brain and calm the ache building inside me. She rubbed the tip with the pad of her thumb, and I squirmed with a groan, my ass buckling from the seat.

"Two can play this game, big guy. How well can you hide the fact I'm about to bring you to your knees?"

"Wilde, you should be the one on your knees right now," I said through clenched teeth.

"Later, Tuck. This game isn't over just yet. If you win, you'll be able to ask anything from me."

I planted my fork into my steak with more force than necessary, stabbing the poor piece of meat. Even chewing it had become painstaking as she pumped me faster under the table, eating her chicken salad next to me as if nothing was happening. As if I weren't about to explode all over myself.

My willpower, no, my sanity, only held by a flimsy thread.

"How are you doing, Tuck?" Addison gave me a side glance, and the animalistic beast in me begged to unleash himself, flip her over the table, yank her panties down, and ram into her until the next morning.

I inhaled, flexing and unflexing my fingers at my side. "Great. No idea what you're talking about."

She moved closer, tasting the flesh of my neck with her tongue.

I loosened my tie, suffocating with need.

"Getting bothered, Tuck?"

"Nah. Just hot in here. Wanna go for a walk and ditch dessert?"

Her smirk reached her eyes, and mischievousness filled them in the low light of the restaurant. "Never threaten a pregnant woman to forfeit dessert." Her squeeze on me intensified.

"Jesus, we…we…huh…we should go. Now."

"Are you forfeiting? If you do, I win. The last time we made a bet, it had unexpected repercussions." She gestured to her abdomen. "And I believe I won."

I curled my hand around her neck and crashed my lips on hers, hungry and unable to resist her any longer. "I won," I murmured against her lips. "I got the girl, didn't I?"

Addison moved to her feet and discarded her cloth napkin on the table. "Meet me in the restrooms by the back door in two. I'm calling it quits tonight. You get a free pass. This time only, though. Don't get used to it." She winked, and it almost killed me on the spot. "I need you inside me. Stat. It can't wait until we're home later."

Having Addison in my life meant living precariously, and as always, I was all in for the danger—and for every wild, unpredictable side of her.

———

"If we accept this offer, we gotta move out within two weeks, is that it?" I asked, just to make sure I heard Elisa right.

"Yes. The offer is above the asking price. I'm not sure we'll get another one like this. You two can discuss and decide if you'd like to move forward. We need to give them an answer by tomorrow at noon." She placed a stack of papers in front of us. "Go through it. Sleep on it. I'll be in touch in the morning."

She left, and I sat back beside Addison at the table. "What do you think?" she asked, stars in her eyes. "It's… wow…it's incredible."

"Babe, I'm gonna make a counteroffer. Buy us more time. You're seven months pregnant. No way are we moving so soon."

She rose to her feet and straddled me, toying with my hair and massaging my scalp with her fingers. "Tuck, you're not turning this down. Unless you've changed your mind and want to stay here—which I don't mind—or there's something else bothering you about their offer, don't refuse because of me. And before you suggest a moving company, I'd like for us to do this together. Pack boxes. Put labels on them. Do normal *couple moving in together* stuff. The movers can take care of the heavy lifting because obviously, I won't be able to do it. I wanna set up the nursery. Paint the walls, assemble that crib, and buy tiny clothes. Together. Build our life on a solid foundation."

I rubbed my palms over my face, trying to stay cool-headed and think without letting my emotions take over. "If we do this—and I said *if we do this*—then you'll need to decrease your weekly work hours. No more overtime. Moving is exhausting. You need rest. The doctor warned you. You look like you're about to pop any minute, and you still have eight weeks to go. I'm serious, Wilde."

She leaned in to kiss my lips. "I love it when you wanna make sure I'm safe and sound." With a hand caressing her belly, she stared at me in the way I could never get enough of. "Tuck, be honest with me. Do you really wanna sell this place?"

"I do."

"Then it's settled. Everything will work out how it's supposed to. Trust life."

"I trust *you*."

"Well, it's even better," she said, "because I want what's best for us. Let's call Elisa back. You know the townhouse just a couple of streets from her house? I can see us living there for a little while. It even has a backyard and a park across the street."

I picked up my phone and dialed my friend.

Addison's hands traveled under my shirt while I tried to have a coherent conversation with Elisa, her fingers tracing the ridges of my stomach. Her sensual perusal of my body electrified all my nerve endings. She teased the corner of my lips with her greedy tongue. My body powered up at the sensations traveling through me.

Dropping to her knees, Addison unbuttoned my pants and reached into my boxer briefs. Before I could stop her, she licked the length of my dick and purred as she wrapped her lips around it. *Jesus fucking Christ.* I tilted my head back, struggling with my breaths and my words. She worked me faster, sucked me deeper, her tongue and hands busy making me see stars. I offered her a pointed look as I asked Elisa to repeat what she had said for the third time.

Fuck, Wilde, I mouthed.

She dug her fingernails into the back of my thighs and gave me that devilish look I always failed to resist. When she increased the pace, the bobbing of her head and pressure of her tongue drove me insane and propelled me toward my release.

I hung up and stopped Addison with a hand. "Wilde, it's a very dangerous game you're playing right now."

"You love it when I play dirty," she whispered before moving to her feet and licking the length of my chest, followed by the side of my face, and offering me a sheepish grin. Standing up, she hurried away from me. Jumping over the couch, I caught her and enveloped her in my arms. Together, we tumbled onto the piece of furniture in a mess of tangled limbs, my body shielding hers to soften the deliberate fall.

Shifting position, I pinned her beneath me, my mouth teasing hers with gentle pressure. Her tongue darted out to entice mine, but I leaned back. "Tell me what you want?" I asked, panting as if I had just run ten miles.

"You."

Before I could say anything, she tore my shirt open, sending buttons flying around us.

"Hey. I liked that shirt."

"With the sale of your condo, you'll be able to afford a new one." She winked. Devil. Not missing a beat, I used both hands to rip her sweater from the front.

"Hey. I loved that sweater."

I winked. "With the sale of the condo, I'll buy you a dozen more like this one."

Her round, perky breasts allured me, and I leaned over her, ready to indulge in them.

Her inquisitive hands explored under the torn fabric across my chest, and she squeezed my nipples. "Has someone ever told you that you have great nipples?" she asked, her voice laced with lust.

"A woman. Once. And she seems to have some button-ripping fetish. I always end up naked when she's around."

"Oh, what a vixen she must be."

Her eyes were a dark sea of blue now.

Her cheeks bore a light flush.

I attacked her mouth. "You have no idea."

Her fist returned to my dick, and she pumped me with world-shattering strokes.

A sudden knock on the door yanked us back from being lost in each other.

Addison frowned, and I soothed the wrinkle between her eyes with the pad of my finger.

"Elisa," I croaked out. Caught up in our little make-out session, I'd totally forgotten I had called her back.

Another knock.

Forcing ourselves apart, I went to open the door, assuming Addison had retreated to the bedroom to change.

No. Instead, Elisa walked in on us, her eyes flaring, surprise etched across her features. "What happened to you guys? It looks like you've been mauled in the fifteen minutes I was gone. Am I in the right apartment?" She shook her head. "Never mind."

"Give us a minute," I said.

I led my woman to our bedroom and pushed her against the closed door after I kicked it shut. "When we're done here, I'll make you pay for ruining my favorite shirt." I kissed her harder, and she became putty in my hands, kissing me back with fierceness.

Plunging my hand behind the elastic waistband of her jeans, I ran one finger against her soaked center, rubbing it back and forth just to monkey around with her composure.

With hurried movements, I slid her pants and panties down her legs, then freed my pulsing dick.

In one slow thrust, I entered her, not a care in the world about our guest waiting in the kitchen. A gasp left her mouth.

She rolled her hips, tightening her grip on me.

I nibbled the length of her throat with my teeth as she tipped her head, her back arching, and her swollen breasts begging to be cared for.

I bent down and licked the swell of her skin spilling over the delicate lace of her bra.

Once I got her ready and needy, I pulled out.

"Tuck, no," she whined. "Give it to me."

"It's a promise, sweetheart. To finish you later. Give me twenty minutes and you'll be screaming my name so loud people on the rooftop will wish they were you, or they will call the cops on us."

She strangled my cock with her hand and used just enough force to get me to submit to all her wishes. "Good boy. You better deliver."

I pressed my mouth to hers one last time before stepping back. "I will."

Rummaging through my closet, I called, "Have you seen my gray shirt?"

"It's in the hamper with the clean laundry."

I shook my head. "Wilde, how many times do I have to say this? My suits and dress shirts, dry cleaning. I love it when they're pressed and ready to wear, not wrinkled balls."

A new surge of desire pulsed through me as I watched her in nothing but her jeans and that sinful bra.

"Oops. Tuck, you're too high-maintenance. You must learn to let it go. Laundry is laundry."

I sighed and picked a simple T-shirt from a drawer. "I like my clothes a certain way."

"And your housekeeping. Your fridge. Your car. This baby of ours won't care if your couch is leather or the rug is some imported thing that cost a pretty penny when it spits up or spills milk. One day, you'll thank me for helping you be less stuck-up."

"Stuck-up? Me?"

She kissed me. "Yes. But you're getting better at it. I still have faith in your abilities."

From the moment we met, I knew Addison Wilde would be the end of me. Every day with her proved me right. She was wrong about me. I wasn't *that* high-maintenance, just a little picky about certain things. She was talking nonsense.

Dressed, decent, and ready to move forward with our life, we joined Elisa in the kitchen, perched over the stack of papers she'd left earlier.

Me, stuck-up? Nah.

Two weeks later, we were waiting for our things to be delivered to our new—well, temporary—house, a twenty-minute drive from the city, while finishing the second coat of soft moss-green paint on the nursery walls. As predicted, moving had been rushed and exhausting, but now that my bachelor lifestyle was officially behind me, I felt lighter than I had before.

"We never really chose names," I said, stepping back to admire the work.

My woman had on a denim overall, with no shirt underneath, because I forced that new rule after she compelled me to work shirtless, a bandana tied around her head, her ocean-blue eyes vibrating as she scanned the room.

"I thought we did. That time in Green Mountain. Have you changed your mind?"

"No."

"Me neither. See? Settled. Super easy." She paused and turned to face me, her blinding smile contagious. "We did it. I'm proud of us."

Before I could stop the words from pouring out, I got down on one knee and said, "Marry me. I'll never love anyone else the way I love you."

I braced myself for the answer that had always followed my proposals in the past, but deep down, I hoped this time it would be different—that I'd finally hear the right one. I knew we were it, and I really wanted Addison to be my wife. She was my person. I could feel it in the marrow of my bones.

"Tuck—"

I felt my heart drop in my chest as she looked at me, surprise and something else flickering in her eyes.

Her lips moved, and I froze, holding my breath as anticipation coiled tight in my chest.

Chapter 16
Addison

I blinked, my heart racing in my chest as the words I'd been waiting to hear for a while rushed out. Like a complete idiot, I stood there, frozen, trying to process everything they implied.

Tucker's eyebrows bunched together, and the fear that crippled his expression shattered me. Hurrying in his direction, I kneeled—well, more like slouched—on the floor before him and circled his neck. "*Yesss*. A thousand times, yes."

My lips danced against his, and I hoped they conveyed the depth of my feelings for him.

"You sure? Last time you said yes, you freaked out afterward and ran away."

I brushed my fingertips along the side of his face, memorizing the contours for the millionth time and leaving a blotch of green paint on his dark skin in their wake. "No more running away ever again. You're stuck with me now.

For better or worse." I kissed his chin, his jaw, the corner of his mouth. "Tucker Philips, I wanna be your wife. Let's stick to the original plan."

"Which is?"

"You, me, our closest friends, Vegas. And a party once the baby is born."

"Jesus, I love you so much. Once this little nugget comes out of the oven, we'll set a date."

"Oh geez, are you trying your hands at *poetry* now?"

"Maybe."

I burst into a train of giggles, which ended in a contraction. "Forget it. I hope poetry isn't your mysterious project. With practice, you'll get better…or not."

"No offense taken. I'll forgive you. Someday."

He plunged forward, his tongue cherishing mine in luscious strokes, and his hands roaming all over me.

"I wanna marry you now," I whispered. "Don't you think we've waited long enough. No doubt, you're the one for me. I've known it the first time I laid my eyes on you. And after you sang that song to me in that bar, I was a goner. Big time."

"And yet you resisted for months."

"You can't deny I was worth the chase," I said in a teasing tone. "It would have been boring had I made it too easy on you. Gotta keep up with my rep."

"Woman, you're the most perfect headcase I've ever met. Lucky for me, you're *my* headcase. Are we really getting married?"

"Yes, and we're not waiting until Mini-Tucker is born. We're already a family. Let's make it official."

———

The next morning, we were having breakfast when I surprised my man with two plane tickets to Vegas. He rounded the table to secure his arms around me, one palm splayed over my middle—the same manner he did every day—and his chin propped against the crook of my shoulder. Our little one was having a blast in there, kicking and stretching.

"Oh, so you two have been planning this nuptial behind my back?"

I grinned, so big it hurt my cheeks. "Yeah…huh…no. Not really. Remember, I had a debt to pay."

Tucker remained silent, waiting for me to explain.

"Vegas. Our bet in Nashville. I thought neither of us actually won, but a while back, you said you did. In all honesty, you're the only one who brought a girl back to the hotel that night. And since you had to wait months for me to admit my feelings for you, I'll give you the win. This time only, though. Don't get used to my accepting defeat so easily. I'm usually a much-tougher player. Today, I'm paying my dues. Two tickets. Presidential suite with a view of the Strip. The flight is tomorrow morning. If you agree to elope, Nick and Dahlia will join us to be our witnesses."

Tucker blinked, holding my hands in his. "Yes." He pushed my hair back and leaned in to kiss me but stopped halfway. "Question. Are you sure it's safe for you to fly?"

"I called Dr. Pettyfer two days ago.He said everything looked good at the last check-up and that, as long as it was a short flight, he wouldn't object, even less, especially if it was to make an honest man out of you."

"Wilde, you secretive woman. You planned this. When I asked you yesterday—"

"I had already planned to ask you this morning. You just beat me to it."

"Sorry I ruined your proposal."

I flicked my wrist. "Even though I was looking forward to asking you, I love that you did it first. I've been thinking about it for a long time, and I finally got the nerve to reach for one of my dreams."

His mouth descended on mine, tasting my lips. "I love it." He trailed kisses along my jaw and down my throat.

Shivers passed through me. Arching my back, I gave him the unspoken agreement to play my body the way he wanted to.

"Let's reward you with an orgasm, my second-place prize offering, and then we'll go dress shopping. You're going to be the most beautiful bride ever."

His lips returned to mine, and I shook my head against his mouth. "No. The groom isn't allowed to see the bride before the wedding day. It's bad luck."

"Tell me you don't believe in that shit?"

"Nah, but it's still fun getting you all worked up over what I'll wear. Dahlia and Nick arrive tonight. She's bringing a few options from her store. We'll spend the evening at her hotel, just the two of us, so she can make some adjustments."

Tucker grabbed my ass cheeks, and I purred, unable to resist him as I rubbed myself against him.

"That's perfect. Nick will be able to help me put together the last details of the nursery. That way, if you go into labor sooner rather than later, everything will be ready tonight."

"Who knew talking crib and rocking chair could get me soaking wet?"

His fingers ventured under the straps of my overall, but I pushed them away.

"Not so fast. Wedding night, Tuck. No sex until then."

"Jesus, now I'm happy we're getting married tomorrow.

I gotta say that not tasting you until you're officially mine is kind of a big turn on."

I kissed him, deepening the connection, as I fastened my arms around him.

"Wilde, there's something missing in that genius plan of yours?"

"What?"

He released me and left the room, only to come back two minutes later.

Dropping on one knee, he opened a white velvet box showing me two matching pink-gold bands. I always knew pink was his favorite color. "Addison Wilde, would you marry me tomorrow?"

I cupped my mouth with a trembling hand, tears flowing down my cheeks while I nodded. "Yes, I will."

———

I was saving my Mini-Wilde newest design when a contraction hit me. I exhaled and pressed each side of my thirty-eight-week baby belly with my palms, rubbing the taut skin, trying to dissipate the discomfort. When I met with my OB-GYN two days ago, he said he believed I wouldn't make it to the forty-week mark. Mini-Tucker already weighed over nine pounds, and I looked like I could explode at any time if someone poked my stomach. Yes, I had gotten that big. I blamed my husband for all of it. Every time I went out, people still asked me at least once a week if I was carrying twins—or triplets. The new story of my life.

"If you could please stay put for a few more hours," I told my unborn child, caressing my baby bump in a protective manner. "If I want this onesies collection to be a success, I gotta finish it before you decide it's time for you to get out. Otherwise, I won't be able to order the samples in time for you to show them off. Daddy asked for one of each in all available sizes."

My baby kicked, the imprint of his feet, elbows, or knees tenting my skin. I pushed against it, and hero she pushed back, both of us relishing our little private game. Soon, it would be a different one, and I felt myself growing more ready each day for this new challenge.

A mix of excitement and anticipation to meet this little human that Tucker and I had created together danced through me every single day.

On my feet, I printed my newest design with the special printer my husband got me—I still couldn't believe we were married—and plugged in the iron press to heat it up, ready to see how it would look in real life on a blank onesie I bought for our baby. *A Little Wild* written in colorful letters looked amazing on the tiny piece of cotton fabric.

I covered my stomach with it. "This one is yours. The first tangible item from my baby collection." Pride filled my heart, and flutters invaded all my senses.

I moved to return to my seat when another contraction hit me—stronger and longer than any I'd felt before. Bent forward, I balanced my weight with one hand on my desk, the other massaging my tense belly.

"Guess you love it," I said through gritted teeth as I calmed my breathing. "There are nicer ways to show me your approval, you know?" The tension left, and I went back to work, but soon, another contraction hit me, followed by another.

I swallowed through the pain and called out, "Tuck—" My jaw clenched as the pain radiated across my back. Okay...they were coming closer and closer together. "Tuck," I screamed again.

He came running, storming into the room and squatting between my legs. "What's wrong?" His palms closed around our baby in a sweet protective gesture. "Mini-Wilde giving you trouble?"

"I think it's time," I said.

He watched me with furrowed brows. "For what?"

"This baby wants to come out. Now." Another contraction.

"For how long have you been having those?" he asked once it relaxed.

"Since yesterday, but they were far apart, and I thought they were just the fake ones. But now they're less than ten minutes apart, and they fucking hurt."

"Why didn't you say something?" He pushed my hair back and kissed my forehead. "I'll get your things and then come right back for you. Can you wait just a minute or two?"

I nodded. Tears pooled in my eyes. *I am going to be a mama.* Reality came crashing down on me, and for a second, I forgot how to breathe on my own. This was the most exhilarating and scariest thing I'd ever done in my life. I knew the endgame, but nothing about all the suffering and pain to get there.

Tucker wiped my teary eyes. "Hey, I've got you. We'll do this together. You're the strongest woman I know. Everything will be all right. I promise."

He jumped to his feet, and I grabbed his hand before he could walk away.

"Thank you. I can't do this without you. You're my rock, Tucker Philips. I love you."

"You're my inspiration, Addison Wilde. I love you so much right now." A wide, ridiculous smile painted his face.

"Just right now?" I teased.

"Nah. Always and forever."

————

After the nurse checked if I was dilated enough, the doctor told me to get ready. Our baby would come within the next few hours. I watched Tucker watching me with a *too large for his face* grin.

"Wilde, you've given me things in life I never would have gotten anywhere else. A family. You've made me a husband, and now a father. You've shown me how to love. How to trust someone, even when it meant risking my heart—because it could all be worth it. I'll never be able to thank you enough. All I can say is that I love you so freaking much."

He kissed me before helping me change into a pastel-blue hospital gown.

He snapped a picture with his phone. "This is the last mile. The finish line. And you look beautiful."

"Tell me that later when I'm all sweaty, my hair disheveled, and ready to murder someone."

"Deal."

The doctor came back to check on me for the umpteenth time almost eight hours later. "The effacement is slower than we expected. Even for a firstborn," he said, tossing his latex gloves into the nearest trash can after examining my cervix.

"What does that mean?" my husband asked, worry coating his tone, his hand holding mine with a strangling grip.

"The baby is large," the doctor said, scanning Tucker from head to toes. "Let's just say it doesn't surprise us, but your contractions aren't strong enough, and your cervix hasn't dilated as expected. Before we consider medications to speed up dilation and strengthen contractions, I'd like you to walk for at least the next hour—or until your condition changes. At this stage, I can't send you home, and it's too early to be talking about a C-section."

Fears tangled around my heart, but exhaustion made it hard for me to process all his words. "I'm so tired. How can those contractions not be strong enough? They hurt so bad."

"It happens. Let's just do this for now, and we'll reassess afterward. There are other things we can try. As long as the baby's vitals remain good, there's no reason to worry or rush the delivery."

"O…okay," I agree, too weak to argue.

Tucker helped me to my feet, and after I went to the bathroom to empty my bladder, he secured the hospital gown at the back. Knitting our fingers together, he led me out of the room.

Silent tears rolled silently down my cheeks.

"Hey, Wilde. It will be all right, you hear me? It happens often. I asked the nurse while you were in the bathroom."

I nodded, too exhausted to even stop the flood blinding my vision.

For the next sixty minutes, we paced the hospital hallways, only pausing when a contraction hit me. Each time, Tucker massaged my lower back, easing the pain.

An older woman stopped us as we passed the room where family members waited for their loved ones to give birth. "Oh, lucky you, you're expecting multiple. Are they twins or triplets?"

A new surge of tears drowned my eyes as I pivoted to bury my face in Tucker's chest and broke into sobs. I blocked the conversation out while Tucker explained to her there was only one baby in there.

"I'm so fat. I don't wanna be pregnant anymore. Can you get this baby out? My entire body hurts. I'm so sleepy I could fall asleep anywhere if it weren't for those damn contractions ripping my belly in two."

My husband rubbed circles over my back with his hands."Shhh, it's fine, sweetheart. I'm right here with you. I know I can't do a lot, but I'm not leaving your side."

As if I got stung, my head jerked up. "No, it's not fine. How can it be? We fucked while we were both wasted, and I took the morning-after pill, yet this baby found a way to stick in there. What are the chances? We're either the luckiest or the unluckiest people on Earth. I took the fucking pill, and it still decided to stay. Now I look like a whale, and people keep reminding me how fat I am. And just to fuck it out a tad more, this baby has now decided it won't come out."

"Addison," he said in the softest voice he could manage. He rarely called me by my first name, only when he was being emotional. Or overwhelmed. "You're neither fat nor a whale, you're pregnant. And that weight won't stay on forever. We already discussed it. The doctor told you not to worry about it. I know it must be hard, but even if you can't see it, I'm telling you, *you are* beautiful. Take my words for it. I'd never lie to you."

I pressed my face between his pecs and let his words sink in.

"We'll get that baby out today. Or tonight. We're not going home without our little one." He lowered down before me in the hospital hallway, pressing both palms to my belly. "Baby, I love you. You know I do, but let's come out. I wanna meet you. Give your mama a break. Do we have a deal?"

As if the baby could hear him, it kicked, followed by another contraction.

Tucker rose to his feet and worked out the tension in my back with firm, steady hands. "You've walked long enough. Let's see what the doctor thinks." With his strong arm, he held me up against him, supporting me, while we returned to the room.

In bed, I surfed between different conscious states, barely registering the nurse strapping the fetal monitor back around me and reading my pressure.

"The heartbeat is strong," she told me, rearranging the pillows under my head and the covers around me. "You're doing great. Sleep while you can. Try to stay on your left side. I'll be right here if you need me."

She exchanged a few words with Tucker, but in my drowsy state, I couldn't make out their conversation.

Every two or three minutes, the contractions felt like lightnings ripping me apart, but in-between, I found some rest.

Sometime later, Tucker woke me with kisses peppered across my forehead and soft caresses over my tense abdomen. "Wilde, the doctor gotta check your cervix now. Can you move to your back?"

I nodded, having a hard time escaping the dreams I'd lost myself in.

He helped me flip around and intertwined his fingers with mine.

"Okay, here's the thing," the doctor said, a somber expression drawn on his face. "Our goal is to avoid exhausting you or the baby. Before we consider an emergency C-section, I'd like to try medication. I know you wanted a natural birth and preferred to avoid an epidural, but at this point, this is the most logical next step. I need to warn you, though. The contractions will intensify. They'll be stronger and closer together."

"Huh…okay," I said, the enthusiasm in my words missing.

"Both vitals look good. I'm confident we can achieve

full dilation. If there's no progress within the next few hours, we'll reevaluate your options. For now, given the baby's size and the width of your pelvis, we'll consider this a high-risk pregnancy. That's not uncommon and nothing to be alarmed about. We'll simply monitor you more closely. Do you have any questions?"

I shook my head, unable to comprehend what he said or the gravity of the situation, my brain not registering any of it.

Tucker pressed a kiss to my forehead. "I'll be right back." Seeing the pained twist of his lips sent zings of discomfort through me. Tucker would sort it out. Whatever it was, he'd make sure neither the baby nor I would be hurt.

I nodded and let go of his hand as the space between us grew and our fingers could no longer touch.

We'd been here for over twenty-eight hours when I gave the last push, almost fainting from exhaustion. Tucker smiled through his tears. I forgot all about my sleepless nights, the rocky ride of the last day to get to this moment, my sore inner thighs, and everything else when the doctor handed him our son after my husband cut the umbilical cord. Tucker placed him in my arms, and the sound of my baby's first cry awakened a primal need to protect him deep in my core.

Yeah, I'd be a tigress mama. An emotional surge I had no control over whirled through me, and I cried like I hadn't done in a long time as I counted his tiny toes and fingers, all perfectly formed. Twenty. The count was perfect..

"All there," I croaked.

More tears cascaded down my face.

Tucker and I'd created this little human being together.

"Good job, mama," the nurse said, cupping her heart with her hands. "You did amazingly well."

My gaze never left the small bundle lodged in the crook of my arm while I stroked his cheek with my finger.

A fresh batch of tears clouded my eyes, born of pure, raw happiness. From a joy I never knew my heart could contain. The look on my husband's face as his eyes ping-ponged between me and our baby boy took my breath away. It broke me. And revived me. I knew, in that instant, that everything would be okay as long as we were together.

I pushed the top of my gown down, and the nurse positioned the baby, only dressed in a white knitted hat, his dark skin rosy and his eyes round, on my bare skin.

Tucker leaned in to kiss me. "I'm so proud of you, sweetheart. He's perfect. And he has your eyes. You did great. Today sealed the deal. You're definitely the strongest woman I know." Yes, our baby was indeed perfect. Tanned skin, dark hair, and blue eyes.

"I love Lucas," I said, deciding on the name Tucker liked the most.

"No. He's a Jamieson. A Southern soul. You were right."

"You sure?" I asked, drying my wet eyes with my fingers, the tab still running.

He bobbed his head fast. "Jamieson Nicholas Philips. It sounds fierce. And badass. Just like you."

Chapter 17

Addison

We secured little Jamieson in his car seat. Tucker adjusted the knitted cap over his head and the pacifier in his mouth that he sucked like his life depended on it. Watching them, my eyes leaking fresh tears, I let out a nervous puff of air. The moment we left the hospital parking lot, I would be on my own, responsible for most of the care of our child. Tom would be there, of course, but he wouldn't fully understand what I was going through—the disconnection that had settled deep within me.

My emotions were a tangled web growing inside me. In the hospital, every time I held him, Jamieson wouldn't stop crying. But with my Tucker, his tears would vanish in an instant. A nurse had even nicknamed him the baby whisperer, and the entire staff agreed. How was I supposed to care for someone who couldn't find comfort with me? My baby had spent nine months in my womb, and it felt like he didn't recognize me…or the intimate bond we shared. My husband and the nurses assured me it would get better, but nobody understood the overwhelming sense of failure that washed over me every second I was alone with my newborn child.

"You wanna sit beside him in the back?" Tucker asked, pointing to the open car door with his chin.

"No. I'll sit in the passenger seat," I replied in a thready voice, more tears pooling in my eyes. "Next to you."

"Wilde, are you okay?" he asked with a frown. He wiped the streams of tears rolling down my cheeks. "What's wrong?"

"I-I don't know. It all just…it all just seems like too much." I waved my hands before me. "All this… I can't explain. I just feel like crying. My nerves are scraped raw. Everything sounds like a big deal right now."

Tucker pulled me into his arms, strong and powerful, as if he could shield me from any harm and pain. "Sweetheart, what you went through is fucking hard. You're exhausted, and you've barely slept in the last three days. Let's go home, and I'll put you both to bed so you can recover and find your footing again…regain some strength. It'll be easier to deal with everything with a rested mind. Lean on me. I'll always catch you. Let me play nurse for the day."

I nodded against his chest, the leak in my eyes unstoppable.

My husband's comforting hand linked with mine as he drove us home, to our new life as a family.

The entire ride, I pressed my head against the window, staring through it without really seeing anything. Maybe a nap would help. A surge of chaotic emotions washed over me, and the tears I'd been holding back int he last ten minutes erupted into heart-wrenching sobs.

Tucker stopped the car by the side of the road and pulled me to him. "Shhh, Addison. Don't worry. We'll find our balance." Could he read my mind? "The doctor wasn't joking when he said it was a difficult delivery. But you did good…so, so good. Amazing, in fact. It's okay to be emotional. Anybody would be in this state." He kissed my temple. "Wanna go home?"

I nodded against his chest.

His lips lingered on the top of my head until I calmed down a little.

For the rest of the drive, his squeeze on my hand never faltered, and he brought our joined hands to his lips, kissing my knuckles. "We will be okay. Don't ever doubt it."

"I know," I said, sweeping the back of my hand under my runny nose. "I love you."

"I love you so much I'm not sure my heart can contain it all." We parked in the driveway, and he turned to me before opening the door. "Ready?"

"I…I think."

Tucker exited the truck and rounded it to help me out. I felt wobbly on my legs, and he wrapped his arms around me to steady me. "Once we get inside, you go to bed. Husband's orders."

I rested my head in the crook of his neck and nodded, the weight of the world pressing heavily on my shoulders.

"We'll do great, Wilde. I promise."

When we stepped inside our home, everything looked different. So foreign. Perhaps Tucker was right, and sleeping would erase the heaviness inside of me. When we left for the hospital a few days ago, excitement had bubbled inside me. I had been ecstatic at the thought of coming back as a family of three. But right now, I couldn't feel those sparkles of joy. I dragged a hand over my face, my eyes swollen from all the tears I had shed.

Tucker walked behind me as I stopped in the doorway of the nursery, winding one arm around my waist and pressing his cheek to mine after he lowered the car seat with Jamieson at our feet. "We did it, Wilde. I can't wait to introduce him to his room…to everything we are."

I scanned the space we had poured so much of our hearts into. The one we had decorated with love. And anticipation. Right at this instant, coils of fear wrapped themselves around me. As if walking into the nursery would mark the end of me and all that I was. The room felt like my personal prison. One that I would never be allowed to leave. My throat worked hard, swallowing the shards of unease lodged there. The abyss I was falling into was growing bigger by the second.

As if on cue, Jamieson started wailing, and I shut my lids, hating the idea I would have to breastfeed him again so soon. I had just done that before leaving the hospital.

A battle raged inside me.

Saved. That was the only word my brain came up with. My stance relaxed, and I breathed out my relief that I wouldn't have to step into the nursery. Not today, at least. Because we had agreed that, for now, I would breastfeed in our bed.

"Lunch time," Tucker said, his voice teasing. "Come on, sweetheart. Let's open the baby buffet," he joked, without realizing how much his words grated on me.

Maybe he should be the one feeding him. Then he'd know what I was going through. I shook off my thoughts and, with heavy steps, followed him to our bedroom, my resentment rising with every step at the thought of my nipples being sucked raw until I could scream in agony.

I knew I was responsible for feeding our son, but nothing could describe the hour of torment. All I wished for was to be away from here.

I forfeited the idea of sleeping until the next day, and going through the motions, I lay on my side on our bed. Tucker placed the baby in front of me while I unhooked my bra so Jamieson could suckle on my sensitive nipples.

The pain when he latched on sent a chill through me. I gritted my teeth, trying my best to just send my thoughts on a journey far from here, to evade my own mind. And body. Tucker, with a proud smile, lay behind our son, one protective hand resting on my hip bone, showing me, in the simple gesture, just how much he cared for us and how involved he would be in the entire process.

I blinked away the tears burning the back of my eyes. Was this how motherhood would be? Hurtful. So far, since my contractions had started, nothing had been pleasant. Labor had been long, every moment steeped in intense pain. Even in the hospital, everything was agony, and at home, the ghost of those events still haunted me. The nurses promised I would forget the excruciating moments once I held my baby. They lied. Nothing erased the pain. Well, maybe for a few hours. Until some of the ecstasy settled, and it came back with a vengeance.

I sighed and brought my attention to the present, when I had to switch breasts so that Jamieson could latch onto my other nipple. An hour later, I studied the men in my life, Tucker looking at the tiny bundle in his arms in awe, as he patted his back and burped him. Why was his awe not directed toward me? I had fed him, raking over the coals of fire with every suckle. I was nowhere present in the world that was inhabited by father and son.

Something snapped in the depths of me. A hidden fissure, one I never knew was there, tore my heart apart. Where there should have been a bottomless rush of love at their bond, my feelings had vanished. I felt nothing. It felt as if I was standing there in front of them, but neither could see me. They appeared to be a thousand miles away. Far from me. Or was it I who had moved away? My mind was a fuzzy fog I couldn't breach to go back to my physical body.

For an instant, I wished I could disappear. That I could just quit and find solace elsewhere. How could my mind conjure these thoughts? I was supposed to be overjoyed. Ecstatic. I was loved and had a family of my own. One I had wished for so many times in the past. Still, no joy passed through the barrier of my heart. Even though I tried, I couldn't find it in me to feel contentment.

Tucker turned to me, a dozing Jamieson nestled in the bent of his elbow, and kissed my cheek. "I'll put him to bed. Rest. I'll be right back to check on you."

Through my half-lidded eyes, I watched his silhouette, our baby cradled in his arms, disappear through the door. He looked like a natural. Like he was born to care for him. They belonged with each other. I was just the milk factory.

A stray notion crossed my mind, and I clung to it. No matter what happened, Jamieson would be safe with Tucker. Nothing bad would ever happen to him. Besides, he already preferred his daddy over me.

A pinch clamped my heart at the thought I couldn't see myself as being a part of this picture.

Fresh, soul-crushing thoughts kept surfacing in my mind. They'd been coming on and off since the day I'd delivered.

Tucker raising Jamieson on his own, me watching them

but not being able to be near them, locked in a dimension I couldn't escape.

Tucker, living in a house with a white picket fence and a swing set, laughing his heart out with another woman nestled in his arms who looked nothing like me.

My life slipping away from me with nothing I could do to hold on.

A fresh batch of hot tears filled my eyes.

I suffocated, air burning my lungs on its way in.

Was I even awake, or was it all a dream?

Before I could come out of my distressing thoughts, muscular arms that always made me feel safe held me. Words were whispered into my ear. Kisses peppered on my temple.

This reality felt like a daydream. And so distant.

"Wilde? Wilde—"

Tucker talked to me, but I couldn't make out his words.

"Addison," he barked, worry lacing his tone, and I snapped out of my funk.

I blinked, trying to bring my mind back to the present.

Through a curtain of tears, my eyes drifted to his.

He pushed my hair away from my face with his fingers. "You okay, sweetheart? It's just a dream," he said, his voice lower now, protective, familiar. "No matter what it was, it wasn't real. I'm here."

I nodded, unable to speak, sobs clogging my throat.

"I'll stay here with you. Watch over you. Sleep now." He fumbled with the knob on the baby monitor by the side of the bed, molded his tall self to my body, and before long, sleep claimed me. Calmer this time.

When I woke up to my husband caressing my cheek, I felt like he was pulling me out of some place far away. A dark cave I'd disappeared into and where I'd found my peace.

I opened my eyes to Tucker and Jamieson watching me. The smile on my husband's lips should have been burned into my memory forever, filling my heart with joy. It was a mix of reverence and unconditional love. But for a reason I couldn't name or explain, I felt nothing. It was like it was intended for someone else than me.

"Hey you," he said. "Dinner is ready. You slept for over three hours. Our little man has decided to be on his best behavior too to give his mama the rest she needed, but now he's hungry and about to suck on my tits if you don't feed him soon."

Feeding him again? My heart sank at his words.

The intoxicating smile that split his face in two didn't have the desired effect on me. Instead, it caused my being to quiver in fear.

I had to nurse the baby. Again.

Pushing my discomfort down, I forced a small curve onto my lips and placed my hand in Tucker's as he helped me to my feet.

I swallowed. "Gimme a minute. I'll join you in the living room," I said, my voice gravelly from sleep and all the tears I'd cried.

"I love you, Wilde." He gave me a quick kiss, then let his mouth rest on Jamieson's fluffy hair.

"I love you too," I croaked, repeating the words by rote, almost without feeling.

In the en-suite bathroom, I locked the door and faced my reflection in the mirror. I didn't recognize the woman I saw. Dark circles around her eyes, engorged leaking breasts sensitive to touch, floppy skin over her stomach. There were no sparks in her eyes. No satisfactory grin shaping her lips. No sign of the woman I used to be. I buried my face in my palms.

What had happened to me?

Jamieson cried, and I turned the tap on to drown out the sound.

Motherhood was worse than everything I thought it would be. My gaze returned to my abdomen. Unable to watch my reflection any longer, I pivoted until my back faced the mirror. No way would I ever be able to live with myself looking like I'd stepped into someone else's skin. A body that no longer felt like mine.

Crumpling onto the bathroom floor, I surrendered to the tears I could no longer stop.

"How will I do this?" I asked to no one. "How can I go through with this?"

Rummaging through Tucker's wardrobe after I dried my face, I chose a pair of sweatpants to hide my bulging stomach and thighs and one of his x-large T-shirt to cover the ugly nursing bra. Using his clothes to conceal my new, unwelcome form would do the trick until I found a better idea. If I didn't see the revolting bits, perhaps I could forget about them. For now.

Infusing fake happiness into myself and drawing my features into a neutral expression, I joined my men in the kitchen, Tucker rocking the fussy baby in the crook of his arm, singing to him.

In the doorway, I stared at them.

My baby had the best daddy I could ever ask for. That I was certain of.

But where was my place in all this?

Feeling bad about the dreadful thoughts my mind kept conjuring, I chased my uneasiness away and looped my arms around him, praying it would heal all my invisible, brittle scars.

———

I stood at the edge of the precipice, debating if I should jump, craving the freedom. Could I fly if I put my mind to it? The breeze swept across my face, and the sun warmed my skin. It looked so peaceful down there. Silence. I could hear nothing but the sound of my own breathing. Calmness filled all my senses with peace. From afar, I could see the line of trees and the blue sky. Extending my arms around me, I greeted the open air. Nothing could disrupt my happiness here. I was safe from any harm. Nature shone brighter here. Closing my eyes, I let the world around me imprint its beauty on all my cells. I had become the wind and the sun.

A murmur resonated from far away, disrupting my peace. With my hands over my ears, I blocked the sound. I would let nothing get to me.

I glanced down and asked myself once again if I could fly if I jumped.

My feet brought me closer to the edge. I bent down to get some momentum when soft lips sprinkled kisses over my cheek, and I woke up from my slumber. I wouldn't fly today.

"Wilde, time to go. We have yours and Jamieson's first postpartum appointment in two hours. I let you sleep in for as long as I could, but if you want to be ready on time, you should get up. It's almost ten, and our little one is famished."

My body felt like it had been carved in concrete. Heavy and inflexible.

With clenched fists, I rubbed the sleep from my tired eyes.

Tucker lay beside me and kissed my neck.

I kissed him back, but listlessly. I couldn't seem to feel anything for him anymore. All his requests sounded like orders or demands. For the past few days, I had been hoping the doctor would prescribe some magical pills to restore my energy and my happy demeanor—the one I'd lost after giving birth. That he would tell me it would all get better. Because I missed the girl I once was, the one ready to become a mother, the one who worked her ass off to make sure everything would be perfect the day she welcomed her bundle of joy into this world.

"Can you feed him while I take a quick shower?" my husband asked, handing me our son.

"No." I took a step back, recoiling and twisting my arms behind me. He frowned, and I quickly recovered, shrugging.

"What?" Tucker watched me with a confused expression.

"Huh…sure. Never mind. Gimme a minute. I'll meet you in the living room."

"Don't you wanna do it in the nursery?"

I shook my head and pinched my lips to avoid grimacing. I couldn't walk into that room without feeling a clamp around my stomach and hyperventilating. Even though it had been two weeks since I got home, the feeling only grew instead of fading. I decided to avoid it, but I didn't tell Tucker—he would worry or ask questions—and I wasn't in any state of mind to answer them. I couldn't explain what was happening in my own head.

Pretending I had to get a glass of water, I shunned holding the baby for a little longer. Only once I was sitting on the couch did I tell Tucker to bring him over.

With the baby set on a half donut-shaped nursing pillow pressed against my chest, I fed him. Even after two weeks of doing it every few hours, the entire thing still felt oddly uncomfortable and unnatural to me. My fingers itched to brush Jamieson's soft hair or rub his back, but I couldn't bring myself to touch him…or to connect with him the way I should.

I kept my hands at a safe distance, close enough around him to make sure he wouldn't roll off the pillow, but not so close that I would have to feel his warmth under my palms.

In the doctor's office two hours later, I put my best poker face on and answered his questions with as much enthusiasm as I could muster. He wouldn't pin me as an unfit mother. Not today.

"I was just wondering," I said, inhaling deep to find the courage to open up about what was bothering me. "Is it normal that I'm so tired all the time? Getting out of bed is hard. I mean, really hard. My energy reserves are low. And my emotions are all over the place."

"Addison, giving birth is not easy. It takes time for your body to adjust and find its balance again. You went through a long and difficult delivery. It can explain your symptoms. Some mothers need a little more time than others to recover. Postpartum is a personal journey. Don't be too harsh on yourself, just take it easy. As long as you rest and eat healthy, you'll be fine. And your husband seems like a hands-on father."

"He is."

"Then lean on him when it becomes too much. A lot of mothers put pressure on themselves and get overwhelmed because they can't do it all. Take it slow. Jamieson looks healthy and is growing according to charts. You guys are doing it right. When it all becomes too much, step back and take some time for yourself."

His words instilled flecks of hope in me.

It wasn't me, just my body taking longer to adapt to the schedule of feeding a newborn every couple of hours. For the first time, I believed I'd be all right. Time. I needed more time. Things would get easier.

In a slightly better mood, I offered to grab some food on our way home.

"You look beautiful," Tucker said as we entered our home an hour later. "Let's put Jamieson to bed and spend some time together. I've missed having you all to myself."

Tucker and I lived on opposite schedules, and the few hours each day I was awake were spent feeding our son, so we hardly ever had a chance to be together anymore.

He looped his hands around my waist. The image of my loose skin flashed in my mind, and I flinched before stepping back. I didn't have time to reel in the scowl on my face before my husband noticed it.

"Wilde?" Tucker asked, a wrinkle forming between his eyebrows. "What's wrong?"

I swallowed. "Nothing. Just hungry. Can we eat now?"

He scratched his nape. "You sure? You'd tell me if it was more than that, right?"

I forced a curl to my lips. "Yeah. Sure."

The deep-dish pizza didn't taste like usual. I forced a slice in, washing the small bites down with a sip of water so Tucker wouldn't bitch about the fact that I didn't feed myself enough.

I cleared the table and put the dishes in the kitchen sink. When he attempted once more to wrap his arms around me, I decided not to pull away this time, before he could be alarmed by my change in behavior and my refusal to indulge in the affection he offered.

Minutes after we settled in the living room, my head dropped onto his lap, and before I knew it, I had fallen asleep, wondering how long it would take for me to get my groove back. When I woke hours later in our bed, I couldn't remember him putting me there.

The next week passed in a blur too. It had been three weeks since I gave birth, and instead of feeling more energized with each passing day, I felt increasingly exhausted. Even showering felt harder with every passing moment.

I woke only to nurse the baby or feed myself the bare minimum, my stomach in a near-constant knot.

When I crashed after breakfast, I begged my dreams to take me to that cliff edge. Where I felt free—and at peace.

Slowly, each day, I drifted further away from my own life.

Chapter 18

Addison

"Please make the baby stop crying," I asked out loud, trying to drown out the annoying sound by covering my ears, and then retreated to our bedroom.

Tucker followed me close and grabbed my elbow to spin me around. Frustration blistered inside me as his grip forced me to look at him. "Babe, he's twenty-six days old. He's not a robot. You can't just turn the switch off." I groaned something while he continued, "And he's not *the baby*. He's our son. *Jamieson*. He has a name. I don't understand why you can't say it. You chose it, and it fits him perfectly. Why are you calling him by any other name under the sun but his?" He sighed. "Talk to me, Wilde."

I gestured around me. "I'm exhausted. That's all. And my tits are leaking. Gimme a break, okay? I'll get better at this *mommying* thing. You're not the one who popped him out of your body. Time. I need some fucking time to myself. Not attached to a milk-sucking human twenty-four-seven."

"Addison—"

The look in Tucker's gaze broke me, but I really needed to be by myself. Sleep it off. And just be in the moment. Was it too much to ask?

"I'm tired of people telling me what to do. Didn't you hear me? I'm not just a milking machine."

"I never said that." He restrained his annoyance. I could hear it in his tone. "Where is this coming from?"

I threw my arms over my head. "Just forget I said anything."

He inched closer. "What's going on? Talk to me."

"I'm fat and…and…ugly. I look like I've just gone through war. Or left an asylum. I need time. This entire thing is asking too much of me."

He rested his hands on my upper arms. "Why didn't you say something sooner? We gotta talk about these things."

I stepped back and escaped his touch. "I don't wanna talk. I wanna sleep. And go back to how things were… before the baby. Before I became—"

The baby's cries intensified.

"Coming, Jamieson," Tucker said as he turned on his heel. He stared at me over his shoulder. "This conversation isn't over. I understand everything you're saying, but it doesn't make it okay. Or acceptable."

"Whatever," I said, entering the darkness of our bedroom—I didn't even bother opening the curtains in the morning anymore—and slamming the door behind me.

Once alone, my breathing resumed. The knots in my stomach loosened. The weight pressing down on my shoulders cleared. And the suffocating prison I felt closing in on me released a little.

My clothes were rumpled, my hair dirty and tousled, but I had zero cares in the world. All I wished for was to sleep for a day—or a dozen. Tucker could feed the baby. I had pumped milk like a stupid cow for hours earlier. He could also do the night shift. Sue me, but I disliked the bottle, diapers, naps, and *do it all over again* routine. Elisa came over yesterday to play nanny for the afternoon and ended up doing my makeup and helped me change into real clothes. A much-needed upgrade to the sweaty-and-stained-shirts look I'd been wearing lately. Still, I refused to let her see my abdomen, too ashamed of how it looked at the moment. So far, it hadn't given me any hint that it would return to a respectable shape anytime soon.

I scrolled on my phone for a little while, and once Tucker got the baby to stop hollering, sleep claimed me, and I just abandoned myself to it.

In my dream, I found my way back to the edge of that precipice. The only place where I found serenity. Peace washed through me as the breeze swept across my skin.

Hours later, the morning light filtered through the crack between the curtains as I stretched my arms beside me.

The sheets were cold on the left side of the bed, which meant Tucker had been up for a long time already.

Feeling less groggy, I took a long and hot shower, letting the stream wash away every remnant of my sleep. I had become quite good at avoiding my reflection and looking at my postpartum body. As long as I didn't acknowledge it, my brain could keep pretending it didn't exist.

I put on black pants and a loose-fit off-shoulder shirt and met my husband in the kitchen, hoping wearing clothes that belonged to me for once would make me feel good about myself.

"Wow, you look great," he said, placing a cup of tea in my hand and leaning in to kiss my lips. "And smell great too. Feeling better?"

I shrugged.

The baby cooed in the seat Tucker had set on the countertop, and my gaze lingered on him for a second before returning to the food in front of me. Using my fork to avoid my husband's heavy stare, I pushed the scrambled eggs around, playing with them. I could sense the questions, the annoyance, the incomprehension—all pouring out of him.

Not hungry, but refusing to engage in a conversation I knew I wouldn't win, I brought the food to my lips. My stomach churned at the scent, and my gag reflex flared as I tried to swallow.

"Sweetheart, you've been eating almost nothing since you gave birth. You gotta fuel your body with something other than caffeine. Dr. Pettyfer said it would help with the milk production too."

My fork hit the plate with a loud bang as I pushed it away, done with breakfast. "Don't call me sweetheart. I hate it. And I already told you I'm not a milk-factory. They sell baby formula at the store, so if you're unhappy with my services, feel free to buy some."

Tucker pulled the seat next to me and angled himself so we'd face each other. He grabbed my hands in his, and even though the gesture repulsed me, I exhaled and plastered a fake smile onto my lips, trying not to start another war. Yeah, war. Because all we did lately was argue.

"Since when do you hate it when I call you *sweetheart*? You never complained before." He tipped my chin up with a finger, encouraging me to stare at him. "I think we should make an appointment with your physician, just to make sure everything is fine."

I sprang to my feet and jerked away from his touch. It felt as if millions of needles were prickling my flesh every time our skin connected.

"I'm okay. Exhausted maybe, but fine. No…no need to worry." I went to our bedroom to get heels and my purse and applied some lipstick, looking at my reflection in the entryway mirror. Our place was beautiful. Wide windows, hardwood floors, archways. Everything I'd adored when we first moved in. Now I couldn't care less about where we lived.

I smacked my lips together and fixed my hair, ready to bolt out of here.

Tucker joined me, a sleeping baby nestled in his embrace, alarm flashing in his dark eyes. "Where are you going?"

"Work. I've missed enough weeks already. I sent my boss an email two days ago, and he said I could come back whenever I was ready. Don't wait for me. I may come home late. I have a lot of work to catch up on."

The baby woke up, and his blue eyes found mine. I cocked my head, wanting nothing else than to escape this prison I lived in—and his innocent gaze.

Tucker stepped before me, blocking the doorway with his broad shoulders.

"Let me go," I ordered.

"No."

I folded my arms over my chest. "I gotta go. Move."

He handed me the baby. "Take him. Here and now, take your son. You haven't entered his bedroom once since we came back from the hospital. You've nursed him only a handful of times, and every time, your face is painted with disdain. You've never changed a diaper or given him his bottle."

If I had steam coming out of my ears, Tucker would have been able to visualize how upset I was right now.

"You don't kiss him, hold him, or comfort him. Never. Not once."

"I'm tired," I said.

"Stop. It's your go-to excuse to justify the fact you're not bonding with him. Stop feeding yourself lies. I understand that giving birth hasn't been easy. On top of that, you're going through all these physical and psychological changes, and your hormones are all over the place. Also, you've been bleeding for over two weeks straight. It's not easy. I. Am. Aware. But that doesn't explain why you're not connecting with our son. Why you keep us at arm's length."

I shook my head, shame hanging heavy over me. Why did I feel like such a failure right now? Why did I feel like I'd win the *worst mama of the year* award? Before Jamieson was born, I was looking forward to be a mother. I had always been envious of Dahlia and Jack, and I'd been wishing to be a mama for as long as I could remember. But the images I'd pictured in my head looked nothing like the real thing.

I'd always thought I'd be the mother taking long walks through the park, happy to push a stroller around. I believed breastfeeding in my bed, lying on my side like those pictures in maternity brochures, playing dress-up with my little one, and singing lullabies every night would make me happy.

Nope. Reality looked nothing like those fantasies.

"My breasts weigh tons. My nipples are too sensitive. I

have to wear absorbable, thick granny panties… The skin of my belly is super saggy. My hair is falling. The shadows under my eyes aren't fading. You can't relate to any of these things. I'm the one who carried him for nine months. Were you the one who was torn in two when he finally came out of me? Through my fucking vagina. After over twenty-four hours of unbearable pain. How would you understand any of this, Tuck? Enlighten me. Sorry if I am not jumping around with overflowing joy. Not that I could, anyway. My bladder is probably screwed as we speak. Get in line if you wanna wreck my existence too."

Right then, I just emptied all the gloomy thoughts that had been swirling in my head for weeks now.

After I gave birth, I fell in love with our baby. Hard. I would've given my life for him. Hours later, a distance had grown between us that I couldn't seem to patch. After we were discharged from the hospital, I had convinced myself it was normal to feel a bit out of it after what I went through. Thanks to a new set of hormones, my emotions ran wild. I was exhausted, crying over nothing and everything, and sore. Then we got home, and that gap widened. Before I could comprehend why, all the excitement of being a mother faded into routine. I lost the connection I had shared with the baby. I didn't recognize him as a part of me anymore.

I slept for longer hours, trying to go back to the blissful state I'd experienced at first. In vain. The more days passed, the more lost I felt. And the larger the distance grew between the baby and me.

Now he felt like a stranger. Not the one I carried around for nine months. Not the precious little in-construction human being who kicked my stomach and whose knees and elbows I pushed back when they pressed against my taut skin. The baby resembled Tucker and me in the best of ways, yet I felt nothing while around him. No, all I felt was emptiness—and the desire to get the hell out of here.

Tucker lifted the baby against his torso, rubbing his tiny back. Deep down, I prayed to be as hands-on a parent as he was, because I could recognize that my husband had been doing a remarkable job so far. He was a natural. This man turned out to be the most amazing father.

Right now, though, it didn't seem important.

His lips descended to kiss the baby's soft, dark hair. No, I couldn't say his name. No matter how hard I tried, it refused to cross my lips.

"Addison, we're having this talk right now. Why didn't you confide in me? I've been patient and have given you space, but it's getting worse every day. The more you close yourself off, the harder it will be to come out of your shell. I'm not going anywhere, Wilde. So, better get used to having me around and in your business because I'm not letting go this time. Perhaps you really can't see it, but I know you. And this"—his finger motioned to the length of me—"isn't you. I'm not asking you to be a perfect parent, but I need to at least see you try. Now you're not even doing shit-anything. Sorry, Jamieson. You can't fail at being a parent if you're not even trying. All you do is stay detached, keep your distance. Completely. I heard every-thing you've just said, and you're right. I didn't deliver a baby or carry one around fro none months. And I can't understand how leaking tits feel. But I'm willing to learn and to put myself out there. Whatever else is bothering you, please talk to me about it." His tone hardened. "In case you still have doubts about me and my involvement, I won't let you down. You better be honest with me. Truth, remember?"

I wished I could cry, the emptiness inside growing

deeper with every passing second, but even the tears refused to come.

Tucker brushed my hair back with a gentle touch. "I'll put him to bed. Wait for me, don't go. Gimme a minute." He paused. "Okay?"

I huffed and nodded, walking back toward the kitchen. I filled a cup with a dose of caffeine—I'd never been that much of a coffee drinker, but now it had become my drug of choice. The idea to add a little pick-me-up to my cup crossed my mind, but I didn't have the energy to reach for the liquor cabinet by the back door. Why were all these thoughts racing through my mind? Now I was even considering adding booze to my morning drink. Great. Tucked was scared to turn into his parents, but so far, I was the one about to score high on the bad-mother charts.

My husband came back and sat next to me, stopping my train of gloomy thoughts.

I hoped I could see hatred in his eyes—or fury—so, I'd feel something, but all I read were concern and unconditional love.

Neither of us spoke for a long minute.

I sucked in a jagged breath, breaking the tense silence. "Back when we started hanging out together, we said *truth always*. Here's the thing. I don't love him, Tuck. I know I'm not supposed to say that, but that's the truth. When I look at him, I feel nothing, except maybe annoyance and disdain. All he does is cry or suck at my tits. I need a freaking break. Some fresh air away far from him. He's always in my space. I-I'm suffocating. I had some time to think, and I feel like I wasn't meant to be a mother. You're much better at it than I am. So, kudos. You win—whatever this is between us. And I won't argue with you. You wanna spend time with him, deal with all his needs? Fine, go ahead, but I'm not gonna do it. I want nothing to do with all this baby crap. Happy now? I've laid all my darkest secrets on the table. Can I go now?"

How could all these cruel words come out of my own mouth? When did I become a robot, unable to feel anything?

I moved to get up, but his muscular hands kept me seated.

"Babe, I know you're not being serious. You're not speaking with your heart right now. Nobody said having a baby would be easy. That you'd get everything right on the first attempt. For God's sake, I've ruined a dozen diapers, and shit spread everywhere before I figured out how to put it on the proper way. And every once in a while, I forget to burp him after he's finished with his bottle. I don't pretend to be perfect at it, but I'm doing my fucking best. I'm trying. I'm putting myself out there."

"You don't get it, do you? I. Don't. Care. I prefer going back to work than spending more time at home. I feel useless, and I'm not interested in the job. I just want to be left alone."

How could Tucker be so good at being a parent? How could he connect in the same way I feel disconnected from the baby?

I always thought mothers were instinctively better at nursing their children and understanding their needs. Then why was I so incapable of loving the baby the way he deserved? Why had Tucker been doing a better job than me since day one?

Warmth enveloped my chest. Awesome. Now my breasts were leaking, and I was soaked. I was uncomfortable and sore.

I crooked a finger to pull my bra away from my chest to give my breasts some room to breathe. A new feeling of failure coiled around me.

I wanted to tell Tucker he was right because a part of me knew he was, but those confessions died on the tip of my tongue.

I had turned into the worst version of myself imaginable. Darkness swirled in my mind. Exhaustion washed over me. Unable to stand any longer, I kicked off my heels.

"Happy now? I won't go to work because I'm already too tired to even get there. I've turned into a sloth. Even pregnant at thirty-seven weeks, I had more energy. I could have run a marathon. Or built a house. Now it's fucking hard just to get out of bed or take a shower. And that sound. Gosh. That high-pitched sound he makes when he cries for no reason… It…it gets on my last nerve."

Tears should have come. They should have flooded my face. But no, they refused to show up. Instead, anger bubbled up inside me.

Tucker pulled me against his chest—the same way he always had whenever I needed his love and reassurance in the past. This time, though, his arms around me felt like fuel for murder.

I pushed him away, but he just tightened his squeeze around me.

"Stop. Relax. I miss you, Wilde. So damn much. You're pushing both of us away when you should lean on us instead. To get through whatever you're going through. Jamieson and I, we love you. All we want is for you to get better. To come back to us instead of living a parallel life like you're there but not there at the same time. It's too soon for you to go back to work. I object."

"No. It's not your call. I'll be happier there. Being here is asking too much of me. I already told you. And the baby…nah, forget it. I am no mother material."

"Addison, Jamieson is your son."

"Maybe, but I didn't choose to be a mama. It just happened. And I…and I blame you."

"Okay, so now I'm guilty of the best thing that has ever happened to us."

"I don't have a dick, so I didn't put him inside me all by myself. The semen was yours. Can I go now? There's a happy hour after work tonight. Don't wait up for me."

"Wilde…"

"Don't Wilde me. If you wanna be a father so bad, just take care of him yourself. After all, he's your child too. See that as bonding time. All the books I've read say it's important for the father to get involved in the child's life from the beginning. Go ahead. Enjoy your time together. I'm out of here."

"No."

"Why do you make everything so complicated? You should just let me go."

"Never. You're stuck with me forever. Remember those vows? Because I do. *Addison Wilde, in front of our best friends, I promise to love and cherish you forever. You're my soul mate, my other half, my best friend. When you have doubts or are afraid, I'll be by your side, holding your hand. Together, we're it, sweetheart. We can face anything. We can be anyone we want. We can accomplish great things. I love you. Here, always and forever.*"

A first tear hung from my lower lash as Tucker recited his wedding vows. My heart cracked. Breathing became harder. Wrenching sobs escaped me as my husband held me against him.

"Shhh. Cry it out. It's okay. I'm here, and I've got you."

I shattered in his embrace. I had poured my heart out to him, and it hadn't made me feel better—only worse.

My own words replayed in my head. *I don't love him, Tuck. I know I'm not supposed to say that, but that's the truth. When I look at him, I feel nothing, except maybe annoyance and disdain.*

How did those words even come out of my mouth? Who was I? What had happened to me?

Lucidity and shame washed over me all at once.

Tucker and the baby would be better off without me.

I had already failed them so much in just a few weeks. No newborn deserved a shitty mother…a mother like me. A mother who just couldn't care.

When Tucker's arms slackened around my shoulders and my tears ran out, I rushed to our bedroom and locked the door behind me. With my back pressed against the wall, I pondered my options. I had very few choices. The only one that made sense told me to run—to set them free from me, to get the hell out of there.

Tucker turned the knob. "Addison, let me in. We're not done."

I wiped the tear residues off my face with my sleeve and swallowed the giant lump in the back of my throat.

The baby started crying, and I thanked him in my head for forcing Tucker to leave me alone.

"I'll be back." He sounded torn at the idea of stepping away. "Shit," I heard him say under his breath before he added, "Coming, little guy. Missing me already?" The softness lacing his voice, the tenderness, the love, I wished I could master that too.

He walked away, and the more distance he put between us, the easier I breathed.

Left to my own devices, I grabbed a bag from the closet and filled it with basic necessities. I changed into a pair of jogger and put tennis shoes on.

Tiptoeing out of the bedroom, I reached the entryway, slid my purse over my shoulder, and penned a note on a piece of paper.

I'm sorry. You'll both be better off with-out me.

Addi

I removed my wedding band and placed it on the console after pressing it against my lips.

A split second before the door closed behind me, my husband's panicked voice echoed from inside our home. "Wilde, wait—"

Once on the sidewalk, I hurried away, almost at a running pace, toward the nearest train station. I had no clue where I'd go, but anywhere far from here seemed safe.

I walked for minutes—or maybe hours. At one point, I had no idea where I was, lost in my drowning thoughts. The sun shone at its zenith in the blue sky, and I kept my head low to avoid being blinded by its rays. A car slowed beside me, but I ignored it.

"Addison Wilde, get in the car. Now," Tucker said in harsh voice through the rolled-down window. "Enough with the running away. You told me once you'd never do that again."

I kept my eyes trained forward, refusing to meet his gaze.

"Addison, we'll get you help. You're usually a bubbly, crazy number, and these days, you're a shadow of yourself. Can't you see something is off?"

I kept my mouth shut, refusing to acknowledge any of his words.

"My mom left… You know that. She ruined me for the longest time. Until…until you came along. I won't let you do this to our son. Never. You hear me? Whatever it is, we'll figure it out, but you won't leave him like that. And you're certainly not leaving me either. We're a team. None of this makes sense. Get in the car."

I continued my escape, only to realize I'd been walking in a circle. Great.

Tucker passed me and parked on the side of the road. He jumped out of the idling car to meet me, gripping my upper arms as I averted my eyes. "Where do you think you're going? What do you think you're doing? Enough now. Get. In. The. Car."

From the corner of my eye, I noticed the baby watching me through the window from his car seat. His big blue eyes fused with mine. He smiled at me, unaware of all the commotion around us, as if I mattered to him. How could he? I hadn't been his mother in so long. Or more like ever. But still, he didn't break eye contact, as if to tell me he believed in me or something. Hurt stabbed my heart, and for the first time since we left the hospital, something passed between us. Something I couldn't name—except that it brought fresh tears to my eyes.

Tucker caught me just when I thought I'd collapse on the sidewalk, drained.

"Wilde, I've got you. Here, lean on me. Come back home. Come back to us."

The baby let out a loud, happy cry as if he agreed. Could he really sense everything going on? Could he feel I was fading away?

"Will you accept my help?" Tucker asked, his arms tight around me, and his mouth kissing the top of my head.

I nodded.

I had almost left my baby. I had almost walked away from my own life…from my heart.

"Tomorrow you could go to the spa, get pampered, and catch up on some rest. I called your doctor. He'd like to see you next week. Pregnancy is hard and delivery, harder. You're exhausting yourself. You don't have to return to work so early. We…we talked about it. We have enough money for you to take time off, to enjoy Jamieson's first few months…and…for us to be a family."

I held on to him like a lifeline. "Don't lose faith in me. Please. Don't…" Once again, I became a sobbing mess as my husband hugged me before helping me inside our car and buckling my seatbelt, my hand shaky and my body too numb to take care of itself.

Chapter 19
Tucker

I drove us back home and put Addison to bed before feeding a hungry Jamieson. With him strapped to my chest in one of those baby wraps, I cleaned the kitchen and set myself behind my laptop, working on the secret project I'd been keeping from my wife for the last few months. Something for her. For the three of us. I had no idea if she'd like it, but my instinct told me she would. Anyway, with everything going on right now, we all needed an escape. A place in this world to call ours.

Losing myself in work kept my mind from dwelling on how my life had taken a turn for the worse over the past few weeks. Our fairytale came with a sour aftertaste.

My son snored against my torso, and I relished the sensation of our bodies connecting and comforting each other. In the last month, he had become my anchor. My rock. The one thing keeping me sane.

Right now, my baby required my love and care more

than ever, his mother unable to provide for him the way she should be. I wasn't even mad at her for zoning out—too worried about her mental and physical health. I questioned myself every second of every day, wondering how to reach her, how to help her, how to heal whatever it was that made her refuse to give Jamieson the attention he deserved.

But the weight of it all had grown heavy on me.

I pinched the bridge of my nose, fighting to keep my breathing steady, a truckload of emotions whirling inside me.

I couldn't lose it. Jamieson and Addison both required my support. My unconditional dedication. I'd just never imagined doing this parenting thing all by myself. Sleep had become a luxury I couldn't afford anymore. Between work and taking care of the people I loved the most and everything around the house, I could barely hold it all together.

When I'd talked to Addison's doctor earlier, he said something about depression. Could that be it?

My heart sank in my chest as I grabbed a framed picture of us on our wedding day. My wife looked so beautiful in her long white dress, cradling her huge belly, her hair curled, and her smile genuine. The sparks in her eyes didn't lie.

How did she go from being radiant and full of hope to being sad, disconnected, and miserable?

How did all the zest for life that once illuminated her gaze transform into empty abysses?

I traced the contours of her silhouette with a fingertip. "Whatever it is, sweetheart, we'll find a way back to you."

I turned the frame over and read the words she'd written there, the ones I knew by heart.

To my husband

This last year has been a rollercoaster I never saw coming, but I wouldn't change the ride because it brought me to you. And you're everything I've ever wished for.

I'm sorry I've been stubborn for the longest time, but now I'm certain that I wanna spend the rest of my life with you.

We never do anything in order, but that's what makes up so perfect for each other.

I love you now and for the rest of my life, and I can't wait for us to be a family of three.

Your one and only sweetheart, A. xx

I reread it a few times, a smile etching itself onto my lips while tears burned the back of my eyes. With a protective palm caressing my son's back, I dialed my best friend.

"Hey, man. How is it going?" he asked when he picked up.

A cocktail of emotions balled up in my throat, blocking my airways.

"Is it Tuck?" Dahlia asked. "Put him on speakerphone. Or better, ask him to switch to video chat. I wanna see my nephew."

I said nothing, fighting to keep my tears at bay as an incoming notification for a video chat filled the screen of my device.

"Hey guys," I said, plastering what I hoped would resemble a smile on my lips. "How is it going?"

"Oh, he's sleeping," Dahlia cooed. "He's so tiny. How did I forget Jack was that small once? Oh God, they grow up so fast."

My smile reached one side of my mouth, and I rubbed the column of my throat, trying to ease the commotion storming inside me. "Yeah. So small."

I glanced at my best friend, and he watched me, a wrinkle forming across his forehead.

"Tuck, don't bullshit me. I know the look. Something's happened. What is it? If it has anything to do with your secret project, I went there two days ago. It looks amazing. It should be done by the end of the month. My guys are doing great work. We should pay the place a visit together soon. A boys' road trip. With our sons. Wow, I love the sound of that. Both of us dads now. Who would have thought? Anyway, it's been a long time since we did something together."

I mustered another smile, the words stuck in my throat. I liked his idea, but for some reason, it made me wanna curl into a corner and bawl my eyes out. Probably not the answer he was expecting.

"Fuck, it's not that," Nick said, question marks now swimming in his eyes.

His wife backhanded his chest. "Careful, tiny ears close by."

"Sorry, Jamieson," my friend said. His focus returned to my face. "Do I need to fly to Chicago to pry it out of you, or are you gonna tell me what's wrong? You look defeated. Stained and wrinkled clothes. I know for a fact something is definitely wrong."

I didn't want to complain, to draw my friends into this, but I had exhausted all my resources, and I was tired. I had to confide in someone, or I'd burst at the seams.

In a way, I had Addison to thank. In all the months

we'd been living together, she had showed me I could let go, that a schedule could be modified, and rules could be bent. That a shirt that wasn't pressed or a pair of paint-stained jeans were not the end of the world. I was grateful she had, or I'd never survive this chaos right now. I sometimes felt that unconsciously she knew this would happen and that she had prepared me fro all of it.

"It's Addi," Dahlia stated, more like a fact than a question.

Moisture rose in my vision, and I nodded, unable to keep my suffering to myself any longer.

"Tucker," Dahlia said, her voice gentle and comforting.

Fuck, I missed comfort—and love—right now.

"She ran away earlier. It…it's bad." My voice cracked. "Very bad. I have no idea what I should do."

"What happened? I was going to call her tomorrow because she's been vague every time we've talked. She's always either too tired or too out of it to chat. It doesn't sound like her."

For the next twenty minutes, I filled my friends in on everything—from the moment we came home after leaving the hospital to when Addison cut me and everyone else out.

"She hasn't stepped in the nursery once. She never holds him, never kisses him, or even looks at him."

Dahlia's hands flew to her mouth. "Geez, I had no idea it was that bad. I thought she just required some time to get used to her new role. I'm so sorry, Tuck. What can we do?"

I traced my eyebrow with a finger. "If only I knew… I've booked her a spa day tomorrow and an appointment with her doctor next week. Now I'm afraid that each time she goes out, she might not come back. That…that she'll abandon us." I coughed, doing my best to clear my clogged throat. "She wants nothing to do with any of it...with either of us. I'm not complaining, but I barely sleep, and I can't think straight. It's just too much. What am I supposed to do? Force her to be a mother when she clearly doesn't wanna be? Or let her be and cross my fingers, hoping she'll grow out of it? That it's just a phase?"

"Man, you should have called us sooner. We're not doctors or shrinks, but we could've given you a hand. Don't shut us out when it gets tough," Nick said.

"Thank you, guys. But you already have your hands full with two businesses and Jack. You don't need my shit piled on top of that."

I sighed and kissed Jamieson's head as he squirmed against me. He opened his eyes, stared at me, and a new wave of warmth filled my chest. Releasing him from the wrap, I held him over my forearm so he could face my friends.

"Oh, he's getting cuter by the day," Dahlia said.

A genuine grin stretched my lips now.

"I know it's hard, but you're doing it right, Tuck. I can tell."

New tears blurred my vision on hearing her words. "Thanks," I croaked. "It means...it means a lot."

"Saturday morning, we'll be there. Let us help you out," Nick said.

I nodded. The thought of having support sounded great right now.

"Let me make a few phone calls. One of my employees once told me that she had dealt with postpartum depression during her last pregnancy. I have no idea if this could be it, but I'll ask questions. Talk to my doctor. See what I can learn. With Addi's family history, we can't rule out the possibility." She relaxed her shoulders. "I'm sorry it's happening to you two, but I'm sure there's a reasonable explanation. Addi would never abandon you or push her own son away if everything were all right with her. This I know for sure. Can you hold the fort until Saturday?"

I bowed my head. "Yes. What else can I do, anyway?" I breathed out. "Her doctor said something about being depressed too. I have no idea what to make of it."

"Gimme a day. For what it's worth, Addi is lucky to have you, Tuck. You're a pillar in her life. I know it doesn't excuse or fix anything, but I wouldn't want anyone else caring for my best friend. I trust *you*."

I swallowed hard. "Thank you, Dah. I shouldn't say those words to my best friend's wife, but I love you. Your heart is pure and precious. Wilde is lucky to have you in her corner too."

I closed my eyes and pressed my lids with my thumb and forefinger, trying to dissipate the ache in my heart. Dahlia's words replayed, and I stared at her.

"Dah, what did you mean earlier when you said with her family history? I'm desperate for answers. If you know something I don't, please share. I'm at my wit's end."

"Listen, if she hasn't told you about her daddy, it's not my place to tell, but I'll say this. After her last breakup, Addi has been worried about her mental health. It has never happened before. She was down, then she got pregnant, and it explained most of her symptoms, so she filed it under hormonal changes."

"I don't understand. What does that even mean? How bad is it?"

"Tuck, depression runs in her family."

I stopped breathing. "I-I...I had no idea. She never said anything. She's usually always so cheerful and bubbly."

"I know. Let's not jump to conclusions just yet. It might

be something else. I'll make those phone calls tomorrow and keep you informed."

"Thanks."

We hung up, Jamieson now fussy in my arms. My heart broke into a million pieces at the thought that my wife was suffering, and I had no clue how bad it was.

———

After I bathed Jamieson and changed him into fluffy onesie pajamas, I searched the chest of drawers in his room for a pacifier. I couldn't find the one he usually had on him. It probably had fallen in the car earlier when we went to get Addison, and with the downpour outside, I had no intention of getting it right now. I was certain she'd bought a few when we went shopping days before his birth.

I grabbed a basket full of baby stuff from a shelf in his closet when I discovered a white box. On the lid was written in gold letters which I recognized as Addison's artsy handwriting:

Baby, I love you to the moon and back.

Curious, I lifted the lid and found a book lying inside. With care, as if it could detonate at any moment, I placed it on top of the changing table.

Jamieson had fallen asleep in my arms, and I switched him to my left side as I flipped the pages quickly, my heart pounding in my chest. My breathing whistled. I felt dizzy and held myself up against the piece of furniture. Why hadn't I known about this book before? How did Addison forget to mention it? With Jamieson now securely pressed against my chest, I stepped back and hit a hard surface, then slid my tall self down the wall until my ass hit the floor.

The title, made of cardboard square tied to the front page with safety pins, read: *How I Fell in Love with your Daddy*.

One by one, starting from the beginning, I turned the pages, my focus on all the words and objects my wife had attached to them.

I used my shoulder to wipe the tears rushing to my eyes. "Baby, mommy loves you so much. You have no idea."

I read the message she'd written on the inside cover.

Dear baby,

I've been making this storybook to give you on the day you're old enough to hear our story. It depicts every moment when I fell more and more in love with your daddy. It's full of keepsakes, memories, little things that make our love story as incredible as it is today.

Tears ran freely down my cheeks now, and I pressed my son's sleeping body against my heart as I continued reading.

Each page had a handwritten note with an item attached next to it, the first one being the hotel keycard from the night of Nick and Dahlia's bachelor-bachelorette party in Nashville. The one I thought I had thrown away with my ripped shirt that night.

This is the hotel card from the weekend your

daddy and I met. He looked so handsome, dressed in one of those suits he wore all the time, with a glint in his eye every time our gazes met. From the time I first laid eyes on him, I couldn't look elsewhere. He was all I could see. Back then, he thought he'd lost his keycard and invited himself into my room. When we came back to the hotel, it was late, and I had forgotten I had put it in my purse. Now I know it was the best thing I've ever done. Because that night cemented something between us.

This is one of the buttons from the shirt your father tore when he climbed that fence after I made us late for the night's events. He was upset and annoyed by me, I could tell, but even then, I was mesmerized by him. When he put on that groom T-shirt—the one I'd designed, far too small for him—my heart leaped at the fact that he trusted me, that he would follow my lead. At that moment, I fell for him for the first time. Then later that night, he sang to me (see lyrics of our song on the next page), and I knew my heart was in trouble, that he'd stolen a big chunk of it. Because even if we were just supposed to pretend to be in love, the chemistry between us couldn't be faked. To everyone else, it was fake, but I knew better. That kiss was as real as it could get, and I fell for him a second time.

This is the speech I wrote for Dahlia's bachelorette party. Back then, for a lot of reasons, my head was all over the place, and I'd forgotten to actually write it. Your daddy, even though he barely knew me, read me like an open book. He figured me out when I had the hardest time doing so myself. He came to my room, sat with me, and didn't leave until I was done with my speech and was happy with it. He believed in me for the first time. To this day, it still means a lot to me—and my heart. Your daddy is a special kind of man. When he loves, he loves hard. He's my favorite person in this world. Along with you.

I kept reading, my lips pressing against the top of our baby boy's head.

This is the menu of Cosmos. One day, I was feeling off. I was so tired all the time and had no idea I was pregnant. Your daddy flew in for a few hours, just to take me out on a date to this amazing restaurant and cheer me up. We zipped around the city on scooters afterward, and up to now, it's still one of the best nights of my life. I fell for him a little more with every passing hour we spent together. I never told anyone, but when he walked away that night, I felt sad. Our relationship made no sense, and we didn't tell anyone about us, but our friendship was everything to me. It still is... Falling in love with your best friend is something quite amazing.

Those are my plane tickets from the time I surprised your father in Chicago. I landed there with only a suitcase and no plans, except to see him, and ended up spending the weekend with him at his place. We chatted for hours, and he opened his heart to me for the first time. He brought me to his special place on the rooftop of his building. When I returned home, I cried for hours, missing him from the moment we parted at the airport. Back then, I wished my heart wouldn't feel so much when it came to Tucker Philips because I was scared of love...of being heartbroken. But I couldn't help it. I fell in love with your daddy all over again. Even though it made no sense to me.

This is the invite to Dahlia and Nick's wedding, where your daddy was not only the best man (I was the maid of honor), but also my plus-one. In all honesty, I would've been so crest-fallen if he had invited any other woman to go with him that day. I was an emotional mess. I was pregnant and had no clue. Those hormones are quite something, I'm telling you. Your daddy worried about me. He cared for me. He held me when I cried and gently brushed my hair while I slept in his lap. It was also the weekend when he told me he loved me for the first time. I told him he was crazy because I didn't want to acknowledge my growing feelings for him. And yes, I was falling for him a lot more than I should have.

This is the bus ticket that drove me out of Green Mountain the same weekend. The time I broke your daddy's heart for the first time because I ran away (I'm telling you the truth because you deserve it). I thought I wasn't pregnant and decided to put some distance between us to assess our growing feelings. I felt it would do us some good. That weekend, your daddy opened his heart to me, selflessly and completely. I already knew I loved him, but I tried to avoid making spur-of-the-moment decisions to prevent another broken heart. If there's one thing I regret doing in my life, it is not listening to my heart sooner. I remember being so miserable without him. You were the sign I prayed for. The one that would lead me back to him and prove we belonged together.

This is the first picture I have of you. It's a sonogram from the day I learned I was really pregnant with you. The day my life took a turn for the better. I should've been freaked out, but I wasn't. The only things I feared was your daddy's reaction. Not that I ever believed he'd be mad or anything, but I worried I would be too late and that he would've forgotten all about me. After a few days, I went to him, and we reunited. From the moment he learned about you, he's been nothing but loving and supportive. He's never left our sides. We moved in together and learned to be a couple. We solidified our relationship, getting ready to welcome you. You're so lucky, baby. I hope you realize it. Your daddy is the greatest man I know. He's fearless, resilient, strong, and generous. I fell in love with him all over again when he carried me in the rain, refusing to be separated from me ever again.

At this point, I couldn't see through my tears, my vision blurry and my shoulders heaving. "See, Jamieson? You've got yourself an incredible mama. I know things are hard right now for all of us, but hang on with me for just a little longer. She'll come back to you…she'll…she'll come back to us. I believe it. Because this woman, she's unable not to love with all her heart. In the meantime, let's stick together, okay? And help her get through this. I'm sorry for everything, but I'm here and not going anywhere. It's you and me against the world. Trust me. I'll fight for you forever."

I buried my face in his mass of dark baby hair, relishing the scent of his honey and lemon shampoo, reminding me of the one his mother used.

With my little boy in my arms, I spent a few hours on the floor of the nursery, my legs bent and my heart heavy. Until my eyelids weighed too much and it pained me to keep them open. After I laid my son in his crib, I went to my room, undressed, and slipped under the covers, wrapping my arms around my wife's waist, craving her warmth and the beating of her heart.

"I love you, Wilde. Never forget it. When you are ready, I'll be here. I waited for you once, and I'll wait for you all over again because what we have can't be explained. It's stronger than love. It's a bond from the core. It's fireworks. Get better, okay? Jamieson and I, we need you. We always will. Fight for us too."

I sealed my lids to prevent a fresh batch of tears from drenching my face and dozed off in no time, hoping Addison and I would meet in our dreams. And we could be happy there, at least for the time being.

Chapter 20

Dahlia knocked on my bedroom door less than ten minutes after arriving. I hadn't known Nick and she were flying in—Tucker hadn't said anything about it. Was it meant to be a surprise? I didn't feel well enough to dress up and be social, so I'd shut myself in our bedroom, avoiding our guests after spotting them in the entryway."Hey, girlfriend, can I come in?" she asked.

"Sure." I smoothed the fabric of my shirt to flatten the wrinkles and adjusted the covers around me. I closed my eyes, probably looking so out of it right now.

Two days ago, I'd spent a few hours at the spa, at my husband's request. I had left after the massage, not in the mood to be around people any longer.

Yesterday, I'd barely got out of bed, too tired to stand up or eat food. Tucker had ordered in dinner, and I'd slept next to him on the couch after I'd gulped a few bites of orange-glazed chicken and rice, which used to be my favorite. Not anymore. It just tasted blah nowadays.

He had kissed me when we finally made it to bed, and for a moment, my body recognized him, and I lost myself in the comfort he brought me. He whispered to me how much he loved me. It had been weeks since we had gotten any sort of intimacy, and for once, his touch didn't repulse me. It actually felt good to be in his arms.

Dahlia sat on the bed beside me, her legs stretched forward, and her back pressed against the headboard. She intertwined her fingers through mine. "How is it going?" she asked.

I shrugged. "Okay."

She draped an arm around my shoulder and drew me closer to her. "No need to pretend. It's me. You've seen me at my worst."

My breath hitched in my lungs, and my head spun.

"I'm numb, Dah. I...I'm not even sure I love Tucker anymore." My heart hurt so bad as I said it out loud. "He's been nothing but incredible, but it just feels wrong being with him, you know. Like he says nice things to me and I can't even return them. When I do, it's like I've rehearsed it, and it doesn't sound genuine."

"What about Jamieson?"

I scratched my temple. "Same with the baby."

"Your son."

"Yeah, yeah."

"Do you recall Jeff after he returned from the war? You were away in college by then, but you visited...and we talked almost every night."

"It seems like a lifetime ago."

"Yep, it does. Do you remember how he was back then? How he had changed?"

I nodded.

"He was lost…and sad. He couldn't figure out how to get better. He…gosh…he had become an agitated and angry version of himself. War had fucked with his mind. He saw images in his head, images that he couldn't get rid of. He never told me what they were about, but I had a pretty good idea. Anyway, for a while, I lost him. It got so bad I refused to let him join me on that second world tour."

She paused, and I was aware she didn't like revisiting those painful memories of her past.

"I…I remember."

"Anyway, back then, he didn't confide in me. Instead, he yelled at Carter, pushed all of us away, his pain overtaking every aspect of his life, destroying every good thing he had going on for him. That's when our lives turned chaotic. He fucked up. I-I did too. Because we couldn't find a way to communicate, to be there for each other. We were kids, for God's sake. I was nineteen. Back then, I made bad choices… All I'm saying is that he needed help, and for the longest time, he battled the idea. Until he decided he wanted to get better… To feel better. To regain the control of his own life…of his own mind. Until he decided fighting for himself, and for us, was worth more than his ego."

Mixed emotions rose inside me. Dahlia's story really got to me. I had witnessed Jeff's life turning to hell, and all the hurt he had caused around him because of something he couldn't control.

"What if nobody can help me, Dah? I miss my old self…everyday…but she has vanished. I can't find her. Perhaps it's just a few bad days, and everything will get better."

"I'm no doctor, and I won't pretend to be one, but Tucker and I, we talked. I won't hide the truth from you.

He's desperate, Addi. He's not doing so great either. He's sad and exhausted and so worried about you. And before you get mad, he never asked me to come over to talk to you. He didn't even tell me you were struggling. He tried to handle all of it on his own, but it's too much. You guys have a newborn to care for. And I…I did my research. Talked to people. Do you know anything about postpartum depression?"

I shrugged. "Not really."

"It's more common than we think. It affects women after they give birth. There are people trained to help you with whatever issues you're dealing with. They can advise you and give you cues and tips on how to overcome the bumps in your road…to heal and get better. We're not in the fifties anymore, when being honest about mental health struggles was considered shameful. Society has come a long way since then. Today, honesty is valued. Admitting when we're feeling down is seen as a strength." She paused for a long minute. "Listen, there's a center an hour's drive from here. Came highly recommended."

I forced the next words out. "Do you think…do you think it's because of him? Of his genetics?"

"Your daddy?"

"Yeah. I have no memories of him at his lowest point, but I've heard the stories."

"I don't know. Whatever it is, we won't let anything bad happen to you. You're not alone, Addi. We'll help you figure out whatever is afflicting your mind."

"Dah, I'm not crazy. I swear I'm not crazy."

"Nobody said you were—and for the record, you're not —but you and I, we've never shied away from the truth either. You gotta get help, Addi. I think it really could be postpartum depression…or something else. I won't specu-late. In any case, you won't heal magically without outside support and medical care. And…and it's not your fault. Nothing to do with you. Just bad luck. Some chemical imbalance in your brain or stuff like that. Perhaps genes are to blame. Perhaps they're not."

Dahlia putting my feelings to words brought hot tears to my eyes. Maybe I wasn't going nuts after all. Maybe there was some explanation for how I felt inside. Could it be something that could be cured? Using the back of my hand, I wiped my teary cheeks, the void in me not feeling so bottomless anymore.

"I'm not crazy, I swear. Do you think they can fix me? Find out why I'm so detached from everything? And so tired all the time?"

My best friend wrapped both arms around my heaving shoulders, combing my hair away from my face. "Yes. Many women go through this. You're not alone. And I'm here… Tuck is here… We love you so much, and all we wish is for you is to get better."

"It's easy for all of you to say. None of you pushed an almost ten-pound baby out of their vagina a month ago."

"No, I didn't. You're right. But I'm a mother too. I know how overwhelming it can be, and how sleeping in two-hour shifts takes a toll on your mood and your sanity. Tuck said you voiced not loving Jamieson, and that's the part that worries me the most, to be honest. Sleep-deprived, normal. Anxiety to do everything right, normal. Mood swings due to shifting hormone levels, normal. Not liking your baby, *not* normal. Preferring to plan happy-hours with coworkers than feeding your newborn, *not* normal. Do you see the difference? I'm not saying the words so you feel ashamed. I'm saying it so you realize something is wrong and you gotta address it."

I let out a sarcastic laugh. "When you put it like that…I sound like a monster."

"I promise you're not."

"You really think they can help me?"

She nodded. "Try this facility. You can enter their one-month program. See how it goes. Just step away for a moment, assess the situation, and see if their therapy and methods are helping you, and if you feel more like yourself afterward."

"Did Tucker put you up to it? Because he's upset about being a full-time parent?"

"Nah. He's just concerned. He loves you. Nick and I called the other night, and he cracked when we started asking questions. He feared it was something he did… something he said. Or that he didn't do enough."

"I really am a bad person. I…we…"

"Just focus on yourself for now. I'll help him out, okay? Nick and I will be there for your men—as much as possible —and for you too. You'll see. I'm sure it'll improve. Give it time. Don't push yourself too hard. The brain is a complex structure, and too many hormones and lack of sleep would do that to you. Now breathe, and let me know if you'd like me to drive you when you're ready."

"What will Tucker say?"

"He's already packed a bag for you. I helped him over the phone when you were at the spa. You know, he cried the entire time. Said he'd miss you so much and all he prayed for was for you to come back to him."

"He *what?* He cried?"

"Don't be mad at him. It was my idea…the facility. If you agree to go, great. If you don't, we'll find another way to get you help. You have my word. When did I ever let you down?"

"I think I should go…"

"I agree."

I said nothing, lost in my thoughts for a long time.

Mental breakdown or postpartum depression, could this be it? Or would they just force me to swallow a bunch of colorful pills supposed to make me believe unicorns were walking on rainbows?

"I'm not getting drugged, Dah."

She smiled and leaned back to look at me. "You think I'm not aware? This place offers meditation and holistic approaches. Pills don't fix everything. They told me they try to avoid them as much as possible. Their therapies are based on more natural ways. It seems like a good fit... They have a garden with beautiful flowerbeds. A stream with a wooden bridge in the backyard. It looks peaceful."

Going away for a month? Would I survive in a place with a bunch of strangers, when even going to the grocery store right now seemed overwhelming most of the time?

"What do you say?" my friend asked, and I snapped back to the present.

"Will he wait for me? Tuck..I mean."

"Addi, he'd wait for you till the end of time. That's how much he loves you."

"But...but...I've been awful to him."

"He cares about you and wants what's best for you."

"Can I...can I see him before we go?"

"Sure. He's in his home office. Nick went for a walk with the kids, so you two have time to talk. I'll come get you in a little while. Take your time. Listen to what he has to say... And don't be too hard on him. The guy can barely hold it together as it is. And, please, don't be hard on yourself. Recognizing you need help is the first step to healing."

Dahlia helped me change and fixed my hair.

Fidgeting with my hands, I made my way to my husband's office down the hall. "Hey," I said, knocking on the ajar door. "Can we talk?"

"Sweetheart—"

He rose to his feet, and I noticed the despair and sadness etching his eyes. How had I never seen it before now? How had I been so out of it that I'd missed the love of my life hurting? Standing a few feet away in front of me, he waited, his head hanging low, his hands stuffed into his pockets. He looked vulnerable right now. And weary.

"Well…I-I've decided to accept Dah's offer to get help." I couldn't breathe properly, the lump in my throat so big I believed I would choke on it. "Go…huh…away for some time. You've been right all along. I'm…I'm not myself. And I might require some professional help to find my way back."

I averted my eyes, heartbroken at the sight of the tears pooling in his.

"I recognize something is wrong with me…and that I might have said things I didn't mean. That could be hurtful toward you…and…huh…the baby."

Tucker stepped forward, closing the distance between us.

"Wilde, I love you so much. All I want is for you to be happy again. To go back to your crazy ways. So you're present when you're with us, mentally…and physically." We stared into each other's eyes, our souls having their own conversation as we stood there, charged particles of air spiraling around us, witnesses to our despair.

"I'm not breaking up with you… It's…it's only tempo-rary, okay? A month. To fix whatever is not okay with me. Don't…don't break up with me either. Please."

He huffed a trembling breath. "Why would you think I would break up with you? I'd never do that." His voice shook, and tears prickled my eyes.

Leaving the man I loved felt like deserting him—just as his mother had before me. The thought twisted my stomach. "Because you've been abandoned before… I-I hate the idea that you might feel like I'm doing it too. I swear I am not."

"Wilde, you're nothing like my mother. You're my best friend…the love of my life. Not only that, but you're the mother of my child. I know your heart. You would never leave us on purpose or due to selfishness."

I stared at him, my words dissolving before they could form on my tongue.

As if he could sense the battle in my head, Tucker added, "Can I hug you?"

I nodded. At first, his arms around me felt stiff and foreign, but soon, I warmed up to them and nestled my body in his loving embrace. Sobs I'd been holding in shook me, rocking my core. Weeks of pain and distress poured out all at once.

"I'm…I'm…so sorry. I'm not okay. I-I don't feel okay. And I have…I have no idea who I am anymore. Wh-where I belong. Or what's going on with my life. I know I've hurt you…and that you and the baby don't deserve my mood swings and absence. But I can't do otherwise. It's like being around you burns me. Like…like I'm lost in space and have no idea how to come back home. Almost like watching my own life through a glass-mirror and having no way to connect with the people on the other side."

Tucker cupped my cheeks. "Don't chastise yourself, sweetheart. I know you. I know your heart. I'll wait for you…for as long as it takes. Because I love you and this will never change."

"I'm not leaving you, okay?" I repeated. Insecurity grew within me at the thought he could fall in love with someone else during my absence. Deep down, I had to convince myself more than him that we'd be all right. "Don't…don't forget about me…please. Don't lose faith in me…or I'll never find the courage to heal if I have to do all this by myself. Or if I have to come back to an empty house."

We both cried, his inner strength pouring onto me and keeping me safe. Protecting me from myself and the rest of the world.

"I'm so proud of you for agreeing to do this, Wilde. For recognizing you need help. I'm sorry… I'm sorry I can't be the one giving it to you. I tried…I really did…but I'm not equipped to do more."

"Don't ever blame yourself. Right now, I'm not sure I deserve you. I'm the one who's sorry. For putting you through hell. It was never my intention. You…you've been waiting for me every step of the way. From the very first day, you've been my hero. Where would I be without your unconditional love and support?"

"Sweetheart, I'll be here when you come back. When you're ready to come home. I love you…so much. Never question it. By the way, we're in this together, sweetheart. Always remember that."

My husband kissed me, and for the second time since I've given birth, I let myself melt against him and abandoned my whole being to the love outpouring from him.

"Can I tell you about my daddy?" I said.

"You can tell me anything. I'll never judge you."

I cleared my throat. "A few times in the last year, I've tried to open up about it, but I was so afraid this could be it. I didn't want you to think I was damaged… Or that I could be damaged. My father… Well, depression runs in his family tree. When I was eight, huh…my parents separated because my daddy wouldn't get help for the longest time. He refused to acknowledge he had problems and that they impacted his life and his family. My parents never had another child because my father worried he'd passed the gene to us…to Phoenix and me. And up until last year, it never occurred to me I could carry it. After my breakup, before we met, I was down…so down. It took me a while to get my groove back. You're the one who snapped me out of my funk. Who painted colors back into my world."

I paused, clearing the fog taking over my brain.

"I'm sorry I didn't tell you before. I really wanted to. Now I'll get better. You don't deserve just a part of me, but all of me. I'm not sure if I want it to be depression or not. All I know is that I don't want to suffer anymore, and I don't want you and the baby to suffer either."

Tucker pulled me into his arms once again. "Whatever it is, we'll fight this. I'm not going away, and I'll lend you all the strength you need."

"Thank you…for being you."

We stood still for a long while, connecting for the first time in almost a month.

"Do you want me to drive you?" he asked.

I shook my head. "Dah will take me. It will be too hard if you're there. To see the pain in your eyes. The hurt I've caused our family. To…to walk away." I stepped away from his embrace. "I'll get better, okay?"

In front of my son's nursery, I stopped and scanned the room, my heart heavy and bruised in my chest. With tentative steps, I walked in. It had been weeks since I entered the room. The last time was before his birth. My heart closed in on itself. Painfully. More tears cascaded down my cheeks. Holding against my chest a stuffed-elephant I picked up from the crib, I let the tears flow. "I'm sorry, baby."

He wasn't here, but I could feel his energy all around me and somehow, I preferred him not hearing my words.

"I'll try to be a better mother…to love you the way you deserve. You won't see me for quite some time, okay? I'm going away, but I'll be back. Wait for me and take care of your daddy. I'm sorry I haven't been a mama to you. It…it was never supposed to be this way. I was so excited to hold you in my arms the first time, and I have no idea where it all went wrong. Things won't change unless I accept help. I know it now. All I want is for you to be proud of me and to be able to rock you to sleep or feed you without having a meltdown. None of this has anything to do with you. It's all on me. My brain is… I don't really know myself what is happening, but something is making me this way. I wanna love you so much, and you have no idea how painful this is —" My tears drowned my last words. I kissed my fingers and grazed the comforter. "Can I keep this one?" I asked nobody, clutching the animal tighter against my heart. "It's my promise to come back to you."

With a giant boulder pressing against my ribcage, I exited the room, closing the door behind me. From the corner of my eye, I noticed Tucker watching me from our bedroom doorway, looking dejected. He offered me a tiny smile when our eyes locked and a nod. Dahlia came back at the exact moment, and they exchanged a few words. My husband left with my suitcase as my best friend joined me.

"Come on, Addi. It's time. Let's do this. For what it's worth, I'm proud of you. Tucker is too. Jamieson would be if he could talk. It's a great example you're setting up for him, even if he can't tell you himself right now."

A loud cry tumbled out of my mouth. A cry of pain. And helplessness. "Will he even remember me?" I asked through my tears.

My friend circled my shoulders with her arms. "You're his mama, Addi. He spent nine months in your womb. He would recognize you, your voice, your body, your scent anywhere, anytime. Would you like to kiss him goodbye?"

I shook my head. "No. I-I can't. It's too hard being around him… I'm a terrible person."

"No. You're stronger than you think. And that's what matters."

I nodded and followed her outside.

I caught sight of my baby tucked in Nick's arms, Jack standing tall beside them. I waved in their direction, and the toddler ran my way, his little arms fastening around my thigh.

"*Addidi*, where you going?"

I caressed his short dark hair. A lone tear traced the length of my cheek.

"I'll be back soon," was all I could muster as a reply.

We broke apart, and he watched me.

Nick stepped forward, but I shook my head. He nodded his agreement and grabbed Jack's hand, leading him to the house.

Tucker kissed me before helping me into the car. "Be brave, sweetheart. We'll come get you when you feel better. When you're ready to come home."

He closed the door, and I pressed my palm against the window. He mirrored the gesture, our stares unflinching.

The sad bent of his lips shattered my heart.

I love you, he mouthed.

I nodded, breaking the contact.

For the first time in a month, a streak of confidence woke up inside me at the thought of getting my life back… back on track…and to regain control over myself.

I would put in the work—because my family was my universe—and I wouldn't let them down. Never.

Chapter 21
Tucker

This was the day. The one when my wife would come back home. To us. When we'd visited her last weekend, she looked stronger and spent over an hour with Jamieson nestled in her arms, whispering in his ear while he watched her with adoration—like he was seeing her for the first time. In a way, he had.

My eyes had welled up with tears the entire time, and I'd snapped too many pictures, knowing one day Addison would like to have them. We had lunch together, by the stream, and she'd told me all about her therapy and her friends.

Dahlia had visited her two weeks ago. As promised, she'd been standing by her friend's side since day one. She had even joined her for a therapy session when Addison said she couldn't have me there because it'd hurt her too much to face me after everything we'd been through and she wasn't ready. I'd never force her to do anything unless it came from her, so I'd respected her decision, even if it hurt. If it meant she'd get better, I could set my pride aside.

I looked at my reflection in the bedroom mirror for the tenth time. Yeah, it would do. Dark jeans and a white V-neck T-shirt. "How do I look?" I asked Jamieson, who sat in a baby chair at my feet. He nibbled on his thumb and made funny noises. "Yeah, you're right. We should go get Mama." I lifted him up in my arms and kissed his cheek. He wore Addison's *A Little Wild* onesie, the late spring heat slightly high to dress him in any more clothes. The custom-designed piece fit him perfectly, and he looked too adorable for his own good.

The one-hour drive to the center seemed to last forever. Nick and Dahlia had called to wish me luck and asked me to keep them updated. They'd also made me promise to call if I still needed their help. In the past month, they'd flown over two weekends in a row to give me a hand. Thanks to them, I had slept through full nights and felt much better than I did a month ago.

My heels dug into the ground as I reached the back-yard of the facility. Addison was standing there, her eyes locked on mine, and the sight of her stole my breath away.

As usual, my woman looked beautiful, but now she also appeared more serene. More put together.

Before I'd left last weekend when I visited, she had even kissed me of her own volition, sending my heart into a frenzied dance.

Addison ran in our direction, wearing a flowery sundress, half her hair tied in a loose braid. She halted a foot in front of us, making no movement to take Jamieson from my arms. Instead, she kissed his forehead, which, to me, equaled progress—a big fucking step forward in her healing process. It turned out Dahlia had been right, and my wife had suffered from postpartum depression, after all. Since she'd been here, she'd found relief in daily meditation, something she had abandoned after giving birth. Small acts of self-care peppered her days, along with a carefully balanced diet, individual and group therapy, and yoga.

One night, Addison had called me and opened up a little more about her father's struggles with depression. How it had affected her growing up. How she had learned to accept the genes that might have triggered her breakdown, even without any certainties.

Standing in front of me, the tilt of her lips drew me in. I scanned the length of her, burning this more joyful image of her to my memory.

Color had returned to her cheeks, and sparks to her eyes.

Right now, I had real hopes we'd be okay…that she'd be okay.

Eating the space between us, I closed one hand around her waist in a protective and possessive gesture, my lips descending on hers, itching to taste her essence. "I've missed you like crazy, sweetheart."

She rested her hand over my thrumming heart. "I've missed you too. And I'm sorry. For everything."

I shook my head. "It wasn't your fault. Don't apologize. I'm just glad you're doing better. That's all I've ever prayed for."

"I will. You gotta be patient with me, but I'll get there. Life isn't as dark anymore. Light is coming back. A tad more each day."

I kissed her again, unable to resist, and she let me. "That's fantastic. I love the sound of it. Ready to go home?"

She bobbed her head. "Oh yes."

She went to hug and thank everyone as I spoke with her doctor and a nurse who offered me some pointers and an envelope containing brochures and the special treatment plan she had to follow. We had weekly appointments scheduled with them for another month, so they could track our progress and help us find our rhythm when navigating daily life on our own.

The road ahead of us was still bumpy, but I trusted that we'd make it to the other end.

The following month went by smoothly. Addison still didn't feel comfortable caring for Jamieson by herself, but she now put him to bed, sang him songs, and held him for longer periods of time each day.

Sometimes, I found her crying in bed or calling herself a failure, but with love and patience, no obstacle seemed impossible to overcome. If we'd made it this far, I was confident we could face whatever life put in our path—as long as we faced every challenge together.

We also spent more time outside, at the park, having picnics and walking around with the stroller, the sun and fresh air great for her mood.

We celebrated Jamieson turning four months with cupcakes Addison baked and a low-key lunch, just the three of us. Our son slept almost the entire time, but this milestone was a huge deal for my wife and me. Even more considering we celebrated it together, as a family.

I scratched the side of my head and swiveled to face my wife after I put the dishes away. "I was wondering if you'd like to join me in the shower. We don't have to do anything. I just missed being with you that way. The intimacy. It's not even about sex, but the connection."

I stayed still, praying she'd say yes, that we could move forward a little more as a couple too.

She fidgeted with her fingers, avoiding my gaze.

"What's the matter?" I asked, holding her hands in mine.

"My stomach. It's still…huh…flappy. And wrinkly. I'm not sure you wanna see me like that. It's not pretty anymore. Nothing like it used to be."

I tipped her chin up with a finger, forcing her eyes to meet mine. "No. Don't go there. Don't avoid me. I'm in love with *you*. All of you. Sure, I enjoy your body, but I'm more impressed that it has created life than the aftermath of such a miracle. In my eyes, you're always beautiful and will forever be."

"You won't find me disgusting? Or not good enough?"

"Never." I intertwined our fingers. "Come on, let me show you how beautiful you are."

Chapter 22

Addison

Tucker led me to the en-suite in our bedroom. The hammering of my heart probably could have been heard from miles away. Until this day, I had always succeeded in keeping my body guarded around my husband, but I knew this moment would come—when he would ask for more, when we would resume our intimacy. So far, the thought had made me so anxious that I had always shut it down. Holding my hand firmly in his, he glanced at me over his shoulder, and the smile he gave me sent sparks of confidence through me. Confidence that I could let go with him. Confidence that he meant every word he'd spoken earlier. Confidence that I was safe with him.

We entered the bathroom, and I flicked off the light switch, plunging the room into semi-darkness, with only a soft glow from the bedroom window illuminating the space.

Tucker turned it back on and rested both hands on my hips. "No. I wanna see you. No more hiding."

His voice sounded so soft, so comforting, how could I resist him? Tucker Philips always had that pull on me. A magnetism I couldn't escape.

"O…huh…okay," I whispered, glancing at my feet.

"Can I?" he asked, gripping the hem of my shirt in a delicate gesture.

I closed my eyes and swallowed my discomfort.

Deciding to let go of my fears, I nodded.

In a slow motion, he peeled the shirt over my head. I battled with myself to avoid covering my stomach, keeping my eyes shut. Shivers traversed me when his fingertips grazed my arms.

I risked a look at him, and it left me breathless. His face gushed with love. I believed his words. That I could do this. With him.

Bending forward, his eyes on mine, Tucker kissed the length of my neck, the valley between my breasts, the soft skin of my belly. He hooked his fingers into my shorts, and kneeling before me, he slid them down my legs. When he glided his thumbs toward the elastic waistband of my panties, he stopped and looked up at me, asking for my permission to remove them.

I nodded, missing the way we used to love each other in the past and the adoration he always showered me with.

He pressed his lips against my inner thighs,and kissed me there, his tongue warm against my center when he laved the seam with gentle strokes.

Chills of pleasure I hadn't felt in so long moved up and down my spine.

My hips rocked forward, chasing the building pleasure only my husband could provide.

Slowly, he stood up, molding his lips to mine. "I love you, Wilde. And I always will."

He unclasped my bra, and the piece of baby-blue cotton pooled on the floor at our feet. With his palms, he kneaded my breasts, never detaching his mouth from mine.

With every movement of his tongue, I felt more confident about myself. Like we could still be us. Even after everything we'd been through.

Hand in hand, we entered the shower, and Tucker took his time washing my hair and lathering every inch of me with the utmost care.

"Can I…can I touch you?" he asked into my ear.

I worried my bottom lip, exhaled, and whispered, "Yes."

"You tell me if it's too much."

I nodded, meeting his eyes.

Feelings I had long forgotten stirred in my core. Goose bumps blossomed across my arms when Tucker's digit followed the path between my thighs, and he circled my clit in slow motions. I gasped, unable to keep all the sensations swirling within me inside.

"Jesus, I've missed this," he said, his voice husky and thick with need.

Coating his fingers with my arousal, he pushed one digit inside me. A soft cry parted my lips, and I shook at the contact.

I dug my fingernails into his biceps, holding him in place and making sure he didn't pull his hand away.

"You like it?" he murmured.

He positioned himself behind me, his erection pressing against my lower back, his fingers increasing their pace, and his other arm fastening around my waist. I relished his sturdiness against me and wished I had let him get this close much sooner.

Pleasure built in my core, little fireworks igniting the deepest parts of me. Flames that were dead rekindling.

Tucker's thumb pressed against my bundle of sensitive nerves and I came undone, my head tilting back and resting in the crook of his shoulder. His mouth found mine, and we kissed like we hadn't kissed in such a long time. My toes curled and my body electrified, another orgasm washing over me, his fingers relentlessly sliding in and out of me at a lazy pace that drove me crazy.

His tongue danced with mine. We fused together, unable to break apart. I didn't need air to feel alive anymore, my husband the only source of oxygen I required.

He groaned into my mouth, and I deepened the kiss, not wanting to break apart from him, scared I would crumble if I did. Tucker was not only my rock but also my better half—the pillar I could always count on.

"Fuck, sweetheart."

I moaned against his mouth when he toyed with my lip between his teeth. He grabbed a handful of my ass cheeks, and I curled my fist around his steel-hard manhood.

I worked him in slow strokes, but he stopped me with his hand. "Not today, sweetheart. Let's go slow, okay? I don't want us to skip steps or do things you're not ready for."

I pursed my lips to argue, but he kissed me, making me forget everything as he spun my world in the most wonderful way and reminded me why I had to fight my demons. I didn't want to exist in a world where I couldn't share his love—it was magnificent and earth-shattering all at once.

Because this, what we had, was the fuel of my life, and I wouldn't trade this for anything else. Flickers of the darkness that had been surrounding me for months parted away. Burying my face into my husband's chest, I had the certitude we'd be okay. That I would get better and we would find our peace. Together.

———

We exited the shower, and Jamieson's cries reached our ears through the baby monitor set in our bedroom.

Tucker kissed my temple and dried himself up. "Take your time. I'll go get him."

I stopped him with a hand on his forearm. "Let me."

He frowned. "Are you sure?"

I bowed my head before meeting his eyes. "I am. Please. I can do this."

He tucked my hair behind my ear. "I know you can."

I started dressing up when I spun to face him. "Why don't you take a nap? I'm sure you could use the rest. We'll be all right, Jamieson and I. If something's wrong or if I can't deal with it, I'll come get you. I promise."

Tucker studied me like he was searching for answers in the words I didn't speak out loud. "Fine. I'll take you up on your offer. Thanks."

He linked our fingers, and they brushed together until I stepped too far away from him.

A fresh surge of excitement stirred in my heart. I could do this. If I could let Tucker see the vulnerable side of me, my body that I had to learn to love again, I could take care of my son without panic rising within me.

"Hey you," I said, picking up the fussy baby. "I'm here now. You'll be fine. You and I, we'll be okay." After I changed his diaper, I went to the kitchen to make him a bottle.

Sitting in the rocking chair by the giant window of the nursery, the sunlight chasing the shadows away, I fed my baby by myself for the very first time. Basking in the late spring glow, I caressed his cheek with a finger.

He wrapped his tiny fingers around the bottle and fixed his blue eyes on me.

"I'm sorry I've been away for so long, but I'm here now, and I won't leave ever again. I might not be fully myself again yet, but I'll get there. I know I'm asking a lot from you, and it was never my intention to lose myself after I gave birth. It just…it happened. And it makes me so sad to think I've failed you. From this day on, I never want you to feel like you can't count on me. Gimme some more time, okay? I'll prove to you I can do this."

His baby hand let go of the bottle and wrapped around my finger. He tightened his squeeze, and a single tear leaked from my eyes.

"Jamieson, I love you… Ogmygod, I love you so much. And I…and I always will." My lips lingered on his forehead.

He babbled, pushing the nipple of the bottle out of his mouth.

"You agree with me?" He blinked and returned to his milk.

We basked in our tiny bubble a little longer, until he fell asleep in my arms, as if he truly trusted me.

Strong emotions spiraled through me, suffocating me. I pressed a hand over my thundering heart, trying to calm its frantic beating.

I can do this. I can do this. I repeated in my head. Those crippling thoughts didn't appear as often as they used to, but sometimes they caught me off guard, and I froze, panic settling deep inside me.

I breathed in. *One. Two. Three.* And breathed out. *Three. Two. One.*

I was slowly returning to a state of calm and control

when I caught a glimpse of him standing in the doorway, an adorable, sleepy expression on his face. The last remnants of my panic melted away at the sight.

"Are you okay?" Tucker asked, hurrying to my side, clearly noticing the lingering traces of alarm on my face. "Hey, you're doing fine. It's okay… Just breathe." He lifted the baby from my arms and placed him in his crib before returning to my side. "Wilde, you did it. You spent," he checked the time on his watch and kneeled beside me, "an hour alone with him. On your own. It's a big step."

"An hour?" I asked, my words now mixing with hot tears.

He bobbed his head. "Yes. It's huge."

My entire body quivered, and I had no clue how to stop the tremors.

Tucker stood and helped me to my feet, and after closing the curtains, held me in his arms against his heart. "Do you wanna talk about it?"

I shook my head. "Not now." I cocked my head to look at our son. "I did it," I muttered, mostly for my own sake.

My husband never let go of me. His lips captured mine, and once again, I let go of my fears, inviting his strength to hold me a little closer.

We stepped out of the nursery, a hint of a smile touching my lips.

Yes…I had done it.

Chapter 23

Tucker

Jamieson had just turned five months old when, one morning, I sat my wife down after breakfast. She had our baby propped on her lap, kissing the nape of his neck, his laughter warming my heart—and the sight of them together fulfilled my wildest dreams. Once again, I immortalized the moment with my phone. Our family was fragile but strong, and we were determined to grow and heal together. This was the priceless promise linking us all together.

"How are you doing? For real?" I couldn't conceal the worry in my gaze. We had that same exact conversation almost every week.

Addison extended her arm to reach for my hand. "I'm getting there. I was thinking of spacing my therapy sessions."

"You are?"

"I talked to my therapist, and he agreed. If it gets too overwhelming, I'll return to a weekly schedule. What do you think?"

"If you're confident about it, I'll support your decision. Try it. We'll see how it goes. For your information, I agree you're doing much better." I leaned in to press a kiss to her forehead. "I'm proud of you. Always am." I studied her. "Wilde, you know that secret project I've been keeping from you?" She nodded. "I'm ready to show you, but for that, we have to go on a road trip. The three of us. If you feel you're strong enough to go on an adventure."

She straightened her posture, eyes brimming with curiosity. "Oh, it sounds exciting. What is it? I wanna go."

"Do you trust me?"

"Always."

I kissed her lips and laced our fingers together. "Jamieson already agreed to it. We just have to convince you now."

We exchanged grins, and my fingers threaded through her hair as I leaned forward to claim her mouth when she rose to her feet. I locked my arms around her, holding her close to me, Jamieson resting between us. "Sweetheart, I've missed you so much. I've missed *us*."

She pressed her hand against my chest, just over my throbbing heart. "Thanks for believing in me. Even when I didn't believe in myself. It means the world to me. And for the record, I love it when you call me *sweetheart*."

"Sweetheart, I've always known. My heart belongs to you. Forever. I'm just happy you found your way back."

"Can we go today? I'm really excited about doing something together, the three of us. Like families do."

I nodded, pressing my forehead against hers.

"But first, let's put Jamieson to bed because I really

want to make my husband feel good right now. I've been dying to thank him the proper way."

I tilted my head back. "You sure?"

She slid her hands under my shirt, her fingertips grazing my abdomen, and shivers traveled along my spine. "Yes."

I took the baby from her arms. "Then you won't have to tell me twice. This little guy is due for a nap, anyway. Meet me in the bedroom in five."

I turned around, the sound of her snicker doing nasty things to me. Things I hadn't let myself feel in such a long time.

When I entered the bedroom, Addison stood in the middle of the bed, wearing nothing else but a new set of lacy lingerie I'd never seen before, looking like the temptress she had always been. My temptress.

"Jesus, Wilde." I removed my clothes as fast as I could and stood before her, my dick hard as a flagpole, drooling at the sight before me, enjoying every delicious curve of hers. "We should take our time."

She shook her head. "Nah. I'm not made of porcelain. And it's been so long. I'm missing the connection we share when we love each other. Don't go slow or gentle. Just love me like you used to."

"In that case, spread those legs. I have months to make up for, and I'm starving. Wanna play with me?"

"Always, *Tuuuck*." Need laced her voice, and it almost shattered me, my restraints already weak.

"God, don't say it like that, or I'll come before we even get started."

"Then don't make me wait, big guy. I'm soaking wet right now."

I plunged forward, and taking my sweet time, I savored every inch of her flesh.

When my tongue connected with the apex of her thighs, Addison wriggled underneath me, her muffled cries my undoing. My fingers joined my mouth, cherishing every bit of the woman I love.

"Oh, Tuck. *Yesss.* I love you."

Those words. I could never live my life fully without hearing them from her.

She pivoted on the mattress and positioned herself over me, reaching for my cock. It'd been forever since he got playtime of his own, and I almost came from her attention alone. When her lips circled the tip, I jerked my head back, the sensations surging through me, too intense to bear. Heat swirled in my balls. My spine tingled with an upcoming release. "Be careful, sweetheart. The guy—" She sucked me into her mouth, and I could barely hold it together anymore. "He hasn't had a lot of attention in a long while. I have no idea how long I can last if you're being your vixen self."

Addison licked me in long, moist strokes. "I'll be gentle with you, big guy," she said between chuckles. "How did we survive so long without this?"

Lifting her hips to switch position, I lunged forward and flicked her clit with my tongue, pushing my fingers back into her tight channel and moving them back and forth.

We both lost ourselves in the intensity of our desire.

Every whimper from Addison induced a growl from me. Her pleasure wet the lower half of my face as I devoured her, making up for all the months I couldn't.

She rolled her hips over my mouth, purring around my dick, never releasing her grip around it. Each jerky movement of her hands chipped away at my last shred of control.

Increasing the tempo of my fingers, Addison cried as

she came on my tongue. "Tuck, fill me now. I wanna feel you."

She would never have to beg me.

Shifting on the bed, she locked her legs around my hips, and I pounded into her with rhythmic strokes.

Her folded legs fell on either side of her, and I changed the angle to be able to increase the connection of our bodies.

She molded her hands to my nape and pulled me to her, kissing me without restraints.

"I love you," I murmured against her lips.

"Then fuck me harder," she said with a sharp intake of air.

"No. I wanna love you." I kissed her back. Intertwining our fingers, I brought our linked hands above her head.

We moved together. No more walls existed between us. Flipping her on her knees, I entered her from behind and cupped her ass as I rammed into her with everything I possessed. Her eyelids, half-masted by the pleasure coursing through her, broke me when she looked at me over her shoulder. A new surge of desire took me hostage.

The sound of our mixed breathings and of flesh hitting flesh filled the silence. We pleased each other until neither of us could draw a full breath in.

Leaning forward, I peppered kisses along her spine, shaping my upper body to the delicious curve of her back.

Pulling out, I turned her around until we faced each other, and with my body upright, she wrapped herself around me. I cupped her head while I slid back where I belonged, and we kissed some more.

We moved together, unable to break apart even after we both climaxed.

"Now I'm ready for that road trip," Addison whispered

against my shoulder as we lay together, entangled in the bedsheets a while later.

"Pack a bag for four nights. We're not coming back here this weekend. We'll spend at least two nights there…if you like it."

She frowned, though the corners of her mouth were smiling, and detached her body from mine. "On it."

I jumped to my feet, my heart beating fast in my chest at the idea of showing her the project I'd been working on for months. "I'll take care of the baby stuff. Meet me downstairs when you're done."

I kissed her reddened lips and put my clothes back on.

———

We arrived in Nashville in the evening after stopping several times to feed Jamieson or change his dirty diapers. The sun hung low in the sky, and a warm breeze brushed our faces as we stepped out of the car.

With our son strapped to my chest in the baby wrap and my wife's hand nestled in mine, we walked down the sidewalk.

My heart felt lighter in my chest. The sight of us matched the images I'd imagined countless times.

Just before we entered a door, I whirled around to face her. "Listen, it's a two-part project. When I started it, we weren't a couple yet, but somehow, along the way, and with everything that have happened in our lives, this just made so much more sense than it did back then. Because it fits who we are and what we're aiming for. Love, a low-stress lifestyle, nature, and family time. You'll tell me what you think, but I believe this could be it."

Excitement bubbled up inside me at a dizzying pace.

Never before had I made plans this big for anyone other than myself. I really wished Addison would get on board with everything.

"Even though it started as my project, it's ours now. And truthfully, it was always meant to be ours. If something bothers you, you tell me. You don't agree and want to forget all about it? No worries. It has great resale value…I already checked. But I'd appreciate it if you at least gave it some thought before saying no."

My wife watched me with a smile that made me feel virtuous in her eyes.

"Ready?"

She sucked in a breath and nodded.

We entered the space Nick and his guys had been renovating for months. They finished shortly after Jamieson's birth, but I had to wait a long time to show the one person whose opinion mattered the most. The weekend Dahlia visited Addison at the center, Nick, the kids, and I had driven here to finish the final touches. Beside me, my wife gasped, her eyes perusing the space around her. High industrial ceilings, plank floors, stainless steel countertops, black wrought-iron chandeliers, and a wooden stage with a lit-up *Wild and Country* marquee sign at the back.

"What is it?" she asked, now facing me.

"Our own bar. Or event venture, I should say. *Wild and Country*. A bit wild, a bit country. It's you and me."

"How? I'm speechless. It's amazing. You did all this on your own?"

I shook my head. "I had lots of help. Nick has been taking care of all the remodeling and improvements. Dahlia has helped with the decor since she works with Nick on some of his projects, and Riley, you know, her ex-manager? Well, he loved the idea so much that, when we asked for his expertise with the stage and sound system, he decided to buy shares—and he's now a partner in the whole venture. So now it's our big project, but it also involves your friends. Carter agreed to play on opening night and o hold his next album launch party here as well. His way of supporting you. Or us, I guess."

Addison watched me with rounded eyes.

"Oh, and that's not all. Follow me."

I held her hand, leading her to the third floor.

"This," I said, motioning her through the open space, "is your own event business. One day, when you're ready. The rooftop is yours too, where you'll be able to throw baby showers, bachelorette parties, or weddings. Or anything you'd like. Sky is the limit." We crossed a set of barn wood doors. "And this is your office. Your own Little Wild headquarters. There's a crib, a playroom, a highchair, and everything else if you decide to work from here with Jamieson. My official office is downstairs, but I've set up an extra desk here for the days we want to work together. Or have dirty office sex."

She blinked, mute.

"Wilde, are you okay?"

"Tuck... I'm more than fine. I'm...huh...I'm impressed. Wow. I'm over the moon right now. It's all I've ever dreamed of. Right here, you've made my wildest wishes come true. You did all that for me?"

"I did it for you...and me. For us. The rules haven't changed, though. You'll start working again when you're ready. When you can deal with the hours and hectic schedules, and not a day before. I won't let you."

"Are we moving here?"

I cradled her face with my hands. "That's the plan. If you're on board. I fell in love with a girl when I visited this city over a year ago, and it seemed fit to continue our story here. I know how much you love this city too, so it wasn't a hard choice to make."

Addison rested both palms on my chest. "Jamieson, you knew about all this?" she asked him. He smiled, drool covering his chin, and she kissed his chubby cheek. "Thank you. Both of you."

"Ready for part two?"

"Oh, this wasn't part two?"

I shook my head. "We can take the car, or we can walk for fifteen minutes. What do you prefer?"

"Let's go for a walk. It's a beautiful day outside."

Hand in hand, we made it to a giant tree-lined street with craftsmen-houses. We halted in front of number twenty-two.

"Is it—?" Addison asked, watching the powder-blue property.

"Our new home. If we do this."

The expression on her face told me she longed to explore me, and I nodded with a chuckle. "Go ahead. Go wild, sweetheart. Nick's team has been working here too, and he said he can change anything you don't approve of or don't like."

I heard a loud cheer seconds after she walked in, and the grin on my face just grew bigger.

My wife rushed back outside, watching me with a heartwarming expression on her face. "How did you know?" she asked.

I shrugged. "I'm pretty good at reading you by now. And Dahlia. She still had the journal you two did that summer where you sketched your dream house with pictures from magazines. We used it as an inspiration."

"Are we spending the night here?"

"That's the idea. If you like it."

"You're kidding, right? I *lovvve* it. When can we move in?"

"Whenever you're ready."

"Can I go back inside? Take a look around?"

"It's all yours. As I said, go wild."

In a sweet gesture that melted my heart, Addison released Jamieson from the wrap around my torso and lifted him into her arms. He wiggled his arms and kicked his legs, ecstatic to be freed and in his mama's embrace. "Jamieson, this is your new home. *Our* new home. I'm sure we'll be very happy here. Wanna show me around? Daddy said you've already visited the place before, and I'd like you to gimme a tour."

Our son flapped his arms again in a happy dance, and my wife kissed his small button nose.

Right now, everything in my life made sense again, and nothing we went through was in vain.

"Tucker, there's a swing set in the backyard. Come take a look," Addison yelled from inside the home as if I hadn't put it there myself.

Even my heart smiled at her enthusiasm.

We watched the stars from the back deck after we were done with dinner. My wife sat onto my lap, her arms circling my neck. "Think we will be okay?" she asked after a moment.

"I'm confident. We're already halfway there."

She kissed me, slowly and seductively, moaning against my mouth when my tongue slipped between her lips and stroked hers.

I skimmed the skin of her back with my hands after I bunched her sundress over her hips. Moving my hands to her front, I kneaded her soft breasts and pinched with her diamond-hard nipples between my fingers.

"Oh Tuck, we never did it outside. Think the neighbors will complain?"

"Sweetheart, I got the house with the biggest lot and tallest trees so we would have all the privacy we deserve. One day, we'll build a treehouse and have a pool. This is our piece of heaven. Only ours. And I'm allowed to fuck my wife anywhere I see fit."

She peeled the dress over her head, offering me the perfect view of her naked body, the one that had created life. And that had kept her safe while she had lost herself for a moment. I bent over to suck one of nipple into my mouth as she dug her fingers into my scalp to prevent me from moving away as she purred her pleasure.

"Tucker, I love you. I promise here and now to show you every day for the rest of my life. I've been a mess for so long, but you always stayed by my side and believed in me."

She whimpered as I cherished her other breast.

"Get better. That's all I'm asking for. And let me in. Even when it's tough."

She bobbed her head.

I checked the time on my phone. Three minutes past midnight.

"Happy birthday, Wilde."

"You remembered?"

"I recall everything. About you. With you. We have plans tomorrow night—well, tonight, I guess. But right now, let me love you the way I long to and give you your first present. It begins with *cli* and ends with *max*."

Addison freed my pulsing erection and positioned herself over me as I pushed her panties to the side. She welcomed all of me into her warmth, rolling her lips over me while her lips tasted mine. With passion and hunger.

"Tuck, I can't wait for this new life of ours to start.

Everything is perfect. I don't wanna change anything. You're way too good for me."

"Wilde, you freed me. You freed my soul. And my heart. I'll forever be grateful you entered my life." I got to my feet and with her long legs wound around my waist, I discarded all my clothes.

Laying her on the outdoor couch, I loved my wife with everything I had—and a whole lot more.

Right there on the deck with only the stars as witnesses.

Epilogue
Addison

A year later

"Okay, what's the big surprise?" I asked as Tucker guided me, his strong hands acting as blindfolds. "Where's Jamie? I don't hear him. Are you sure he's fine?"

My husband moved around me, and without removing his hands from my eyes, kissed me. He sucked on my lower lip, and I melted against his hard chest, the one keeping me safe every night.

"Wilde, stop worrying. Jamieson is fine. Enjoy your birthday. I'm taking care of everything."

I nodded as he stepped back.

"We're here. Don't open your eyes until I tell you."

Why was he being so mysterious? Earlier, Dahlia had come home and helped me choose a dress for tonight. Two months ago, she'd expanded her business and now had a satellite store in Nashville, but the headquarters remained in Green Mountain. We saw each other every few weeks when she came to town.

It took me eight months last year to feel confident and strong enough to resume work. And thanks to Tucker, I was now my own boss. Like I'd always dreamed.

And it fulfilled me in every way possible.

Tucker quit his job before we moved to Tennessee. The bar was a success, and he had never looked back. He said he had never been so happy. Gone were the pressed suits and silk ties. My husband now worked in jeans and plaid shirts most of the time and had never looked so hot. The Southern lifestyle suited him. A lot.

Our lives were blooming, in all the ways that mattered.

My heart pummeled in my chest when I heard hushed voices around me.

Tucker trailed kisses down my neck, and I shivered. He linked our hands together and said, "Open your eyes, sweetheart."

A high-pitched cry escaped my lips when my eyes traveled around the backyard. "Tuck, what is it?" My jaw dropped in surprise, and I pressed my chest, just above my heart, with my hands.

All around us were dozens of white rose bouquets, round wooden tables with white and golden centerpieces, and garden chairs in pastel colors. The late afternoon sky was painted in pink and orange stripes.

Warmth filled me. I tried to take it all in, wanting to immerse myself in the beauty surrounding me.

"I'm not sure I understand," I said, my voice shaky with emotions.

My friends, my family, and everyone I cared about stood near a small makeshift stage in our backyard.

"Tuck?"

I turned on my heel, and he wrapped his arms around me. "Addison Samantha Wilde, we eloped to Vegas two years ago, but we never had a wedding reception. In front of everyone we loved, I wanted to make this moment the one you deserve." He dropped to one knee, and I gasped. "We exchanged wedding bands when we got married, but I never actually put a ring on you." A small black velvet box appeared in his hands, and he flipped it open. "I've been in love with you since the minute our eyes met for the first time. Our journey has been wild and crazy, but I wouldn't change a thing, except for letting you walk away that day. Would you do me the honor of marrying me all over again?"

"Ohmygod, yes. *Yes, yes, yes,*" I said, bobbing my head nonstop, a river flowing down my face.

"Is that a yes I hear?"

"It's a million times yes. I love you." The teal Montana sapphire mounted on a platinum band fit perfectly on my ring finger. "It's magnificent." I fanned myself with my hand, trying to prevent the tears from ruining my makeup.

On his feet again and with his hand around my nape, my husband brought our lips together. Fuzzy feelings danced in my belly. My heart swelled bigger than it ever had before.

We exchanged vows in front of a pastor, and everyone cheered as we kissed some more.

Carter and Dahlia stepped onto the small stage, sitting on wooden chairs, a single microphone in front of them. They looked just like the kids who sang for their friends and families in her backyard all those years ago.

"Addison. Tucker. This song is for you," Dahlia said with a wink. They played some of their most famous Carter Hills Band songs. It had been years since they'd shared a stage together—and now, here they were. For me.

More tears shone in my eyes. would carry the memory of this day with me forever.

They finished their set, and my husband let go of my hand. He climbed on the stage and grabbed a guitar someone handed him. Sitting next to Dahlia and Carter, they sang "A Girl Like You," the song Tucker had sung to me in that karaoke bar the weekend we met. After the first chorus, my husband jumped to his feet, ripped open his dress shirt, exposing the too-stretched and tiny pink groom T-shirt he wore that same night, and resumed the song, now on his own.

My eyes stayed glued to him.

How could I look anywhere else?

How could I want to be with anybody else?

I had no idea he played the guitar. He had never hinted at it.

The grin on my face was probably three sizes too big, and I wasn't even sure my feet were still anchored the ground anymore.

Carter and Dahlia joined in for the last chorus.

My friends and family all cheered and applauded, but I stood there, frozen, my heart bouncing in my chest, my breaths short and shallow, and my insides about to turn into fireworks.

"I love you, Wilde," Tucker shouted into the microphone before joining me.

I blinked, unable to speak, my words dissolving as they formed. Nothing I said would be enough to express how I felt.

Nearing me, tugged to me to him, and I sank my head into his chest, listening to the beating of his heart.

"You play the guitar?" I asked once I landed back on planet Earth.

"Got private lessons. Back in Green Mountain…after

you left. A good friend of yours is quite talented." He kissed the tip of my nose. "Wilde, I just played on a stage with Carter Hills Band. How crazy is that?"

I shook my head, unable to stop grinning. "You were great up there. And so sexy. That T-shirt, it really suits you. Big guy, you might have just become my new favorite country star. Don't tell Cart and Dah I said that."

He silenced me with a bruising kiss.

We all sat for dinner, eating in the twilight, the food delicious, and the laughter and chatter of all our friends and family around the table precious.

My mama, whom I tried to see more often since I'd moved back to Tennessee, brought Jamieson over, and with our son nestled between us, we danced as my friends sang their greatest hits under the moonlight.

I needed nothing more in life.

My heart was full.

And I was blissfully happy.

I was still wild and crazy, but I had found my perfect match. Someone to follow me in all my over-the-top ideas, always there to catch me when I fell or to propel me forward when I required a push in the right direction. We had each other's backs always, for better or for worse.

"I can't believe you did this," I said to Tucker, enjoying his warmth all around me, as he held me tight to his chest with one arm and held Jamieson with the other. "This is so romantic."

"If you didn't know by now, I'm gone for you. You once said love, soul mates, and weddings matter to you. They matter to me too. When it's with you."

"Then let's get out of here for a while because I gotta test that theory."

After putting Jamieson in his crib, we retreated to our

bedroom, undressing each other as if our lives depended on it.

"You're so beautiful, sweetheart," Tucker said in a husky voice as he leaned forward and circled a stiff nipple with his tongue. "Do we have to go back out there afterward?" he panted, pointing in the direction of our backyard.

I nodded. "You invited all those people. You just can't throw them out now. It's not even ten o'clock yet."

He drew in a sharp breath. "You're right, but let's love each other first because I couldn't bear to see you in that dress for another minute and not do anything about it. Now spread your thighs, woman. I need my fix."

I fell with a soft thud on our mattress, Tucker fucking me with his tongue before I could even comprehend what was happening.

"Oh God," I moaned. "Best birthday ever." I fisted the sheets around me as my hips shot off the bed, rivers of heat flowing inside me, as pleasure built deep in my core. My body went rigid, and a thousand volts rushed inside me, making me beg for more. I came in a series of seizures. Tucker rose to his feet, and I climbed his body, monkey-style. His thick erection pushed inside me, and with his fingers digging into my ass cheeks, I rolled my hips over his.

"Sweetheart, I'm not done with you. I have a lot more to give you." His mouth feasted on mine, and we kissed until my lips swelled, my toes curled, and I had a hard time breathing on my own.

Moving me up and down, he speared into me in luscious strokes. I came undone all over him, and the satisfied expression on his face brightened the entire room.

"Happy birthday, Wilde."

Once the waves of bliss lessened, my husband laid me down on our bed.

Kneeling between my legs, he flipped me onto my front, placing a pillow underneath my stomach, and positioned himself so he could slide back inside me, my body humming at the sensation of his fullness. With a hand flat on my lower back and the other one kneading my breast, he rammed into me until all I could say was his name and all I could see were stars.

I turned over, and he thrust into me, lust brightening his eyes.

He stared at me with adoration—and that smile. The same one he'd offered me the night we first met. The one I'd never seen aimed at anyone else.

We came together, entangled, never breaking apart, breathing the same air, intoxicated on our love. His heart pounded strongly against mine. With one hand, he held my face and kissed me. His mouth ventured lower, sucking and teasing my skin with his tongue. "I wish we could celebrate you birthday every day, sweetheart. Ready for your cake?"

I nodded, unable to speak, still overwhelmed by the after-orgasm bliss running through my bloodstream, my body not responding to orders anymore.

"*Mamamamama*," followed by a cry startled us both, breaking the enticing slumber in which we were drowning. Jamieson was awake, telling us he wanted to go back to the party. Like us, he loved people, music, and gatherings.

We dressed, and I fixed my hair and makeup before joining our guests in the backyard. Dahlia came to me minutes later, a big, round chocolate cake in her hands, friends and family in tow. They crooned the birthday song, my baby snuggled in my arms, and my husband pulled me to his side, keeping me close and safe against him. Like he always did.

His warm breath tickled the shell of my ear as he whispered, "Make a wish." I squeezed his hand, closed my eyes, and prayed I'd be as happy as I was tonight for the rest of my life.

———

Four years later

"You sure you're ready for this?" I asked my husband as I smoothed his jersey, my fingers lingering on his abdominal muscles for longer than required. "This is a big job. You can't lose patience or throw a fit. You gotta be a role model. This is serious shit."

He cracked a smile and devoured my mouth. I lost myself in him when he deepened the kiss, his strong arms holding me against him.

"All the events in my life have brought me to this moment, sweetheart. As long as I know you'll be rooting for me—for us—from the sideline, I can move mountains if that's what you want. Don't worry about me."

Something, or rather someone, caught our eyes on the kitchen floor.

"You should worry about him, though," Tucker teased. "He's trying to fit his left foot in his right shoe. Again."

I slapped his hard chest and stepped back, squatting. "Honey, try the shoe on your other foot. Yeah. This one." I paused. "Better?" My baby jumped to his feet and looped his little arms around my neck.

"Love you, Mama."

"Oh, I love you too. Now go get your brothers. You don't want to be late on your first day."

Tucker helped me up to my feet, looking picture-perfect with our ten-month-old baby girl cradled in his arms.

"Oli, Spence, Jamie, we're leaving," I said as Tucker went to buckle Nelly in her car seat.

My little men stomped down the stairs looking fierce and happy in their matching black jerseys, the ones I'd designed for the occasion.

"You're beautiful, Mama," Jamieson said as he walked past me. My sweet boy, always making sure I was well. Like he could sense things had been rocky back in the day. He adjusted his baseball cap over his tousled curly brown locks. He was his daddy's spitting image, except for his eyes that were like mine. Vibrant blue.

His brothers joined us.

"I love you guys. Now hurry up," I said as I locked the door behind us. "Daddy says he's fine, but you know what fine means." I scrunched up my face, and my sons and I shared a laugh.

"Yeah, we know," Jamieson said with a loud huff. "Are we going to Aunty Dahlia's this weekend?"

"Yes. We're leaving tomorrow morning. I have a big surprise planned for Daddy's birthday, but don't tell him." His small fingers snaked around mine. "Now let's go. I can't wait to see you in action."

Tucker never really had birthday parties growing up, something I learned before Jamieson turned one. Every year now, I planned something special for him. Last year, we spent a weekend in Chicago. This year we were going to Green Mountain. I had rented one of Carter's cabins and had a caterer coming over, a bounce house for the kids, and a whiskey tasting for the adults.

With my hands clutched in front of me, Nelly in a baby wrap, I paced along the field and looked at my guys kicking the ball, or at least trying to. They were all focused, doing their best to remember everything their coach had taught them.

The twins saw butterflies, and their attention shifted to the flying insects.

"Oliver. Spencer. The game is here," the coach said, pointing to the soccer field. At three years old—I got pregnant a month after my birthday slash wedding reception—they weren't interested in playing ball, but the coach had insisted on teaching them the game early. I didn't disagree because the four of them in matching jerseys were a sight warming my insides.

The coach ran after my boys, holding their hands in his, showing them where they should be positioned on the field.

Our gazes locked, and he mouthed, *What should I do?*

I tilted my head back, unable to stop laughing at his expression.

Ha. Ha. Not funny, he mouthed.

I pinched my lips together, my forefinger and thumb almost pressing together, then blew him a kiss.

He grinned, and my pulse picked up like it always did every time we were together. Even after all these years. We had found our rhythm in life. And moving to Nashville had been the best thing we could have done. The new beginning we'd desperately needed after the storm that tore through us. These days, we were blissfully happy. The kids were thriving. We had family and friends around, and above everything else, we had each other. Good days, bad days, we were it. A mix of chemistry, fireworks, and love, as Tucker once said—and I couldn't agree more.

The man I loved winked at me, and I knew the promises this simple gesture bore. In that instant, I loved the coach something fierce.

———

Thank you for reading Tucker and Addison's heartbreaking and beautiful love story.

Did you know?
You can meet Carter Hills and Riley Burns again in almost every book of the Carter Hills Band universe.

Choose your next read today:

Read False Promises: Carter's story
Read Cruel Destiny: Dahlia and Nick's story
Read Last Hope: Riley and Devon's story

Curious about the rest of their friends?
Read Fallen Legend: Sam Stevens's story
Read Midnight Spark: Aisha Jone's story

All available on your favorite book retailer and on emmanuellesnow.com

———

FREE bonus chapter
Want even more? Your bonus chapter awaits here
emmanuellesnow.com

ACKNOWLEDGMENTS

Wow, who would have thought *Wild and Country* (now titled *Breathless*) would be my longest book so far? Not me, I swear. I hadn't planned to write Tucker and Addison's story, but I got to know them better in *Second Tear* and couldn't miss the opportunity to present them to you.

And yes, what a wild ride these two put me through. I love their energy, their loyalty, and mostly their hearts. They are two people we would all love to have in our friend circle. They are passionate and strong-headed. I wrote the first draft of this book on a whim before I even finished *Second Tear*. Both Addison and Tucker were living in my head, and they wouldn't let me finish the other book first. Yeah, they can be loud—and pushy. But in the best of ways.

Tucker and Addison's tale isn't your typical love story, but it was one that had to be told. If you've ever suffered from postpartum depression, remember you're not alone. Just please don't isolate yourself. There are people who can help you through this. My heart is with you.

I wrote this book in two countries, six provinces and as many states, a dozen cities, living at home, at other people's houses, and hotels, trying to put the final touches to it.

I have many people to be thankful for.

First, my husband and children. I love you. I think those words sum it all up. I'm so happy each time you get excited about my newest literary project.

Shalini, one more project we can proudly say, "It's a wrap." And Tucker, wow, he was a love-at-first-sight main character, right? Big dick energy and all. What's not to love about him? Thank you for all your hard work and for being there for me as a friend along the way. I'm happy we're doing this together. Always.

Mom and Dad, thank you for having us over when we had no home and when all our plans changed overnight. This was really generous, and I truly appreciate it. Mom, thank you for reading my postpartum depression chapters and using your professional background to confirm that I was right on track with Addison's struggles.

Jo and Catherine, thank you for having us over when, once again, we had no place to stay after we've decided to drive across the country with our kids and all our belongings, with no real plan. I know they're six of us and it can be wild, but you showed us what true friendship is all about.

Jacynthe, Virginie, thank you for always encouraging me and making me a better person.

To my readers, thank you from the bottom of my heart. Seeing my books in your hands, and reading your positive comments and encouragements are always the greatest joys an author can experience. So thank you! Truly.

To my ARC team, you guys rock. I'm always excited to put a new book out there because I can't wait to hear your feedback. Many of you have become friends over the last few releases, and I'm happy to be able to share these stories with you. Thank you for your love and support!

To the bloggers, Bookstagrammers, BookTokers, and Youtubers, who love and share my work, I'm super thankful for all of it. None of this would be as great if it weren't for you. You make me proud to be the author that I am when I see you loving and sharing my work.

To all y'all, cheers!
Emmanuelle

WANT MORE EMOTIONAL LOVE STORIES?

WHICH COUPLE WILL YOU PICK NEXT?

False Promises

★★★★★ "The angst, the utter heartbreak, and protectiveness I felt for Carter during this book is unreal!"

★★★★★ "Emmanuelle Snow really knows how to tug at all of your emotions and does such a great job of bringing her characters to life!"

A gripping story of sizzling passion, lust, and the price of fame.
Start Carter Hills's story now

———

Sweet Agony

★★★★★ "If I could give more than 5 stars, I would."

★★★★★ "This is not a romance, it is a story about first love, first heartbreak and growing up."

A compelling tale of love, friendship, and self-discovery that will tug at your heartstrings.

Start Dahlia's story now

————

Cruel Destiny

★★★★★ "Wow. Just wow. If that could be my review, that is all I would write."

★★★★★ "Emmanuelle has done it yet again. She found a way to slip into my mind and heart with her words and the creation of characters you can't help but fall in love with."

★★★★★ "This book broke my heart in the first twenty five percent and sewed it back together."

A story of healing, second chances, and the risks of opening your heart to someone new. Can they trust each other with their hearts, or will their pasts keep them apart?

Read Nick and Dahlia's love story now

————

Wild Encounter

★★★★★ "This is by far one of the most well-written

book I've read this month. It is dynamic, intriguing, interesting, unafraid to go there and most of all touching."

★★★★★ "I personally wouldn't call this book JUST a romance novel because it's so much more. I 100% recommend it no doubt in mind."

A tale of passion and perseverance that will leave your heart racing and your spirit soaring.

Read Tucker and Addison's love story now

———

Last Hope

★★★★★ "This book was not only about the darkness but it was about pure love, hope, spice, family, and friendships on point with just the right amount without overpowering the storyline at all."

★★★★★ "Devon and Riley's story is a beautiful one with a lot of emotions. The subject matter is intense but it is handled very gently."

A tale of resilience and second chances in a world where love and danger intertwine.

Read Riley and Devon's love story now

———

Midnight Sparks

★★★★★ "The characters, the love, the humor, the steaminess, the emotions… it's everything I hoped and more."

★★★★★ "I think that is one Emmanuelle Snow's sexiest novels yet."

Welcome to the island where Holiday magic meets unexpected romance and a chance at a fresh start.

Read Gavin and Aisha's love story now

————

Fallen Legend

★★★★★ ""The love that grows, not only through tough angst but through unconditional moments had my heart. This is a spicy and riveting book"

★★★★★ "Emmanuelle Snow doesn't just tell a story, she creates an entire world."

A poignant and uplifting journey of hope, love, and the power of second chances.

Read Sam and Madison's love story now

————

Snowbound

★★★★★ "5 big stars from me for this amazing story. Absolutely loved it!"

★★★★★ "Emmanuelle Snow's stories are always full of angst, and Snowbound is no exception."

The intertwined lives of two strangers bound by fate in the midst of a snowstorm.

Read Anderson and Abigail's love story now

All available at emmanuellesnow.com

ABOUT THE AUTHOR

Soulfully Beautiful Love Stories

USA Today Bestselling Author Emmanuelle Snow is an author of contemporary YA and women's fiction love stories, who gives life to strong characters who'll fight with all they have to reach their life goals and find their own happiness. She loves her characters to be relatable and realistic.

Emmanuelle is in love with love. Especially complicated, deep, and passionate feelings that make a relationship extraordinary and complex all at the same time.

In her spare time, when she's not writing or reading, she likes to go on road trips—with her four kids and her own soulmate—watch movies, paint, or do some DIY, always with a cup of green tea in her hand and listening to country music.

She splits her time between beautiful Canada and the small US towns she adores.

Find all of Emmanuelle's books here:
emmanuellesnow.com

———

ALSO BY THE AUTHOR

CARTER HILLS BAND UNIVERSE

(suggested reading order)

Carter Hills Band series

False Promises

HEART SONG DUET

Blindsided

Forevermore

Whiskey Melody series

Sweet Agony

SECOND TEAR DUET

Cruel Destiny

Beautiful Salvation

BREATHLESS DUET

Wild Encounter

Brittle Scars

Upon A Star Series

Last Hope

Midnight Sparks

Love Song For Two Series

EMMANUELLE
USA TODAY BESTSELLING AUTHOR
SNOW
LAST HOPE
Upon a Star series - book one
LOVE
HOPE

LAST HOPE

RILEY

Our eyes met. Something passed between us. Attraction. Recognition. Yearning. Maybe a mix of all three. And much more. I brought the tumbler to my lips, relishing the burning sensation of the whiskey as it slid down my throat.

A gear shifted inside me.

My heart did one of its moves. The one where it got all bothered and excited.

I fastened my grip around the glass in my hand.

The woman pushed her long, curled blonde hair over one shoulder, giving me a perfect view of her lickable, slim neck. *Lickable?* Was that even a word? I pushed the thought away. I was a man on a mission.

The vampiric side of me—the one I hadn't known existed until now—emerged in full force.

I blinked.

The temptation to bite the soft flesh of her neck multiplied by the second.

The woman smiled, and all my restraints broke loose. They caught fire and burned to ashes in the dark night.

I gave her a subtle nod as I continued staring, hoping for a slight hint of encouragement from her.

Her red-painted lips pursed as she mouthed *Hey* in my direction.

Smoothing my palm over my trousers, I made a beeline for her, my steps light and focused, not allowing the sea of people to break our eye contact. The air around us heated up. We were outdoors, but it felt as if someone had cranked up the thermostat. Slowly, I raked my fingers through my brown hair, gelled to perfection tonight, doing my best not to mess it up. From an outsider's point of view, I bet I looked in control—the opposite of how I really felt. No one in the business needed to know how unruly my heart was behaving. Or the tremble that had started in my fingers. The flickers of excitement that burned in my core.

A server passed by, and I discarded my tumbler before grabbing two champagne flutes from his tray.

In two long strides, I reached the woman in the red lace dress. Her smile reached her eyes when I offered her the sparkling alcohol. "To a great night and even greater company," I said as we clinked our glasses. "I'm Riley." I held out my hand for her to shake. Our palms met, and a jolt of heat surged through me, setting my insides ablaze in a way no woman ever had. Her touch alone threatened to make me combust.

"I'm Devon."

I lifted our joined hands to my lips and kissed the back of hers.

Her soft chuckle resonated through me. "I can already tell you're a gentleman."

"My mama taught me well. So, what brings you here, Devon? I've never seen you at one of these country music parties before."

"Oh, you go to these a lot? This is my first time. It's

quite intimidating. A friend of mine invited me, but she's running late."

I followed her gaze across the rooftop bar. Country music singers, songwriters, and musicians counted for more than half of the patrons here, and together, they'd won enough awards to fill an entire room. Woven through them were music producers, managers, movie stars, and their dates. Yeah, to someone unfamiliar, the crowd could easily appear impressive.

My man, Carter Hills, waved at me when my eyes drifted to him. I raised my glass in his direction. He was not only one of the biggest artists here tonight, but also one of my protégés and closest friends. Over the years, we rose to the top of this industry together, our friendship growing stronger with each album. We had each other's backs. Always.

"All these people, they aren't as intimidating as they look once you get to know them. Most of them are pretty great actually. Down to earth, and genuinely nice. Don't let their success make you nervous. Looking great is part of their job description. But there's much more to them. Well, to some of them at least."

The woman snickered and clutched my elbow, balancing her weight on her four-inch nude stilettos. "You seem like the kind of man who knows a lot about the country music scene, am I right?"

I took another sip of my drink and shrugged, my eyes trained on her face, enjoying the tilt of her red lips. "You could say that. I've been around these folks my entire life, but an active part of their world for almost a decade."

Devon's gray-blue eyes flared. "You're a country singer? Ohmygod, I'm sorry if I didn't recognize you." A flush crept along her neck and cheeks. The same neck I was still dying to feast on.

"Nah. I'm not. Believe me, you don't want to hear me sing. It may burst your eardrums. No kidding."

She grinned at me, and my heart swelled in my chest. "Who are you then? What's your superpower?"

"I'm a manager." I pointed to Carter, now deep in a conversation with Rita L. Sterling, a music producer. "I manage this fellow's career, amongst others."

Devon moved closer and lowered her voice to a whisper as if she feared someone would hear her. Not a chance with the chatter and music surrounding us. "Is that Carter Hills? I'm sorry. I'm not a groupie, I swear, but I thought I recognized him earlier when I walked in."

"Yeah, that's him. I can introduce you later."

She shook her head, the blush on her cheeks darkening. "No, you don't have to. I-I'm nobody here. I'm not part of this world. This night is surreal, I—"

A waitress bumped into my side and lost her footing, sending an entire tray of red wine glasses crashing all over me.

Time seemed to slow. I blinked as my clothes absorbed every drop.

"Oh, shit. I'm…I'm so sorry. It's…oh gosh, it's my first night here. I'm so, so sorry. I-I messed up. Wh-what can I do?" she asked, her eyes glistening with tears as she righted the now-empty wine glasses on the splattered tray. "Ohmygod. I ruined your shirt, sir. This is…this is so unprofessional. I'll get fired over this. Wait here, I-I'll be right back. I will…I'll get my purse. Dry-cleaning is on me."

I wrapped my hand around her wrist before she could run away and leveled my eyes with hers. "Stop. Breathe. It's just a shirt. I own a dozen more just like it. You won't get fired because nobody will say anything to your boss. I might even have been the one who bumped into you. I should've stood on the side of the deck. See? I'm standing in the way."

The waitress raised her watery eyes, studying me as if there was a *but* about to come out of my lips. There wasn't.

"What's your name?"

"Daph…Daphne."

"Well, Daphne. Breathe in. Breathe out. It'll help to calm your nerves."

She filled her lungs with a deep inhale.

"Yeah, like this." Her shoulders dropped. "See? Much better. Listen, now you go back there," I pointed to the bar, "fill this tray up, smile, and get on with your night. Don't let this little incident affect you. You're doing a great job."

She blinked and swallowed hard, a quiver of a smile trembling over her lips. "How-how can you tell? You don't even know me, sir."

"It doesn't matter. I'd recognize a hard worker anywhere. I have a flair for finding good people. It's my superpower." I fished a business card out of the inner pocket of my now damp jacket. "If waitressing doesn't work out or you're ever looking out for a job, gimme a call. I might be able to put in a good word for you. Don't worry. The sun always comes out after the storm."

"Wow…huh…thank you. I… This… That's the nicest thing someone has ever said to me." She clutched my business card, pressed it against her chest as if I'd just promised her the world. With a shy smile, she turned and walked away, chin raised and back straight.

Warmth filled me. Daphne would be okay. She just needed a pep talk. And I happened to be good at those too. Perhaps I possessed more than just one superpower after all.

Devon leaned closer, and her eyes widened in stunned disbelief. Her perfume wrapped around me, tipping my senses into a dizzy haze. She smelled like spring and rain. Fresh and flowery. I burned the fragrance to my memory. Even my heart seemed to enjoy it as it expanded in my chest and drummed faster.

"Wow. That was… That was amazing. Most people would have screamed at the poor girl or threatened to get her fired. Instead, you boosted her self-confidence. That's very noble of you. You are a good man, Riley."

I looked down and pinched the fabric of my stained shirt to unglue it from my chest. "Thank you. It was just a clumsy mishap. Now, would you excuse me for a minute? I need to freshen up." I grimaced as she grinned at me, the gleam in her eyes captivating me.

Her smile grew wider, and she gave a gentle nod. "Go ahead. I can't wait to see how you manage to come back still dressed in these clothes. This should be interesting." She wrinkled her nose at my drenched state and said, "Yeah, very interesting."

I smiled. Like a fool. There was no way I could hold it back. Falling under this woman's charm felt like breathing. Easy. Natural. And imperative. "Wait and see. I may surprise you. I always find ways to turn impossible situations around."

Devon chuckled. "I'm sure you do. While you are in there cleaning up, I'll order us more drinks. Whiskey?"

"On the rocks," I said, holding back a grin. Did Devon notice what I was drinking earlier? If so, it made her even more attractive. I dreaded walking away from her, not ready to escape the magnetism that had settled between us. "I'll be quick."

We eye-fucked each other for a few seconds, my pulse spiking at the way her eyes brought her whole face to life.

Full lashes, high cheekbones, straight nose, heart-shaped lips. She was every shade of beautiful. With just one glance in my direction, this woman had captured my heart the moment I first saw her. It made no sense, but I wasn't about to overthink it.

So far, our encounter was the highlight of my night—of my day, maybe even my week.

With a sigh, I broke eye contact.

In a hurry to get back to her, I weaved through the bar crowd, my jacket now open, my soaked shirt sticking to my abs, and the front of my trousers molded to my thighs. Nothing about being wet and dressed up felt good. I was pretty sure even my socks were damp. I frowned at my predicament, wondering how I was supposed to get through the night in clothes soaked with red wine. It wasn't as if I had a change of clothes in my car or something. It wasn't as if I could just run home and change, even though I lived less than ten miles away. Tonight, I had no intention of letting Devon out of my sight, even for just a few minutes.

In the men's room, I peeled off my once-white shirt, gave it a disapproving look, and dropped it in the trash. A complete loss. I couldn't save it even if my life depended on it. After dabbing my trousers with paper towels, I turned the undershirt around and tucked it into my pants. I used more paper towels to soak up the excess wine from my jacket and put it back on. The look wasn't perfect, but in the dark bar, nobody would look too closely to notice.

I eyed myself in the mirror one last time, fixed my hair and the lapel of my jacket, and with determination in each step, made my way back into the night, looking for the woman in the red dress.

———

Read Riley and Devon's story,

Last Hope, now

emmanuellesnow.com/products/last-hope

Author's bookstore at emmanuellesnow.com

"Once again Emmanuelle Snow has created such amazing work. I went through an emotional journey with this story, I had happy tears, sad tears and laughter. It was just so heartfelt and pure. I couldn't put the book down." ***(Goodreads)***

"I always love it when an author is able to make me feel all kinds of emotions. And with 'Hope and Country', Emmanuelle definitely managed that. This read was romantic, fun, sad, heartbreaking and wonderful." ***(Goodreads)***

Read ***Last Hope*** now
emmanuellesnow.com/products/last-hope

EMMANUELLE

SNOW

FALLEN LEGEND

a love story

Love Song for Two series - book one

FALLEN LEGEND

SAM

Fisting my hands at my sides, I paced the room, a ball of lightning bouncing around my chest. This was a nightmare. A disaster about to happen. How had I not seen this one coming? How could I have been so blind?

My nails dug trenches in my palms, drawing pinpricks of blood, but I would keep my composure. I had to.

The lump in my larynx rubbed against the chaffed walls of my throat.

I reeled in some of my wrath and tried another approach. My voice came out a ragged whisper, but calmer this time, putting my pride to rest. And urging my sanity to stay in the game. "Lisa, you can't be serious. Listen, there must be something *I* can do. Can we talk about it first? And what about the kids? How am I going to explain any of this to them? We'll get help... You can't just leave like this."

No emotions—rather not the ones I wished to see—crossed her hardened features. No *I'm having second thoughts.* Or *you might be right, we'll get help.*

My wife had turned to stone, unmoving and unreadable.

Hoping the pain would numb the one ripping my chest in two, I tugged at the roots of my hair. How could I have been so clueless about the woman I'd been married to for the last four years?

She pushed another shirt into her bag, ignoring my words.

Maybe I could reach out to the mother inside her. "Lisa, your leaving will fuck them up for the rest of their lives. Abandoning your own children, really? That's not what motherhood is all about." I halted and turned around to face the woman, who I thought I knew so well, zipping up her royal-blue suitcase. The one that had traveled around the world with us for years. Yeah, what a joke.

She finally raised her gaze, and I saw determination pass through her eyes this time. She wasn't doubting her decision to walk away from us, her family. I studied her for a long minute, wishing I could see tears glistening somewhere in them, or regret marring her features. But there were none.

She was done.

When did my wife harbor a rock in place of her heart?

"Is it about the miscarriages?" I asked, praying she'd say yes and that I could call her doctor and set up an appointment to discuss her psychological distress. "I know how difficult it's been on you, but it's been hard on me too. We can get through this. Together. We're a good team. We love each other."

She sighed and shook her head, her eyes still showing no sign of hurt or sadness. Or anything. "That's the thing, Sam. I don't love you. I did. Once. But both miscarriages were eye-opening. I need to find myself. I'm twenty-eight. For the last six years, I've followed you around the globe. I liked that. For the last four, I've played wife and mommy. And I enjoyed it…at some point. Being a parent is your thing. We had babies because you wanted to be a daddy… I never asked to be a mother. In all honesty, I thought it'd grow on me…" She shrugged. "But it didn't. I crave fresh air. To be free to do whatever I want. Whenever I want it. And being a parent isn't just what I hoped it'd be. I'm sorry, but I'm over it."

I blinked. What? Was she serious right now? *She's over it?*

I was having one of those crippling nightmares that felt too much like reality. This was it. No woman in her right mind would say such horrible things about her own children. About her family.

Her flesh.

Her blood.

My Adam's apple bobbed, and bile rose in my throat. Tinted with disgust and disdain.

My wife was delusional.

Who should I call to get her some help?

Could her state of mind be ruled a mental breakdown? Did she require psychiatric professionals? Or a vacation? No matter what, she looked sane.

Lisa smiled at me as if quitting on us was just a daily occurrence and not something about to wreck our entire world.

My shoulders fell, and so did my heart. I inched closer when she moved to her feet. "Can we talk about this? Please. You at least owe me that. We've been through so much together. Did you forget everything?" I asked, forcing my voice to sound even, trying my best to keep my anger under wraps.

She offered me another twist of her lips. This time, she

looked diabolical. Who was this woman? Where did my wife go?

"I owe you nothing, Sammy. The ride has been fun, but I'm not playing this family game anymore. I'm out. Oh, and I'll send you the divorce papers in a week or two."

My eyes sprang wider.

What the actual fuck?

"Divorce papers? Don't you think it's a little early to talk about divorce? We haven't even fought about anything serious in the past, and now you're talking about dissolving our marriage. Tell me you're kidding. Where are the cameras? The crew? Is it for a celebrity prank TV show?"

My wife—or soon-to-be ex-wife if she had her way—huffed, as if anything I said sounded childish. Asking her to stay seemed to scrape on her nerves.

"C'mon, Sammy. I'm moving to the other side of the world. I won't return. Ever. Come to terms with it. Nothing you do or say will change anything." She sighed again and shook her head, looking desperate. "I. Am. Not. Coming. Back. Ever. This"—she pointed around the room with her finger—"is over. You and I, we're done." A car honked outside. "Now move, my cab is waiting." She pushed past me, rolling her suitcase behind her.

I stood there, frozen. None of this made sense. The dream had lasted long enough. I could wake up now. *Please make this nightmare go away.*

My heart stuttered, and I snapped back to the present when the sound of little feet neared our bedroom.

I spun on my heels and watched Lisa as she stood in the doorway, a mask of annoyance painting her frigid face.

My heart froze. Ice frosted the blood inside my veins, and I held my breath.

Mikaella, our four-year-old, ran our way in her one-piece unicorn white PJs, her wild, curly light-brown hair looking like a bird's nest, a fluffy baby-pink blanket hanging from her tiny hand.

She stopped before Lisa, her round golden eyes traveling from her mama to the suitcase beside her. "Going on a trip, Mama?" Sparks shone in our daughter's eyes, and she lifted a finger. "I love going on the plane. *Nneeeaowww*," she said, her hand imitating the aircraft. "The ladies always gimme chocolate. Justine *lovvves* chocolate too. She always eats mine. Can I bring Miss Froggy with me? She's never been on a plane. She wanna come. You said she could come next time. You promised."

Lisa looked at our daughter, her gaze empty and back held taut. I prayed to see an emotion crossing her flat gaze. None made an appearance.

Mikaella tugged at her hand. "Mama, can I pack by myself? I'm a big girl. Can I bring my purple dress? And my ballet shoes? Can Boa the raccoon come too? And Holly? She always misses me when I'm gone. She hates being a doll. She wants to be a real baby…or a lady. And drink tea."

Lisa finally said something. My ears scorched the moment the words left her mouth. "Mama is going on a trip by herself, Mika. To Thailand. You can't come, I wanna be alone."

Tears pooled in our baby's eyes. She tugged at her mother's hand once again. "But I wanna come. Justine wants to come too. She'll be sad if you leave without her. Mama, we'll be good, good girls. And be silent if your head hurts."

Lisa ruffled her hair. "Sorry. You're not coming. I gotta go. Be nice to your daddy. And take care of Justine. Can you be a big girl, Mika?"

Our daughter nodded, a wide smile now brightening her sweet face. Lisa ignored her and stalked away when the cab honked a second time. My heart sank deeper in my chest at the sight of my wife padding away from our baby girl.

She turned to face me once at the top of the staircase. "Bye, Sammy. Have a good life." She removed her wedding ring and placed it on the banister.

My heart tumbled down my chest until it hit the hardwood floor. Smashed and bleeding.

I stood there, acid filling my throat and dissolving the words I wanted to speak.

Mikaella's sobs brought me back to her. "She didn't kiss me goodbye. Mama. *Mammma*. Come back. I'll be a good girl."

I rushed to my daughter and lifted her in my arms, both of us needing each other's love and affection now more than ever.

I brushed her hair with my fingers, dried her tears, and hugged her closer so my heart could soothe hers. Because I had no clue how to heal her pain with words.

I followed Lisa down the stairs. My eyes zoomed in on the front door. My head pounded, and my chest cavity filled with piling rocks as the sound of the revving engine outside faded away. What just happened?

Two hours ago, everything was fine. Or I thought it was. We bathed the girls, read stories in bed… Where did it go wrong?

My stomach heaved. Lisa left. She fucking left.

"Shhh, sweet pea. It'll be okay. We'll be okay… I'm here…"

In that instant, I didn't even believe my own words.

I fished my phone out of my back pocket to call my wife. We needed to talk—before she left for good. Before she regretted any of it. Before it was too late to fix that rift keeping us apart.

Beep. Beep. Beep.

The last thread of hope holding me together burned to ashes.

Chills lined my back.

Lisa had disconnected her number.

Reality hit me. It wasn't a prank or a spur-of-the-moment decision. It was premeditated.

How long had she been planning her escape?

How long ago had she decided the girls and I were inconveniences in her life?

Oxygen could barely make the journey from my lungs to my brain anymore.

My wife had vanished in the night without giving me any kind of explanation. Or a way to reach her.

I buried my face in the crook of Mikaella's neck, hiding my numbing emotions from her.

My head spun. A weight I'd never carried before grew in my chest, crushing my organs. How would I ever be able to tell my baby girls their mama had ditched them for a reason I still didn't get?

The last fragment of my heart broke free as my baby's sobs doubled, now heart-wrenching, coming from some place deep down her little body, her sadness drenching my shirt. "I want Mama. I love the plane. She didn't kiss me. I want a hug…from her."

My eyes glazed over.

My little girl tilted her head back and stared at me, her lower lip trembling and her face a map of confusion and sorrow.

She cupped my cheeks with her hands and blinked. "Daddy, why are you crying? Do you miss Mama too? Did she forget to kiss you goodnight?" She wrapped her baby arms around my neck and fastened her hug around me. "Don't cry, Daddy. I'm here. I love you. Don't cry, okay?"

I pulled my daughter against my heart. "I love you too, sweet pea. I'm not going away. Ever. You hear me, Mika? I'll never leave you. I promise."

We held onto each other until she relaxed in my embrace, and sleep claimed her.

I tucked my daughter in, doing my best to avoid waking Justine, my two-year-old, sleeping in the adjacent bed. In one corner of their bedroom, sitting in a rocking chair, I watched my children fast asleep, their steady breathing a bandage around my hemorrhaging heart.

With a slow look around, I took in the pastel-pink walls, the glittery matching unicorn bedspreads, the dolls sitting around a small wooden white table with tiny porcelain teacups in front of them, the net with over twenty stuffed-animals hanging across the ceiling, the fairy lights casting a golden glow wrapped around the princess-inspired headboards.

Would we ever be okay again?

My eyes landed on the family picture framed on the wall we took last Christmas.

Our smiles looked so genuine.

I studied Lisa. Was she faking being happy the entire time?

I slouched forward, my face landing in my hands, my shoulders heaving as sobs rocked my body.

The fresh wound ripping my chest in two widened. How did I go from having a picture-perfect family at dinner time to being a single dad mere hours later?

How did I not see my world crumbling? There must have been signs leading to this moment. How did I miss all of them? How could have I been so blind?

That's the thing, Sam. I don't love you. I did. Once.

My life was built on a lie. It was a fucking illusion.

Lisa faded into the night like she never existed.

That was when the truth hit me, like a ton of bricks weighing on my fractured heart. I was on my own and had no one to connect to on this journey.

My daughters had become motherless. Not because their mama died, but because she chose to leave them behind.

Not because she was incapacitated, but because she couldn't love them the way they deserved to be loved.

I cupped my thundering organ with both hands. Every cell in me hurt as the truth of my new reality, *our* new realities, crashed on me and settled in my soul.

My girls' lives would never be the same.

My life would never be the same.

Tonight, I'd lost not only the mother of my children, but also the woman I loved. The one I'd been sharing the last few years of my life with. The one I traveled the world with, went through great moments of joy and hardships with. The one I promised forever to. The one who said in front of our dearest friends and family I was her only true love.

I perused the bedroom for the final time, my eyes locking on my babies fast asleep.

They had no idea that by the morning, nothing would ever be the same.

That the light of a new day would carry a truckload of sorrow in its wake.

How would I ever be able to do this on my own? Be a single dad.

How would I ever be able to explain the harsh truth to my girls without shattering their hearts in the process?

Closing my eyes, I let darkness descend upon me because right now, I had no clue how to do this by myself and survive the heartbreak at the same time.

Read Sam Steven's story,
Fallen Legend, now

emmanuellesnow.com/products/fallen-legend

Author's bookstore at emmanuellesnow.com

"Emmanuelle Snow doesn't just tell a story, she creates an entire world." ***(ReadaholicDeb)***

"Emmanuelle Snow has done it again! This powerful, heartwarming, slow-burn love story will break your heart on page one and slowly piece it back together. ***(Goodreads)***

Fallen Legend is book one in the
Lonesome Heart duet.

Read the first part or the complete duet now

emmanuellesnow.com/products/fallen-legend